First Draw

The Hell Hole Saga:

Book I

I0617870

S.L. Kotar and J.E. Gessler

Ahead of the Press Publishing
St. Louis, Missouri

Library of Congress Cataloguing-in-Publication Data

First Draw
The Hell Hole Saga: Book I
 / S.L. Kotar and J.E. Gessler / authors
/E.J. Rossi / illustrator

ISBN   Paperback   978-1-950392-06-3
ISBN   KINDLE   978-1-950392-07-0

Manufactured in the United States of America
Ahead of The Press Publishing
St. Louis, Missouri

Table of Contents

DEDICATION

"First Draw"

All writers are the sum of their parts: for us, many of those facets were drawn from the classic and beloved Westerns that blasted their way across television screens throughout the 1950's and 1960's and even into the early 1970's. There was, for us, the scared Gunsmoke, for which we were honored to play a small role by supplying words and actions for Matt and Kitty, doc, and Festus. There was Wagon Train, and Maverick, The Lone Ranger, and The Big Valley. To James Arness, Amanda Blake, Milburn Stone, Ken Curtis, Buck Taylor, Ward Bond, Robert Horton, Jack Kelly, James garner, Clayton Moore, Jay Silverheels, Barbara Stanwick, Richard Long, Peter Breck, and Linda Evens, we dedicate this book, because you inspired us, touched our hearts and strengthened our souls.

SLK and JEG

CHAPTER 1

The thermometer read ninety degrees, Fahrenheit. The short, squat, sweaty man squinting at the instrument affixed to the wall by a bent nail, spat on the floor. He missed the spittoon by half a mile.

"I don't know why you look at that -- thing," his companion complained. "It only registers two numbers: ninety degrees in summer an' twenty degrees in winter. Whatever a 'degree,' is," he tartly added, staring down at the floor where the Secretary of War's assistant for Law and Order had expectorated.

Greg Thomas ignored both the exasperated comment and the pointed look.

"This thermometer was manufactured in Germany," he instructed, instead. "There is one like it in the Capitol Building in Washington, twice this size."

"The doc here says the idea of reckonin' temperature with a contraption like that will never catch on. He says when it's hot, it's hot. An' when it's cold, it's cold. He don't need some foreign in-stro-mint to tell him when a patient has a fever."

"Fortunately for the air," Thomas remarked, waving a hand in front of his face to create wind, "it has no need of his services."

Failing to derive any cooling sensation from his effort, the Federal man removed his hat from its temporary resting place and fanned himself with the brim. He would get no closer to a breeze all day.

Replacing the haberdashery where he found it, he paced the jail-like confines of the office, temporarily occupied by the United States Government. He had repeated this exact journey two dozen times already, and the hour hand had only reached eleven. Avoiding the oaken desk with the mismatched swivel chair, he finally settled into the corner, facing the door.

His day had begun at 8 A.M. After three hours of futile interviews, his throat felt dry. The thought of the warm, flat beer waiting for him at the Remembrance Saloon hardly provided an inspiration to hurry his work.

Hardly was better than nothing.

"Who's next?" he listlessly inquired. A fly settled on his hand and began drinking his perspiration. It was all he could do to shoo it away.

"There's only one more." John Sparrow's voice held less hope than that of his superior's. While holding the title of clerk, he was known in the parlance as "the local man." If they did not fill the position today, they would have to repeat the entire process tomorrow. And probably the day after. The proposition held little allure.

"What are his credentials?"

The question was asked by rote and answered with dull enthusiasm.

"Volunteered at the outbreak of the War. Saw action in Tennessee and the Carolinas. Fought at Shiloh, Franklin; served under Grant. Received a commendation for bravery at..." His voice fell off. The ink on the form from which he read had smeared. He could hardly make out the words, although the penmanship was neat enough. He did not finish the sentence. It was doubtful his companion noticed the lapse.

"Rank?"

"Private."

"Private?" A note of irritation entered the conversation. "Only a private? I've already rejected two sergeants and a lieutenant today."

The shorter of the two men looked away. There were no windows to his left. It made no difference. The view hardly improved through a pane of glass.

"The applicant was sixteen years old when he enlisted."

That seemed a plausible but not inspired reason for ending the war with the same rank upon which he entered.

"Infantry?"

"Yes."

"Prior law enforcement history?"

From outside came the sound of a horse whinnying, then the indistinct cursing of a man with a Southern dialect. Greg Thomas hated Hays; he despised Topeka. In fact, he had no liking for Kansas. As a territory, it had caused him countless trouble; as a state, it promised to follow in its own footsteps.

Men in Kansas did not understand law and order. They never would. They were heathens, he decided, the lot of them. Twelve years before the

Rebellion, John Brown had chosen Kansas as his battleground, earning the state the moniker "Bleeding Kansas." Men in this godforsaken state could not even make up their mind which side they supported. Rather than let Brown carry his reputation to Virginia, they should have either made him governor, or hanged him.

One dozen years later, nothing had been done to improve the image of the state or its citizens.

Thomas' mood interjected a listless depression to the scene. Removing his Elgin pocket watch, he consulted it for the same reason he had read the thermometer. To pass the time. He wound it absently, pretending to be alive.

"It says here he deputied some before the War; small towns, mostly," Sparrow offered.

The Federal man nodded without real concentration as the inconsistency struck with force. His head jerked up in annoyance.

"Before the War? When he was fourteen, fifteen years old?"

"That's what's written here. It says," the clerk retorted, turning to the second page of the application to quote exactly, "he 'spent time in the Indian Territories; wintered with a tribe one season' when he was trapping. Served as a deputy under Jack Duvall."

"Jack Duvall is dead." Thomas' voice reflected that fact by deepening considerably. Jack Duvall: he remembered him well. No one had been a better lawman than Jack Duvall.

"The applicant has been deputing around the Cimarron since the War ended," the clerk droned. "He mentions...."

But Greg Thomas had stopped listening. His mind focused on the dead lawman. Not until his assistant finished the details did he realize he had not caught a single word of the report. With a slight clearing of his throat, the government man drummed his fingers against the wall.

"Experience with a gun?"

"He left that line blank."

"Can he read and write?" Thomas' interest waned.

"He filled out this application."

The townsman shoved the papers toward Thomas to serve as a specimen of the youth's handwriting. Thomas glanced at it, then nodded.

"Send him in."

The chair creaked as Sparrow stood and crossed the floor. He opened the door no more than an inch and peeked out. Only one man remained in the antechamber. Alerted by the footfalls, a pair of sharp eyes met those of the clerk.

"You," Sparrow barked. No reply. "Come in."

The petitioner rose and approached. He moved the way a man, accustomed to life astride a horse did, with an awkward, uneasy gait. Hesitating at the entranceway, he debated whether to slide through the crack or wait until the summoner moved aside. When the assistant gave no inclination either way, the former soldier lowered his head slightly and used his shoulders to brush by.

The Law and Order minister was not looking up as he crossed the threshold.

"Yes, sir," the interloper reported. The tone reflected an air of expectation, a hopefulness that spoke of his familiarity with protocol.

Thomas broke his gaze from the contemplation of a coffee stain in the wood grain of the desk and found himself staring at the man's belt. With a surprised huff of expelled air, he raised his head back, then back again. Standing before him he beheld a boy of gigantic height.

To hide his discomfiture and the fact he stood a foot shorter than the applicant, Thomas dropped into the oak chair. The hinges squeaked. He did not offer the youth a seat. He did not expect him to stay long.

"What's your name?"

The bright blue eyes of the tall man darted from the paper he had filled out two days earlier to the inquisitor's face. If he thought the question superfluous, he did not say so.

"Kiley. Claw Kiley."

"Claw?" Thomas baited.

"Claudius," came the polite, almost embarrassed correction. The challenge had gone unanswered.

"How old are you, Mr. Kiley?"

"Twenty-three, sir."

There was that of military training about him, and more. An innate tact, a respect reserved; the trust it would be reciprocated.

"You wrote here that you deputized with Jack Duvall."

"Yes, sir."

"When was that?"

"Up until the time of his death."

"Know him well?"

"He was like a father to me."

No mistaking the sincerity in the avowal. It made the government man want to ask him more.

He saw no sense denying himself the pleasure of speaking to someone who had known Marshal Duvall. Which did not mean he had any intention of offering him the job. Or that he actually believed the startling assertion.

"Were you there when he died?"

A hesitation.

"Yes, sir."

"He was gunned down in the street, Mister Kiley. In the performance of his duty. You see the fight?" Kiley nodded. "Was it a fair fight?"

No pause, yet behind the curt nod, a regret, a hurt. A remembrance of helplessness.

"It was a fair fight."

"Jack Duvall was the fastest gun alive."

"He thought so."

Kiley left the "sir" off the end of his sentence. Thomas noted it.

"The man who killed him was a gunfighter. Red McGee." The verbalization of the name after so long a time jogged Thomas' memory. His mouth went dry and he licked his lips with unaccustomed nervousness. "What happened to McGee?"

"He was gunned down in the street."

"Not gunned down, Kiley. Not from what I heard. He was called out. Wasn't that the way it happened?" Kiley shrugged. The fingers of his right hand twitched, as though seeking the feel of a trigger to wrap around. "Called out on the street and shot down. The gunfighter who outdrew the fastest gun alive never lived to tell the tale."

"Something like that." An uncomfortable admission.

"Seems as I recall it was the deputy who shot McGee. You were that deputy, Kiley." Not a question now, but a statement.

"That's how rumors get started, sir."

"Red McGee killed the man you thought of as a father, and you challenged him. Wasn't that how it was?"

"I didn't say so. Sir."

"You had an axe to grind."

Irritation egged him on. Thomas wanted to hear it all. He wanted the tall youth standing before him to speak. To brag of his extraordinary accomplishment.

"No, sir." Silence hung over the room long enough for Thomas to plan his next sentence before the youth finished his statement. "I don't even own an axe."

Blatant audacity. The Federal man from Washington slapped a hand on the desk.

"Who the hell are you?"

"Claw Kiley."

Not "Claudius Kiley." Not "The man who outgunned Red McGee." Just "Claw Kiley."

"You're a gunfighter."

"I can handle a gun."

"You think that's the way to tame a town?"

"I think it's a middle road."

"What's the beginning?"

"Fairness."

If Thomas had been smoking a cigar, it would have dropped from his mouth.

"Fairness?"

"Yes, sir. The duty of a law man is to uphold the law fairly; to see that the rules apply to everyone."

"Is that what Jack Duvall taught you?"

"Among other men."

"What others?"

Another silence, this one longer, before Claw Kiley answered the interrogative.

"Jim Bennett; Dan Cord. There were more. What difference does it make?"

Claw did not want to discuss his past with these men; not coldly, not unemotionally. Duvall, Bennett, Cord. He could have named a dozen others. If ever a man could be said to have twelve fathers, Claw Kiley was that man. Each, in his own distinctive way, had raised him. Molded him. Made him what he was.

Jim Bennett had taught him how to read and write. The first word Claw remembered spelling was "law." Not a mere combination of oddly shaped symbols equating to some obscure concept; it existed as a living, breathing entity.

There's a right way and a wrong way to do everything, son, his memory heard Ol' Jim explain. *With the law, it's fairness what counts. Fairness and an' equal distribution of lead and mercy. You let those folks know you mean what you say an' that you have the backbone to back it up. Your word is what men understand, not some fancy book with gold lettering down the spine.*

You're all alone, Claw, Dan Cord had preached at another time, in another place. *If a man respects you, he'll come to understand the law. The law as you see it. An' in a frontier town, it's the law that matters.*

Claw Kiley had seen Marshal Duvall practice law in the fashion of an artist creating a masterpiece.

The funny thing about law, boy, is that you're never through with it. And it's never finished with you. You live it and you breathe it, day in and day out. It sticks with you where ever you go. You're never shed of it. One day, that law -- or the enforcement of it -- will kill you.

Not you! the boy of six years had cried. He could not imagine the world without Jack Duvall. *No one will ever get you!*

Everyone's 'got,' boy, at one time or another. I'll get mine. You'll get yours.

I won't let anyone get you. There had been tears in Claw's eyes which none of the men sitting around the campfire would have thought him childlike for shedding. The truth of the matter being, they were not dry-eyed themselves, for it was their fate, as well as Jack's, the man described.

You think I'll live forever, Claw? The elder had laughed with resignation.

Forever!

Wouldn't wish that on anyone. A man gets old, Claw. He slows down. He needs to rest. That's what death's all about. Going to rest.

Are you tired? I'll fetch your blankets --

The boy sitting cross-legged at the dying embers of a campfire was old enough to understand death. It had been his constant companion from a time before his birth, when his father had died. No one had ever told him how. Death had touched him as an infant when the fever took his mother. He had seen others who had once belonged to the group sitting around him, die in sundry and unpleasant ways. Yet he was still a child, and with a child's faith and obstinate lack of comprehension, denied the inevitable.

I ain't tired, yet. But I'll get there.

When? A command to speak the unknowable.

I don't know. Maybe I'll never know. Maybe the tiredness'll creep up on me unawares.

Tell me.

That's a tellin' only the Lord can speak, Claw Kiley. You ask the Lord.

I don't know the Lord. The lower lip of the six-year-old protruded and his blue eyes sparkled with moisture. *I know you.*

This boy's education has been sorely neglected, Jack Duvall had declared. *Who's gonna teach him about the Lord?*

Jim Oates had answered. Jim, the itinerant, the perpetual drifter who could never settle down. Of all the men gathered around the fire, Claw understood him least. Jim seemed to come and go at will, disappearing for months, a year at a time, then reemerging with a new scar, a limp, a decade of years added to his stooped back.

The Lord God is the creator of the universe; He's the overseer.

Claw heard one of the others make a low comment under his breath and did not comprehend. He had no awareness of dialects, or Mason-Dixon lines or slavery. He had been taught to judge a man by looking in his eyes. He did not know the word "overseer." It would be years before he heard it again, and then, not in any context remotely associated with the Lord.

The Lord ain't a man and he ain't a beast but he's in every man and every beast. He's in the mountains, the streams; He's seen around droughts an' floods an' famines. They say He's in churches, too. You'll have to judge that fer yerself.

Jim Oates had died that winter. He was thrown from a horse and broke his leg. It was a bad break, the kind where bone shows through. His blood got poisoned, they said, and he died from the fever which wore his massive, sinewy body down to nothing.

Jim Oates had assumed responsibility for teaching Claw Kiley about the Lord because everyone at that campfire knew he would be the first among them to die. After they buried him, with his head resting on the same saddle from which he had been thrown, no one answered the boy's plaintive question about whether the Lord had been in the fever that took him off.

It was the kind of question each man had to answer for himself.

Men came and men went from that little group. It was a small, elite pact of men with nothing in common but toughness and the will to make something better of the hand God had dealt them. Claw grew to know them all, and all, in turn, taught the stripling. Some were trappers and took him away to follow the trail of the beaver up the winding rivers of the uncharted wilderness. Others hunted buffalo alongside the Red Man, who was neither friend nor foe, but just another band of wanderers trying to stay alive.

They taught Claw how to hunt and fish and speak "Injun," and how to live through a winter, when the snow piled high and time hung heavy. They taught him other things, too; things that would take a lifetime to fully understand.

Some were law men and some were lawless. All were good with a gun and they saw to it their common-law boy was adept at handling firearms. Some shot first and asked questions later; others were talkers, chewing off a man's ear while wrangling a gun from his grasp. All were survivors, and each, in his way, had a hand in the making of the youth who stood before Mr. Greg Thomas asking for a job.

How could he explain?

In the end, Claw Kiley could not explain, and so said nothing.

"There's been two sheriffs and one Federal marshal gunned down on the streets of Hellhole in the last twelve months. What makes you think you can do better?"

He really demanded to know why the man known as Claw Kiley thought he would succeed when older, wiser, more experienced peacekeepers had failed.

"I was born and bred for a lawman."

He did not say, for it was not Greg Thomas's business to hear, that the Lord hadn't spoken to him; that the whispered, intangible warnings Jim Oates and Jack Duvall and Jim Bennett and Dan Cord heard before their deaths had been withheld. His time had not arrived.

He understood as a man, what had been beyond the comprehension of a six-year-old child.

His hour would come. But not until he proved himself.

Not until he had walked the dry, dusty streets of his own town, a marshal's badge pinned to his shirt.

He knew his destiny.

It had been inscribed in the ashes of long ago campfires.

"You think you can bring fairness to a lawless country?"

"I don't think it, sir. I know it."

That damned audacity, again. Greg Thomas did not like the tall youth standing before him. There was something about him; something he could not put his finger on. Perhaps it was the restlessness, the sense of wildness he exuded. The calm demeanor, the quiet reserve. To be a marshal, a man had to talk tall, not stand tall. He had to have a roughness, an edge. He had to have lived life, seized it with his teeth, torn off hunks of flesh, consumed it raw.

He had to respect authority. Greg Thomas was that authority and he had the distinct impression Claw Kiley did not respect him.

"Have any money?"

"Enough for stage fare and a box of shotgun shells."

"And if I turn you down?"

"I'll go somewhere else."

"Where?"

"Where ever a lawman is needed."

"Give him an advance on his salary." He directed the order at the clerk.

The pencil-pusher flinched and stared at the government man in stark amazement.

"An advance on what salary?"

"On his U.S. marshal's salary. Give him sixty dollars."

"I'll take ten." Both men looked with undisguised wonder at the newly hired marshal. "I don't want more than is coming to me."

"You'll get what's coming to you -- and more," Thomas predicted. "Send him the rest on the 30th. Sixty a month and found," he added, craning his neck to stare up at the lawman. "That suit you?"

"Yes, sir."

"For how long?"

A rhetorical question.

Greg Thomas rose, feeling no less awkward when standing on his feet.

"If you live up to your height, you'll be a big man -- Marshal Kiley."

The new use of Claw's title presented the first occasion for him to smile. When he did, the grin spread from ear to ear, highlighting the boyish cast to his face. At twenty-three, his masculine features had not quite set, leaving the two office men with the impression of freshly molded clay. The days, months, years would take their toll on Claw Kiley. The next time they saw him -- if he lived long enough -- his face would wear a new set of lines, a road map of wrinkles. Each, in his own way, wondered if Kiley knew what he was getting into.

And then dismissed the subject. They had done their job. It was now up to Kiley to do his.

"Good luck, Marshal."

Thomas stuck out his hand as an obligatory good-bye. Claw took it, fingers closing around the other's fleshy digits.

"I'll be out on the stage today."

"Take your time. Wait a week."

Claw did not have to ask the question; he expressed it in his eyes.

Why?

Thomas shrugged, then nodded toward the door. The marshal understood and left, his long strides covering the distance in a second. Before either could call him back, were they of a mind, he had gone.

Vanished.

As though he had been no more than the ghost of Marshal Duvall or Marshal Bennett or Sheriff Cord.

"I never heard of offerin' a man his salary in advance," the local man announced once they were alone. "Mind if I ask why?"

"Not at all."

Despite the quickness of his agreement, the answer proved long in coming. When it did, the words were spoken in a deaden, almost resigned tone.

"I didn't want Kiley to die without a penny in his pocket. The undertaker'll have to make an extra-long coffin for him. No sense the buryin' man losing out because of my mistake."

"You think you made a mistake?"

Thomas poked a back tooth with a wooden splinter he had picked off a rough area on the front of the oak desk and shrugged.

"He'll either be dead within the year, or the governor in ten. Either way, I won't have done him any favors."

Sparrow snickered and wiped his brow.

"The man who killed Red McGee in a showdown. That's what he'll be known for. It don't matter what he does -- or doesn't do -- in Hellhole. And I met him. Imagine that."

"Yeah," Thomas agreed, squaring his shoulders. He could not shake the impression of being short and insignificant after the interview with the new marshal. "The real irony is, he could make a hundred times more money as a gunfighter than a marshal." He coughed into his hand, an early warning of consumption, then scuffed his foot, figuratively washing his hands of the affair. "Damn fool."

It was as well for his new employer that the "damn fool" did not hear him. While Thomas debated his fate, Claw walked to the stage depot and purchased a one-way ticket for Hellhole. He would not have understood the admonition, but he would have marked it.

And the speaker. For a skeptic.

Claw Kiley had a lot to prove, not only to those who doubted his ability, but to himself.

That he would do.

Even if he had to die trying.

He had proud footsteps to follow.

Ada Duvall, Jack's widow, would have cursed Claw Kiley for the sentiment.

CHAPTER 2

The sky presented an unbroken expanse of blue, as though there never had been and never would be a cloud there to break the monotony. The breeze, had there been any, was defeated by the cloth window coverings draped over the gaping holes which the Overland Stage Line euphemistically referred to as windows.

The shades were drawn to keep the swirling, stinging, penetrating dust to a minimum. A hopeless cause, the necessary action also cast a preternatural gloom over the interior of the coach. Not for the first time did the new marshal of Hellhole wish he had taken the driver up on his offer to sit atop and keep him company.

His refusal had more to do with vanity than wind burn and the scorched face he stood likely to get from long, unbroken exposure to the sun. He had heard it said once that only shotguns, gamblers and prostitutes ever rode with the driver.

Claw Kiley was young enough and proud enough not to want to be thought of as any of those types.

Some would say too young. Too proud. But youth would be served and Claw rode on without complaint.

There would be time enough for that later.

He did not own a watch and his chances of catching a glimpse of the sun for any close approximation of time was doubtful. He therefore had no idea the stage ran two hours late. Had he been aware, he might have worried that the welcoming committee would lose interest and disband before he arrived.

He had a lot to learn.

And a great deal of growing up to do, although in Kiley's case, it might rather be called "maturing," for at six feet, seven inches tall, he had already done all his physical growing.

Which made him a big target.

He had no idea how big.

He would find out.

That, too, would become part of the aging process.

She did not heard the rumbling wheels of the stage, the pounding of sixteen weary horses' hooves on the rutted road called Main Street, nor would she have had any occasion to meet that stage, had she known. The only reason Cougar Bradburn went through the swinging, bat-wing doors of the Lowdown Saloon was to escape boredom. There were two men inside the drinking establishment, both asleep. One hung over the bar, the other rested his head on his arm at one of the green felt-covered tables. Neither had spent as much as a nickel in the past hour, nor were likely to for several more.

Business would not pick up until after sundown, when the shops closed. Even then, there would be little for her to do. Being the dead season in Hellhole no one but the regulars, the occasional gambler, drifter and rag picker ever paused long enough for a drink.

Or the "horizontal refreshment," as the soldier's used to call their trips to the cat house. And probably still did, for all she knew.

"Cougar" Bradburn was a long way from home. As she stood on the wooden boardwalk with the prospect of nothing more drastic to contemplate than the beads of perspiration dripping from beneath her arm pits or down her cleavage, she wondered without much interest, what she was doing and where she was going. Like all the other perpetual wanderers, Hellhole was no more to her than a temporary haven, a stopping-off point before moving on.

In six months or a year, she would have enough money saved for a ticket out. A ticket to where? She did not know and did not particularly care. A ticket to anywhere. San Francisco, maybe. She heard the pickings were good there. But that had been years ago, and the news had been stale, then.

1849.

Not when he told her. The year men rushed to the gold fields in search of instant wealth.

Prospectors'll drop nuggets o' gold the size o' hail into a girl's drink, or pay her wid sacks o' yeller dust fer a trip upstairs. Them good ol' boys'll give her a wild night she'll niver fergit.

That's what he said, her confidant. She never learned his name. Or, over the years since then, she had forgotten it.

Gals is as scarce as hen's teeth in 'Frisco, he swore. *They flocked there from New York City an' Boston an' Philadelphee. A woman,* he emphasized with a chuckle that sounded dirty, *had real prospects in the City on the Bay.*

What made him laugh? she asked, and he replied, *'Cause o' the play on words. Prospects. Prospectors. They go hand-in-hand.* And he had tried to hold her hand. She had not let him, because at the time, she was not a "woman."

But she had been well on her way.

Girls could work a year or two an' earn their fortune. Buy a saloon of their own. Marry the mayor or the man who owned the dry goods store, or the preacher. Become a respectable woman. He said he knew, he had been there.

Perhaps he had.

It hardly mattered. He told a good story and bought a full bottle. That made everyone happy.

San Francisco. It had become a dream. If a girl did not have a dream, she had nothing.

Most girls had less than nothing.

Cougar Bradburn fancied she was not like most working girls. She was prettier than most, with copper-red hair and a face full of freckles which glowed in the sunshine. She had the endowments of a lady and her stature set her six inches taller than most men. She liked the distinction, because in her world, height meant respect. A paying customer would think twice about stiffing her.

She could also read and write and had the innate ability to stare a man in the eyes and tell whether he was worth the bother. She was nobody's fool and she had a dream.

If only she could hold onto it.

Dreams died every day on the streets of Hellhole.

Life stagnated. It withered and died in the oppressive heat and the dust storms. It shrank like the hides that skinners brought in to trade for spending money and whisky. Hellhole, Kansas, belonged to them: a town built to accommodate hiders. Rough, untamed and raw, it represented men and their lifestyle. Two or three times a year, when the buffalo-skinners, or the trappers made their migrations to town, life got good.

Men made merry in the saloons; they purchased pretty, store-made dresses for the girls, and shot out all the windows of the dry goods store when they thought they had been cheated, or just for fun.

They spoke in cuss words and Injun and they brawled like boys over a game of marbles or pig sticker. They had no higher ambition than to be the first in with their furs, or the first back on the trail. The man who could strip the hide off a still-quivering animal was king, and the greatest value they placed on worldly goods lay in the possession of a long, wickedly sharp knife.

During the long layovers when the hiders and the trappers were away, Hellhole reverted to a ghost town. Citizens who lived there year 'round fell into a lethargy. Existence was reduced to a standstill, where even the appearance of a card shark meant welcome company.

There had been talk, once, of the Army moving in, putting an outpost half a dozen miles out of town. Nothing had ever come of it. A year ago, a railroad man came through with a wad of bills thick enough to choke one of Jeff Davis' camels. He talked of the Iron Horse bringing in something he called "civil-i-zation," and of "stockholders" buying up property.

His wild predictions were scoffed at, because no one had ever heard of stock buying anything. Besides, the only cattle anywhere near Hellhole were wild scrubs, and of no use to anyone.

It was 1868 and there was no stage depot. The Founding Fathers had never seen reason to construct one. Hiders came on pack mules and gamblers rode paint ponies. Peddlers and tinware men got off the stage at the Lowdown and went in for a drink. They saw no point being let off at the edge of town and walking back.

Gunfighters and thieves arrived on horseback and left the same way, unless they took up residence of the permanent kind.

Dead men were always carted to Boot Hill in a wagon.

Unless they were left to lie in the street until the stray curs made short order of them.

In either case, none were ever heard to argue about the lack of a proper depot.

The stage had already rolled to a stop before she bothered to turn her eyes toward it. There was a fleeting hope that a tenderhorn with a pale face and a billfold stuffed with Eastern cash would climb down, survey his surroundings and head for the saloon. A faint hope, at best, but claiming only a score of years to her credit, hope had not yet died in her breast.

That set her apart.

That and the dream.

She did not pay the stage any particular attention. She remembered that clearly, for the moment would be etched in her mind the rest of her life. She had only stepped outside for a breath of air.

She would have sworn to it, had anyone asked.

At twenty years of age, Cougar could curse with the best of them.

Two passengers emerged from the door opposite her vantage point. This came as no surprise. The door facing her had been permanently sealed, the latch soldered shut by an errant bullet from a stage robber's gun. The Line had not seen fit to repair the damage. With one door working, management figured no one had cause to complain.

Two men got off the stage. Deprived of any chance at seeing inside the coach, for the shades were drawn, she counted legs. In possession of an education of sorts, she knew two plus two made four. Four legs equaled two men.

The first stranger caught his red and brown carpetbag thrown down by the driver and walked around the back of the stage. Men always walked that way. It was some unwritten law. Never toward the front, where the horses were. She presumed they were afraid the driver would ask their help in unhitching the tired, sweaty, irritable animals.

Women invariably walked toward the front. They had no cause to suppose their assistance would be required.

Nor did they have enough sense to worry that an inattentive driver would fail to secure the reins so the horses would not begin moving of their own accord and trample them.

Therein lay the difference between men and women.

Still out of view, the second passenger paused in the street once he had caught his small valise. She could not imagine why. There was nothing to look at from that perspective. The saloon was across from him.

All roads led to the Lowdown.

Not until the driver resumed his seat and urged the team forward did she get a decent look. He was turning to face her and their eyes met. Locked. A second, no longer. She remembered.

She would remember that look all her born days.

If she lived to be one thousand years old. As old as one of those characters from the Old Testament. Older.

He was the tallest man she had ever seen, but his eyes were what set him apart. They were of a bright blue, the kind which paralleled the sky for intensity. But it was more than that. Much more, although her mind would take seconds, years to calculate the difference.

Call it a sentience.

She might have, had she known the word.

He stretched high as a mountain, broad shouldered and young. He wore a traveling jacket, poorly fit for his lanky frame, an off-white cowboy hat which failed to cover the slight curl of blond hair reaching the edge of his shirt collar, and a gun belt around his waist. The pistol hung low, like a gunfighter, the leather holster thong dangling loose.

He was a gunfighter, all right. A damned good one.

She ought to know.

She had seen enough of them.

Too many.

Knowing what he did, did not tell her the whole story.

Knowing what she did told him only part of hers.

The instant they connected, Claw Kiley became a marked man. His future, as he so carefully planned it, forever altered. He meant to be a loner, as destiny decreed for most who wore the star. He did not want to be a widowmaker. He had seen too many women stand in too many streets, wet eyes staring down at the dead bodies of their husbands.

He had witnessed Ada Duvall set her jaw and clench her fists as she buried her man. Even with the casket closed, Claw knew Ada's eyes were deader than her husband's.

He did not want to see the wasted, haunted, empty stare of the woman he loved standing over his bullet-ridden corpse.

The fact his own eyes would be forever sealed did not register with the young marshal. The imagining was enough. Tragedy waited in the dirt of the dry, wind-swept Kansas town.

Main Street. Back Street. On the floor of the Lowdown saloon. Behind the stable. On the prairie. With a bullet in his back. Shot through the heart. Called out and beaten by a faster gun. Ambushed from behind. Dead of a rattlesnake bite. Blood poisoned from a broken bone sustained in a fall.

A marshal died in many ways but never from old age.

The one absolute certainly in life wore the cloak of the Grim Reaper.

Ten dollars for a coffin, two dollars for the preacher, and the lawman temporarily assigned to take his place, standing beside a gawking hole in the ground, six feet deep. One woman, silently weeping. One man, silently praying he would not be the next to occupy a hole on Boot Hill. One minister repeating words he had memorized and repeated so often they had lost all meaning.

A squalling infant. Another hiding behind the skirts, cloth soiled at the bottom from tramping in the damp earth of the newly dug grave. Enough money for a stage ticket out of Hellhole. Where would they go?

Deep down below.

A macabre rhyme.

Of the kind only lawmen laughed at.

Without humor.

As a charm, maybe. Against it happening to them.

They stood on Main Street, the marshal and the saloon girl, silently communing with one another. Names were not important. They would come later. The dark poem dissipated from his memory like dry leaves blowing in the wind. Last years' dead leaves. Spring would come.

Like love.

Claw Kiley had never meant to fall in love. He knew nothing of it, firsthand.

Cougar Bradburn thought she knew all about love. It meant an upstairs room and five dollars saved to put on a stage ticket west.

They were both terribly young. They had a lot to learn.

A moment, no more. In all eternity, just a second. A heartbeat.

Ada Duvall would have understood. She could have explained love. And then she would have warned them.

Already too late.

She would have said the *law* was a widowmaker. Only one pair of ears would have heard her.

She could have said her memories sustained her. Only one pair of ears would have detected the lie.

The widow of the lawman killed by Red McGee might have pointed upward. Neither Claw Kiley nor Cougar Bradburn would have followed her direction. They were not interested in tomorrow.

Tomorrow would wait. For another day.

The saloon girl pulled at the dress strap which had slipped off her shoulder and disappeared back into the heat of the interior. She expected the stranger to accept her invitation. When he did not, she crossed to a window and looked out.

He had gone.

Vanished.

She wondered if he had ever really been there.

For the first time.

The call of the law had been louder than the silent summons issued by the red-headed woman. From the corner of his eye he had seen the Marshal's Office. His heart gave a thump of another kind, and he heeded that first.

Ada Duvall would never have forgiven him.

The Marshal's Office had been built opposite the saloon and two doors down. Claw walked across the street, leaving a trail of footprints in the dirt. Dust clung to his boots, reached up and adhered to the cuffs of his trousers.

The beginning of a new life.

The death of an old.

He paused outside the office and studied the faded sign fastened to the brick wall by two rusty nails.

United States Marshal, Hellhole, Kansas.

He read the words, repeated them like a prayer. Home. He had found his place in the world.

A bulletin board hung beside the sign, decorated with wanted posters, curling at the edges and faded by the sun. He did not recognize any of the faces staring back at him through ink-weary eyes. The names of the criminals were unfamiliar. He would learn them all. Part of the job.

In a manner of speaking, they were his constituents.

Claw Kiley, United States marshal.

He absorbed the dignity of the sentence. The sense of righteousness.

He had come to bring law and order to Hellhole.

Law and order and fairness.

The fingers of his left hand enveloped the knob and turned it, while his body prepared to slip easily into his office. The door did not open and he hit the immobile wood with a resounding thud. Propelled back, the new lawman nearly lost his balance.

The pride of ownership faded into embarrassed indignation and he turned quickly, looking around to see if anyone had observed his ignoble fate.

No one had.

At least, no one his eagle-eyes detected.

The woman at the window of the Lowdown had disappeared.

With a smile on her face.

As though she had never been there.

Claw tried the knob again, with the same result. Feeling his face grow red with shame, he peered through the curtainless window. No one inside. If the door were locked, it stood to reason the office was empty. He did not wonder why he bothered; he felt too angry to question himself.

Youth would be served.

Marshal Kiley pounded on the window, then banged on the door. None but the ghosts of lawmen past heard, and they did not bother unfastening the latch. Perhaps they considered the effort not worth their while. After all, they might have reasoned, the new man would not be in Hellhole long.

Not in a corporeal sense.

Not in any sense that mattered.

Feeding grave worms had never amounted to much in the scheme of things.

That, they could testify to in the Court of the Deceased.

"Hello!" Claw called. "Anyone in here?"

A spider, resting comfortably in the corner of the window, roused itself and scurried up its web. The fly, recently snared, could wait. The sole prisoner in the jail, its sentence had already been served.

Claw kicked the solid door in a fit of pique, then hopped back, regretting his impatience. Beginning his new job with a sore toe did not fit the picture he had imagined.

If the door were locked, then someone had a key. That stood to reason. He limped across the street and entered the dry goods store. That door, at least, opened to his touch.

It fell under the category of making progress.

The owner behind the counter rested his hand on the stock of a prominently placed shotgun. This did not deter him from his task of rearranging boxes of shotgun shells.

"My name is Claw Kiley. I'm the new marshal in Hellhole. The office is locked. Do you know who has the key?"

Such an announcement was tantamount to saying *I do not have any money. Can you give me a loan until payday?* The man's lip curled into a sneer.

"Don't know that anybody has the key."

"Someone must have it."

"Why?"

"Someone locked the door with a key."

"Maybe they buried it with that last fella."

"Maybe they didn't."

"I don't have it."

The shopkeeper returned to work, preparing his stock for the paying customers.

Perhaps someone had telegraphed ahead that Claw left Topeka without his full months' salary.

And neglected to mention that the new marshal had enough money left after purchasing his stage ticket for one box of shotgun shells.

"Who's in charge in Hellhole?"

"You are, I expect."

"Before I arrived. Who was in charge before I arrived?"

"You could ask at the Lowdown. Bix Bradley owns it. He might have the key."

"Why would the owner of the saloon have the key to the Marshal's Office?"

"I don't know."

"Thank you."

Claw tipped his hat to the owner and walked out, no richer than when he had entered the store.

No poorer, either, in a monetary sense.

Providing a small modicum of comfort.

His education had advanced one grade.

Striding across the dust-dry street, a cur nipped at his heel. Hoping to make at least one friend, Claw leaned back and extended in hand. The dog snarled. Annoyed, he withdrew his fingers while making a threatening gesture. While thus occupied, he did not see the pile of horse maneuver until he had stepped into it.

The dog did not laugh.

Neither did Claw.

Wiping his boot on the edge of an empty water trough, Claw returned to the locked office which would serve as his residence for as long as he marshaled in Hellhole. Feeling foolish, he tried the door again.

Locked.

Eyes slanted in irritation, he took hold of the knob and pulled. No luck. Gritting his teeth in determination, he lowered his shoulder and threw his weight against the wooden structure. The walls shook and the glass in the windows rattled but the door held.

He cursed to himself, for to swear out loud at an inanimate object seemed pointless.

If this were meant to be his first challenge, then so be it. With the will of a man being thwarted by Fate, Claw kicked the door with all his strength. It resisted his blow.

Hands akimbo, he tried flattery.

"It the cells are as sturdy as you are, no one will ever break out of my jail."

Without waiting for an answer, he raised his foot and smashed it against the wood. A sound of splintering, compounded by the twisting of metal, preceded the lock twisting from the frame. The door limped open.

With a sigh of triumph, Claw entered his abode with the pride of a charioteer passing the gates of Rome at the head of a conquering army.

He had not been named Claudius for nothing.

The fact this action mitigated his previous statement remained a moot point.

Inside, motes of dust exploded out of nowhere, obscuring his vision, making him cough. Long unoccupied, the office had the feel of an empty crypt, awaiting its next victim.

Taking in the room at a glance, his attention fixed on a large, framed, hand-colored map of Masson County mounted behind the desk. His territory. He would study it later, memorize the boundaries, come to know the lay of the land: barren prairie, gentle rolling hills, water holes, barankas.

Masson county. He did not know why the area had been so named. After an early explorer, a landowner named Masson, an Indian fighter? Or had some old trapper bestowed the moniker after a jar of preserves he particularly favored?

He would have to ask.

Perhaps "Bix Bradley" could supply the answer.

It never occurred to Claw to question the name "Hellhole." Likely he did not wish to know. Or it may have been that he already had a sense. The bane of hell. Bane, as he understood it, meant irritation. Hellhole, then was a burr on the backside of the devil.

"I like that," he said aloud. Then, turning to the open entranceway with its listing door, he served his first edict. "Be forewarned."

Outside, a wild dog howled. The rabble, it seemed to portend, were waiting for their bread and circuses. A fitting welcome for a man named after a Roman emperor.

CHAPTER 3

Claw originally planned on acquainting himself with the town, but the dismal aspect of the office altered his mind. With a shrug of acquiesce and the youthful enthusiasm of a man who knows he has come face-to-face with his destiny, the marshal took stock of the interior.

The inventory-taking required exactly twelve minutes.

Had he not paused to stare forlornly out the window, he could have completed the task in a little under three.

Enthusiasm, like youth, was not eternal.

There accounted, to wit: one swivel chair, oak; one desk, oak. One pair of stacked wooden receptacles pushed to one corner, the higher for "In," the lower for "Out." Lowering himself into the chair, Claw slowly opened the drawers. There were seven in all: three to either side, one centered. All empty, except for a marshal's badge, placed in the top, left-hand drawer.

The left being commonly referred to as the side of the devil.

Claw did not pursue the topic.

To do so would have tempted Fate.

Pinning the badge to his shirt, he rubbed it with the sleeve of his right arm until it glistened, then grabbed hold of the metal and stared at it.

U. S. Marshal.

He closed his eyes, letting the sensation of power, the euphoria of finally having found his place in life, wash over him. United States marshal. He ran the words over in his mind, carefully pronouncing each, as though they were the beginnings of a prayer.

United-States-marshal.

Truthfully, Claw did not stray from the mark. Those three words would become the mantra by which he lived. They would protect him from debilitating bullets of lawless men, broken whisky bottles of saloon drunks, wildly careening wheels of runaway stages. They would be his defense against drought, high winds, sleet and blinding snow storms, twisted gullies and renegade Redskins.

United States marshal.

The three most important words in the English language.

They would keep his heart, if not his bed, warm at night, because in and through them lived constancy, stability, respect. They signified him as a representative of "civil-i-zation," a man chosen by the leaders of his country to stand tall when everyone around him quavered. They conveyed power, righteousness, faith. In and around those three words were Claw Kiley's religion.

They would protect him from everything but death.

That, he told himself, he understood with a dread certainty.

It was not the first time Claw Kiley ever lied to himself; it would not be the last. But it would come close to being the most dangerous fabrication he had ever heard, ever uttered, ever believed.

He had been suckled on milk bought by lawman's blood; had been lulled to sleep listening to every gruesome story ever concocted on how peacekeepers perished. He could recite the names of sheriffs who had been shot in the line of duty the way priests enumerated the holy deeds of saints.

He had been privy, from an early age, to the bitter joke lawmen whispered to one another about why the badge was worn on the left side of the body, just above the heart.

To give the outlaws a target.

To symbolize marriage.

Ask any lawman's wife. She would hold up her wedding ring finger and point to the gold band. Then she would cast an equally stiff pointer finger at her husband's chest.

Although she had married him, he had married the law.

A gold band for her, a silver star for him.

Precious metals.

No one had to remind her that the badge was not really silver, but nickel.

That irony struck home when she tried to cash in his years of service and found them worthless.

For her job of upholding the man who upheld the law she received nothing but a bill from the undertaker and the remainder of his "sixty a month and found."

It gave the word "married" an entirely new meaning.

Claw Kiley believed, with the faith of a neophyte, that the words and the badge were a troth. That together, they created an aura of protection, a sense of worth and purpose which could not be severed by bullets, knives, saints or demons. He did not think he would live forever. That would be impossible, probably undesirable. But he would survive long enough to bring security to an untamed, untamable land.

No man ever assumed the responsibility of keeping the peace without believing in himself. In his Cause. In his ability to survive against all odds.

Which explained why so many were buried on the plains, the prairies, shoved into outspurs of baranka, or covered with brush and tumbleweeds. Why warehouses back East always stocked tombstones with the emblem of "the star" deeply engraved on top, ready for immediate shipment to all points West. Why reporters wrote lurid copy about "he who walked the streets alone," and why publishing houses printed sensational, yellow-jacketed penny novels detailing how they died.

Dead heroes all.

Dead men, who had believed in themselves just as much as Claw Kiley did.

Brave men who wore the badge and thought the utter need for their services would somehow spare them from the ignoble fate of their predecessors.

Schooled by men whose fame outlived them, Kiley represented the substance if not the shadow of his mentors. They taught him how to use a gun, ball his fists, ride a horse, staunch his bleeding. When they had done all that, they instilled in him a quiet sense of modesty, for brave men had no need of bragging.

Claw represented their legacy to the frontier. To him, they passed the torch. Once, they had been the best. Now, it was his turn. That explained why he stood in a nearly naked office in Hellhole, Kansas, pinning a badge of dull nickel to his light blue shirt. He knew he would be there tomorrow and the day after and the day after that.

If he were not, he would never know it.

Without rationalization, he took comfort in the thought.

Being a realist, Claw could tell his best friend that one day he would not return. He could explain to the woman who loved him that eventually a man with a faster gun would shoot him down in the street. He would pay his stable bill two weeks in advance so his horse would not suffer if he were kidnapped and killed. He would never buy more than a pound of coffee at one time, for it went against his thrifty nature to stock the office for he who would succeed him.

He would not consider himself a liar when he spoke to his best friend, his woman, or when he paid his livery fees. He would be telling the truth.

But only part of it. For deep inside, he prayed to the god of Jack Duvall and Jim Bennett and Jim Oates and Dan Cord. The Spirit in the sky who protected those who wore the badge. They believed, as he believed, in the magic of the star.

Protect me, for I am one of the chosen. I perform your work. I preserve your people.

If only that were true, Claw Kiley would not have been his fathers' orphan.

And Ada Duvall would never have draped herself in black.

No badge known to Man could sustain the life in a body torn asunder by a dozen bullets fired from high-calibre rifles. Or even a derringer, fired at close range.

The god of lawmen was not He to whom the good people of Hellhole prayed. The deity of the lonely and the loner existed for the sole province of the lemmings, those poisonous creatures which died from their own venom. The heavenly patron to whom Claw Kiley's prayers were unknowingly directed put him in a league with aging gunfighters, rainmakers and branc- water faith healers, for they were all cut from the same pattern.

The mold of fools.

Which the frontier gave birth to every day.

And killed as many more. By younger, faster gunmen, irate townspeople dying from thirst and uncured cripples.

To survive a year bucked the odds.

To make a career required a man to walk on the side of the angels.

No one had ever seen an angel in Hellhole.

Or anywhere else in Kansas.

The last sighting of an angel in the United States had been in Philadelphia in 1799. And that, for all intents and purposes, had gone unsubstantiated.

When all the thinking had been done, when the deceivingly heavy feather-weight of the badge had been assimilated into his body so he no longer bore an awareness of it, and the inventory of the desk complete, Claw turned his attention to the rest of the office.

A set of keys dangled from a peg on the wall. Slipping them off with assumed ease, as though he had performed that same task one hundred times, the marshal opened the door to the back and peered inside. He counted three cells, left, right and center. All empty of human occupation. A good thing, for the last man to have gone through that portal had probably done so months ago.

Each cell contained one bunk, a scratchy woolen blanket which might have been cast-off army issue, a flattened and stained pillow with the obligatory faded blue striping and a piss pot. From the emanating stench, he deduced they had done good service, and then, like crippled soldiers, been abandoned by their country.

He would have to clean them. But not now.

Quickly retreating, he closed the door behind him. The keys were replaced on the peg. Instantly, a thin layer of dust settled over them. From all outward appearances, the ring had not been disturbed in weeks.

Moving into the center of the office, he surveyed the contents, or lack thereof. Scrape marks on the floor alluded to the actuality that a table and chairs had once been present, forcing him to conclude that anything portable had escaped long before some unseen hand had locked the door. The fact blankets, pillows and brass receptacles remained behind did not speak well for their respectability.

Or their value.

The fact that the marshal's badge remained behind did not speak well for the job.

Or the nickel from which it had been fashioned.

Or the country it represented.

What it spoke to the new man who wore it was lost to contemplation.

A bunk, built into the wall, sat in a small alcove at the left, rear of the office. From this moment on, until he resigned, retired or died, that bed would be the sole modicum of comfort afforded the lawman. It would shelter him while he dreamed, watch over him as he lay awake at night, eyes wide open, too tired to sleep. It would offer him respite when his sutured body came home from the doctor's office, shot in places most medical men would be hard-pressed to name. It would lie empty more nights than not. Waiting, always waiting.

Waiting for someone to sleep in it.

The identity of the sleeper notwithstanding.

Beds were known to possess very little loyalty.

The only thing this bed could not do, would be to comfort two people at the same time.

If anyone asked her, Mrs. Duvall would vouch for that.

Claw Kiley would never ask her.

He did not have to.

Jack Duvall had already explained the situation.

Marshals Duvall and Bennett and *Sheriff* Cord had all told him. About the creed, the catechism, the one unbroken rule no lawmen transgressed.

Never take your woman *home* with you.

Never let her know.

Never let her see your haunted face, your fear-filled eyes, your shivering, bowel-loosening dread. Your tear-stained, stubbled cheeks. Your shaking hands.

The bed was the only confessor a lawman had. It had taken vows. Been sworn to secrecy. It had no lips; expressed no judgments. It made no more than solitary creaks; offered only a pillow's sigh, or the slight crackle of static electricity from hair touching shiny, worn-down cloth. Those were the only sparks this bed would generate.

Any others would come from dreams.

Like a dead man, the bed told no tales. It served as best friend, worst enemy, harboring nightmares and absorbing cheap whisky. Lumpy and hard, it smelled of sweat and gunpowder residue. Beneath the mattress, a Bible or a pistol. To its side, a pair of boots and over the foot board, a stiffening set of socks. While pretend wives and lovers crept in and out, their imaginary presence kept at bay the child no lawman had a right to father. Under its protective blanket, the bed hid from the world the countenance of the frightened man who would arise at dawn to put on his peacekeeper's face.

Putting aside those issues of larger import, Claw stretched out on the bunk, inadvertently hitting his head against the wall. Not ordinarily a cursing man, the discomfort elicited a growl of annoyance.

"Son of a bitch!"

His feet hung over the bottom by seven inches. There could be no thought of lying flat. That meant curling up.

It was as well the marshal was not a doctor. He did not know the meaning of the words "fetal position," or what they implied.

The idea of sleeping on a bed constructed for someone a foot shorter than he presented an unappealing picture. He would have to see what could be done about extending it. Carpenter's work cost money. He would write to Hays.

That reminded him of his first official obligation. He must telegraph his superiors, notifying them of his arrival. It would give him an excuse to provide information concerning the deficiencies in the office. No doubt they would appreciate knowing there were no pencils, paper, pen and ink; no rifles, no ammunition.

Nor a key for the front door. Which now needed repairing. He decided he would not explain exactly what happened. No point going into extraneous details.

Never overload the bureaucratic mind with too much information, one of his surrogate fathers had once lectured.

Good advice. Being a practical man, Claw knew when to take suggestions.

Pushing off by a hand to the floor, he continued the inspection with considerably less enthusiasm. To the right of the door as one entered the office squatted a bulky cast iron stove. Miraculously, the hinges of the pot belly appeared intact. He did not have to look inside to determine the grate full of ashes and the charred remains of saplings, crate slats and trash.

Small trees were free for the harvesting, wooden boxes came from cluttered alleyways and burning garbage saved the short walk to the window to toss out remnants of an indigestible meal, outdated wanted posters and cartridge cases.

Nothing plus nothing plus nothing equaled one: the savings of a dollar a month off his office budget. He could perform that sum before his third birthday.

A dented coffee pot rested atop the burner. Its black-speckled enameled surface struck a chord of familiarity. Every lawman's office of his acquaintance had one of similar appearance. It made him feel at home.

A faded red rag, presumably a ripped bandana, had been wrapped around the handle used to remove the hot plate. Beneath, on a narrow ledge, were four tole mugs. They and the pot were the only items not covered with dust. That, too, followed protocol. The windows might be covered with grime, the cells a pig sty and the desk a forlorn castoff, but a man must have his coffee. Even dust motes obeyed that law.

Two doors remained unopened. The first, situated at the foot of the bunk and adjacent to the left cell, presented a small storage room the size of a coffin. Empty shelves lined the walls. They would undoubtedly come in useful.

The second door led outside to the rear of the building. Crossing its threshold, Claw found himself in a narrow alley leading to an uncultivated patch of ground. Picking his way through the accumulation of empty bottles, sundry bits of firewood, balled-up flyers and last year's newspapers, he made his way to the outhouse. A half-moon smiled wanly down at him. Out of curiosity and sudden need, he used his elbow to push open the door.

A hole in the ground, half covered by a wooden commode seat, presented itself to his watchful inspection. A pile of wanted posters, wrapped in twine, rested by the seat. It was a toss-up whether the former occupants had used the paper for reading material to pass an uneventful session in the latrine, or to wipe themselves after their daily adulations.

With a disgusted grunt, Claw picked up the bundle, dotted with water spots and curled at the corners, and heaved it up the alley as far as it would go.

He discovered the well to the right of the House of Unspeakable Business. A rope curled around the bar suspended between the uprights. Claw cranked the handle and drew up the bucket. While intact, green slime coated the sides. He made a face, debating whether to cut it off and send it to join the bundled wanted posters, then thought better of it.

No need to be hasty.

He would mention the need for a new pail in his telegram to Hays.

The rope itself had recently been replaced. It bore an uncomfortable similarity to a hangman's hemp. The fact a noose-knot held the bucket nicely aided his identification. On impulse he undid the tie and straightened the kinked rope.

They did not hang men in Hellhole.

He felt a great urge to send it on to Hays but had a sneaking suspicion they would not see the humor in the situation.

Nor the need. Presumably they had enough rope in Hays to hang a dozen men.

Claw failed to realize that Hays had given him just enough rope to hang himself.

Had he known, he would not have seen the humor in the situation.

CHAPTER 4

Standing at his doorstep, the new marshal surveyed his town. From his vantage point, he could not readily identify any structure resembling a telegraph office. Rather than suffer the ignobility of having to ask directions, he began waking.

The central thoroughfare, called Main Street, ran the entire length of the town. Claw's office lay at the eastern end with an open field beyond, as if the building had been an afterthought. A narrow alley separated his place of work from a small shop to the left. Leading to it, a rickety, semi-permanent boardwalk had been installed. No sign in the shop window identified its purpose. Claw could only guess what transpired there. Something which required or received merchandise packed in crates, if the broken boxes and scattered nails he had seen out back were any indication.

Further up the street on the same side were other nondescript shops and a post office. The windows were shuttered as Claw passed. Considering summer business hours generally went until 6 P.M., he could not determine whether the closed appearance reflected the fact the mail center had ceased all operation, or the United States government had no postmaster or clerks to operate their sideline.

Opposite the Marshal's Office but set back almost a street and a half, he noted the livery. He would have to stop there soon, perhaps tomorrow, and arrange to buy a horse. Purchasing an animal from the owner would not only establish good will, it would prompt him to secure his reputation by taking better care of it.

Several hundred yards beyond the stable and flush to the boardwalk stood the Lowdown Saloon. He would no doubt become well familiar with that watering hole.

As saloons went, the Lowdown was typical of the type thrown up in hide towns. The "On Draught" signs displayed in the windows were the same statewide; the swinging batwing doors similar, although these did have the distinction of meeting evenly at the center. He supposed the spacious drinking and gambling room filled with round, green-felted tables, with the bar to his right as he entered and stairs, leading up into rooms "where the girls slept" to the left.

One of his first orders of business would be to make the acquaintance of the owner and establish a relationship. It benefited the proprietor to befriend the law, and the law to have powerful allies. Saloon keepers were not invited to church socials or to sit on banking boards, but they controlled or handled large sums of money. As such, they were men to be reckoned with.

While Claw held a position of appointment rather than election and therefore did not need to cower before anyone in the hope of being re-elected year after year, standing at odds with the men who set the temper of the town meant trouble. Learning to give and take and occasionally look the other way served the type of frontier justice he had come to enforce.

Crossing the street, then heading west, he passed an alley between the Lowdown and its two nearest neighbors before coming upon Hellhole's primary restaurant, the "Regent." Staring through the windows, Claw saw small, intimate tables draped with red checkered cloths. Breathing through his nose, he detected the odor of coffee, lard and roasting beef. It reminded him he had not eaten. He would have to see about dinner before the afternoon slipped away.

Treading cautiously on the uneven boardwalk which swayed under his weight, he bypassed a dry goods store and a gunsmith's establishment. Several vacant lots later, he arrived at a two-story building, the lower level of which seemed to be vacant. Above, if the hand-painted sign were to be trusted, the town doctor practiced his art. The residence of the physician gave rise to idle speculation why any self-respecting man of medicine would set up shop in a place like Hellhole. But in his worldly wisdom, he already knew the answer.

The odds were good the doctor was not self-respecting.

For a man whose life would depend on the skills of the local tonic dispenser, that reality had a decidedly bad taste.

Learn how to take lead out of your own hide, Sheriff Cord had advised his protégée. *It saves the guess work.*

Cheaper, too, replied the ever-practical deputy.

Claw remembered that conversation because Dan had laughed at his eager pronouncement. He had failed to make the connection.

Irony played very little part of Claw Kiley's makeup.

Which probably explained why he had missed the sarcasm in Cord's advice. A man shot in the chest could not operate on himself.

Even if it were cheaper.

Reaching the end of Main Street, Marshal Kiley proceeded north, striking First Street which ran along the same east-west axis. Ten paces took him to the bank, a prominent clapboard and brick building, two doors in front, windows to either side. Situated on a large tract of open land, a hitching rail stood out front, while the wooden sidewalk, in questionable repair, sprawled toward a boarding house in the rear.

Squinting into the cloudless horizon, the lawman determined to take a long, hard at that building. From outward appearances and by reputation, which he already knew as the easiest bank in the west to rob, he could not let it go long. As it stood, the financial institution presented an open invitation. *A preacher,* he decided in annoyance, biting at a hangnail on his finger, *would be tempted to rob it.*

The "Devil's Hole," apparently the best hotel in town, had been constructed just beyond the weed-infested field. A shabby, two-story establishment, badly in need of paint, it offered accommodation for peddlers, passing travelers and the more well-to-do shop owners who rented rooms by the night or the week. As an inducement to make Hellhole a permanent home, it dismally failed. As an advertisement for the uncertain to move further west, it proved a godsend.

Ma Smitt's boarding house sat on an unnamed, dead-end side street. Curtains in the windows attested to the fact the "rooms to let" were indeed owned, or at least operated by, a woman. A sign in the window notified passers-by that "Home cooked meals" could be got at a "reasonable price," and that "Ma" served chicken pie every Monday.

Claw grunted as he patted his stomach. He had eaten enough chicken pie to know that the leftovers from Sunday's baked chicken constituted the prime ingredient.

Dry Street veered off above First Street. Shorter and in worse condition than the other thoroughfares, Claw quickly surmised the name referred to the lack of rain, rather than a dearth of watering holes. Here, the lower order of men drifted. Among others, it featured a seedy-looking saloon called the Wolf's Pelt, a boarding house for those down on their luck or their finances, and a barber shop. Surprisingly, the tonsorial boasted a "bath, reasonable rates," and "haircuts and shaves" by an "experienced barber."

Who had once been an Indian scout, Claw mused without amusement.

Shave and a scalp, two bits.

Strangely, the surmise made him feel at home.

The telegraph office had been squeezed into a small corner lot near the end of the street. Its doors were open. Doubtlessly explained by the fact the operator had no association with the United States government.

Stooping under the low archway, Claw looked around, listened a moment to the click-clack of the telegraph key, then approached the counter where a small, middle- aged man with a card dealer's cap perched on a high stool. The man did not bother to look up until he had finished his message. When he did, his eyes, focused at the level of Claw's badge, opened in wonder.

"You the new marshal?" he asked.

The beginning of a very superficial relationship.

Claw nodded, thinking, perhaps the clerk, who based his entire life on the calculation of words into dollars and cents, would charge him if he spoke.

"Come to send a telegram?"

He nodded a second time. If the marshal later went on to stump the state for the office of governor, the clerk would still think of him as a man of few words.

"You owe me two dollars and fifty cents."

"I haven't told you what I want to send, or to whom," came the somewhat exasperated protest.

"Last marshal died owing me two dollars and fifty cents. He had an account," the clerk apologetically explained, suddenly fearing Claw would draw his gun and point it toward his temple.

"The marshal did not owe you money; your due comes from the Federal government."

Feeling somewhat reassured that his life was not in danger, the key-tapper sniffed. "That may be, but it don't pay the bill that's owing."

Detecting an ill-concealed accent, Claw scowled. "That it don't," he acknowledged, making it clear he took the man's meaning and would not tolerate it. "I came to send a telegram to Topeka. You can fill out a receipt for any previous telegrams and present it to me for payment. At the marshal's office," he firmly concluded. "And see to it you don't pad the 'account.' I can have it checked." Hitching his thumbs in his gun belt, he added, "Owing two dollars and fifty cents, the 'last marshal' must have been a mighty wordy man."

"Yes, sir." Licking the end of his pencil, the operator repositioned himself on the seat. Issuing more of a challenge than an expectation, he blurted, "Can you write what you want to say, or do you want me to take it down for you?"

"What's your name?"

"Billy."

"Billy, what?"

"Billy Brindle."

"Take it down, Billy."

Challenge, thrown back.

"Yes, sir. To Topeka, you say?"

"That's right. Care of Mister Greg Thomas. Write that Claw -- say that Marshal Claudius Kiley -- has arrived in Hellhole and assumed his duties as of --" He glanced at the clock, made a quick calculation, then continued, "ten o'clock this morning."

Billy took the message, then expectantly looked up.

"Is that all?"

If he expected a book, as the former lawman apparently dictated, he was doomed to disappointment. While Claw had more to say, he decided to enclose it in a letter. No sense having his business spread over town before he had a chance to catch his breath.

"That's all. And Billy -- add the price of my telegram to that receipt you're gonna make out for the authorities."

"Yes, marshal."

The naturalness of his acknowledgement caught Claw off guard. He had been many things in his brief life, but the clerk's statement represented the first time anyone had called him marshal. It both began and completed a circle. In the middle of which lay the law. As it should be.

He left with a smile on his face.

The expression lingered as he made his way back to Main Street. Feeling in need of a drink and eager to explore other, newer sensations, he turned toward the Lowdown, pausing at the double doors long enough to survey the premises.

The layout was exactly as expected. Nodding in self-righteous congratulations, he sauntered to the bar with his best man-about-town swagger. Still early, he had the place to himself. With no one else to impress, he casually positioned himself at the bar so the bartender could not possibly miss the badge pinned so prominently to his shirt.

"What'll it be, mister?"

Shot down before he could draw his gun, Claw frowned and moved closer, actually leaning over the polished wood. The bartender backed off.

"A beer."

The barkeep drew his beer from one of the twin taps hidden beneath the counter. The height of the head attested to the heat of the day. Claw recalled that beneath the "On Draught" sign had been no accompanying one, indicating "Cold Beer."

Just as well. If there had been, he would have been forced to issue a citation to the owner, for his beer was as warm as the afternoon. But cooler than his blood, for when he raised his eyes and looked toward the second story, he saw *her* standing there. That woman. His smile of a moment ago widened into one the breadth of the Kansas River.

Twenty feet above floor level Cougar Bradburn peered down at the stranger, noting his peculiar facial expression. She thought she understood the intent, then checked herself. She had issued an invitation before and he had not accepted. If he thought to collect now, he had better get his priorities straight.

And he damned well better have his five dollars ready, she decided. There were no free trips upstairs in the Lowdown. Not when she had to pay Bix Bradley a quarter of her earnings.

Not a "quarter," Cougar reminded herself, making the distinction between two bits and a percentage. A full one-fourth of what she took from every hider, drifter, doctor, lawyer and Indian chief went to the owner. She learned fast how to calculate that fee. And ever faster how to lie about the money she collected.

No man needed to know everything.

A good rule to live by.

She would not get rich off it, but then, she would save herself from getting poorer.

Taking the steps one at a time to show herself off to advantage, she descended, approaching the cowboy with a firm, "Howdy."

She offered the expected greeting. In New Orleans, from where she hailed, a woman -- or a man -- beginning a conversation with the word "Howdy," would be looked at askance. But not on Hellhole. Not in this dusty, brash, isolated hide town. It was "Howdy," or it was silence.

"Ma'am."

The man tipped his hat and moved over a foot, although he stood alone at the bar and had no need to make room. She liked that.

More than she could have imagined.

"Buy you a beer?"

He spoke in soft, polite, respectful tones. She had almost forgotten how to apply those words to a man's voice. Or any other part of his anatomy.

"Sure."

Without being asked, the bartender drew the saloon girl a beer. She slipped her fingers around the glass handle with the same ease she used when slipping an arm around a man's waist and back. Leading him slowly toward a table, she spoke over her shoulder.

"How 'bout sitting down, giant?"

He made no move to follow. Cougar shot him a quizzical glance. A small frown had drawn his eyebrows into a "V."

"I'm not a giant," he explained with just enough pique to make her grin. "I'm the new marshal in Hellhole."

"Really?" she inquired with ill-disguised amusement.

"Really," he replied with sincerity.

"How 'bout sittin' down, Marshal?"

"Like to."

Before the words "Like to" dissipated into the sawdust on the floor, Miss Bradburn changed her mind. Bix Bradley's cut of her usual five dollar fee was one dollar and a "quarter." She could afford to be generous. With the marshal.

Walking with a longer stride, he reached the table first and dropped a hand on the back of a chair. With silent acknowledgement, Cougar allowed him to pull it out for her.

A gentleman.

In her school-book days, Cougar had looked up the precise meaning of that word. And decided she had never met such a creature.

Until today.

Revelations piled up.

"So... you're the new marshal."

"That's right."

From his talkative attitude, she drew the same conclusion as Billy Brindle.

"The last lawman in Hellhole was shot dead in the street."

"So I heard."

"The lawman before him was run off."

"Heard that, too."

"Plan to be here long?"

"The rest of my life."

The boyish enthusiasm elicited a laugh.

"How long you reckon that'll be?"

"No marshal I ever knew ever died of old age." Before she could reply, he added, "Or any saloon girl, either."

"Known many?"

"Lawmen?"

"Saloon girls."

"A few."

She wondered if "a few," constituted the lawman's equivalent of "a percentage."

"I see."

They sipped their beer. His stomach grumbled and she giggled. He blushed.

In order to mitigate his embarrassment, Claw shifted his weight and looked around the saloon.

"Who owns this place?"

"Man named Bix Bradley."

"What's he like?"

She shrugged. "Not much different than anyone else, I guess. Why do you ask?"

Not so much "Why do you ask?" as "Why do you ask *me*?" He understood and returned his eyes to her face. For a moment, the beauty of her features, the red glint of her hair, the soft scent of perfume disconcerted him and he forgot the question. She waited for his mind to return to business and counted thirty before he spoke.

"I've always found you could learn more about a man by askin' those who work for him, than by askin' the man himself."

"I have to agree with you," she replied, flattered by the statement. It had been a long time since her opinion had counted for anything.

All her life, perhaps.

"He's tight with a dollar, has an eye for the girls, deals for the House because he doesn't trust hired gamblers, and he paid the last marshal two dollars a week to let the saloon stay open till midnight."

Claw grunted, wiping an accumulation of sweat from his brow.

"He won't have to pay me."

"That mean you'll make him lock up at ten?"

"Nope. I don't have any problem with him keepin' the doors open 'til midnight. He just doesn't need to bribe me."

"Never look the gift of two dollars a week in the mouth," she sharply retorted, then regretted her boldness and bit her lower lip.

"It's not a gift, Miss --"

"Bradburn. Cougar Bradburn. It's sort of a play on my real name."

"Which is?"

"Caroline," she whispered, feeling shy and embarrassed at the confession.

"I'm Claw Kiley," he introduced. "Short for Claudius. Which makes more sense than makin' Cougar out of Caroline."

"*Marshal* Kiley," she corrected, remembering the scene at the bar.

"First time I've been a marshal. I like the sound of it." Both an admission and an apology. Cougar Bradburn was as unfamiliar with apologies as she was with men asking her opinion.

"You look like a marshal. Marshal Kiley. It suits you."

She wondered how soon she would regret the statement.

"Thank you."

"But that doesn't mean you ought to look a 'gift' in the mouth. Two dollars comes dear. I don't imagine Hays pays you what you're worth."

"Then we have something in common."

"What's that?" she asked. Too quickly.

"We're both underpaid."

She caught her breath, then exhaled slowly. "I'll drink to that."

They raised their mugs and sipped beer. The brew had gone flat. Both were oblivious to the fact. Other, more important things, were on the rise. Things which would have to wait.

Claw reluctantly pushed away from the table then stood, looking down at her.

"I'll be back. To meet this Mister Bix Bradley."

"I'll tell him you stopped by." He had almost reached the swinging doors when she finished her sentence. "Giant."

He paused, then tipped his hat to her and disappeared.

Giving them one more thing in common: a new sense of respect.

CHAPTER 5

Hearing the shouted challenge, her heart sank. With a dread bordering on fear, Cougar rushed to the swinging doors and started outside into the rays of the sun. A man stood in the street, hand suspended between eternity and the low-slung gun belt he wore.

"Marshal!" he repeated in a singsong cadence that spoke more for his youth than his experience. "I know you're in there, Marshal. An' I'm callin' ya!"

When no one emerged, Cougar tried to believe the office empty. Claw had gone out: making rounds, or off to buy a horse. She did not even care if he were drunk down at the Wolf's Pelt. Anything, any excuse to prevent him from hearing the challenge. It came too soon. He had only just arrived. She had just met him.

It was not fair.

And then she remembered. No one had ever told her life was supposed to be fair.

As it should be. She hated lies.

Before her heart stopped pounding, the giant appeared in the doorway of the Marshal's Office, filling the space with his broad shoulders, the height of his body, the strength of his badge. He stared up the street at the man who had called him out.

The gunfighter in search of a reputation met that gaze. The fingers of his right hand twitched. Had he realized the gesture more closely mimicked the spasmodic jerking of a dead man after a bullet, shot at close range, propelled him five feet down the street, he might have thought twice. But he had read -- or someone had told him -- that the nimble flexing of fingers made him appear more threatening.

Only one thing could dissuade the youth, and that would come too late to be of service.

Therein lay the occult power of the Grim Reaper. Boys wanting to be men always believed he had come for another and not themselves.

"I'm callin' ya, Marshal!"

"What you callin' me?" the marshal asked. The inquiry, spoken in so natural a tone, brought a laugh to Cougar's lips.

Almost.

Almost only counted in horseshoes.

"Almost" in a gunfight got you killed.

"I'm callin' ya out!" came the indignant response. "'less you're a coward."

That reply brought the lawman out of his office. Two long strides took him to the center of the street.

"What's your name, son?" Claw pursued, never taking his eyes from the challenger's right hand. The face might be a better indicator, but only the hand action counted. Gamblers read eyes of poker players; those expecting to succeed in a shootout interpreted the muscles in a gun arm.

A pause while the youth pondered the interrogative.

"For your headstone," Claw cajoled. "Hate to bury a man on Boot Hill without putting up some sort of marker. In case anyone comes lookin' for him. Got any kin, boy? Anyone who'll wanna put flowers on your grave?"

A hesitation, no more.

Call it an edge.

Name it survival.

The boy's hand went for his gun and nearly cleared it from his holster by the time Claw's bullet struck. It hit square in the chest, one clean shot. The would-be gunfighter's body staggered back, twisted, then crumpled in a heap, never having time to contemplate the finality of its mistake.

Before the echo of the lone shot had been absorbed into flesh and bone.

Before life's blood stained the street.

Dead in an instant.

It was said life extinguished faster than it took to engender.

No one witnessing the shoot out on Main Street would have disputed that wisdom.

Claw remained frozen, right arm extended, eyes fixed on the corpse. A long beat before he moved. Long enough for the soul of one nameless boy to be accepted or rejected at the Gates of Heaven.

If one believed such things.

If not, long enough for a townsman to have made a move to fetch the doctor.

Either way, the ritual played itself out.

Slowly holstering his pistol, Claw led off with his right leg, making his way toward he whose worth was now calculated in numbers. Notches on a gun; cost of a burial; tongues wagging.

Arriving at the cooling meat, the marshal absorbed the spectacle. His face remained calm but it could hardly be said to look serene. The expression reflected duty; the inner turmoil churned regret.

That, he kept to himself.

The man was dead. Claw positioned himself close enough to see his chest move, had it been. He had aimed to kill and he had killed. Followed the formula. Never shoot a man in the arm, never hope to wing him. Death was the only sure way to prevent an enemy from getting off a first or second shot. Ethics were for preachers and philosophers. Death came to marshals who debated that which lay beyond their ken.

In the Kingdom of the Gunfighter, life belonged not to the fastest, but to he who shot to kill and did not miss.

The common misconception had been explained to him in the cradle. *It's always supposed, Claw, that a man who lives by the gun is the fastest draw. Quick draw is for rodeos and Wild West Shows. Bein' the first to clear leather only assures you the first shot. If you can't hit what you're aiming at, it don't matter what lightning's behind yer gun.*

The odds of lightning killin' anyone are grim. The chances a man hit in the chest will die are great.

Between grim and great stretched a lifetime.

It never stopped men from spreading rumors. Claw had heard them before; he would hear them again.

"He's the fastest gun I ever seen!"

"That boy didn't git his gun out befo' he was dead!"

"I ain't never seen nuthin' like it!"

The townspeople were correct in their judgments. But their opinions meant nothing. Not to the marshal, not to the dead youth, not to the Grim Reaper, commonly known as Saint Peter.

They were incidental but they did serve one purpose. They would draw other gunfighters, like flies to garbage.

Welcome to Hellhole, Claw Kiley.

It had begun.

The crowd swelled. Claw guessed there were twenty: shopkeepers, the gunsmith, the livery agent. The telegraph clerk from Dry Street. Good news spread fast.

Twenty men with nothing better to do than stare at a corpse. Without their saying so, Marshal Kiley knew he had become the new attraction in Hellhole.

Twenty men out of a population of two hundred, high water mark. When the hiders and trappers and buyers arrived, their ranks would swell to twice that. Not much of a town. He had fought Rebel brigades with fewer soldiers.

Hellhole was bigger than some towns. Small than others. One truth remained obvious: it would flourish or wither with the law.

Within a month he would know all their names; meet their wives and children, if they had any. Most would address his as "Marshal." A few would be permitted to call him "Claw." The distinction lay in their relative importance and how they viewed his job.

A few would just call him out. Those he would bury. Beside the boy lying dead on the street.

"Anyone know his name?"

As well, to set his priorities straight out.

"Never saw him before," one observed. A glint flickered behind his eyes. Claw presumed him to be the undertaker.

"Drifted in day before yesterday," another volunteered. "Took a room at Daugherty's."

"What's that?"

"Boardin' house. On Dry Street."

"What's be been doin' with himself?"

"Lookin' fer work."

"Guess he found it," a man in vest and shirtsleeves joked. "Fillin' a hole."

Claw addressed the one from Daugherty's. "Bring his belongings over to the Marshal's Office. Might be his name's on a bill of sale, or a letter. I keep a ledger," he added, fending off the curious stares. "I want it accurate."

"Last lawman gave his personal items to the proprietor," the stranger, who might become an acquaintance but never a friend to Kiley, observed, stuffing his hands in his pockets to mitigate his interest.

"Why is that?"

"To pay fer any tab he had owin'."

"It's been my experience drifters paid in advance."

"That's the way it's always been done."

"That a fact?"

The man shrugged and moved off, the prospect of an easy payday shot to hell.

A small man in a grey jacket and a ribbon tie pushed his way through the crowd and knelt beside the man in the street. Not a man in the legal sense; still a boy. Ultimately, death deprived him of his chance at manhood.

"He's dead."

This, then, was the doctor. The tone of voice, the authoritative way in which he and he alone could pronounce sentence. Another ritual. A judge condemned a man; a doctor declared him dead. The west was filled with do's and don'ts.

"Bring him over to the undertaker's."

Hellhole had no stage depot, no school house, no church. There were saloons, cathouses, several hide-clearing houses and an undertaker's.

All things in their own time.

Priorities.

The physician rose and appraised the marshal. Their eyes met, narrowed, judged and withheld a final determination. They would have to work it out. Slowly. Over time. If there were time. If not, one would not care and the other would go on as before.

"Doctor Ward," the man said, by way of introduction. Claw heard the dialect and winced. Although subtle and couched behind respectability, formality and professionalism, there could be no mistake. Southerner.

In this new hide town, in this bleeding state of torn loyalties and divided political opinions, the Federal man had come. A Northerner. A Yankee. The others; the citizens, the transients who passed a portion of their lives here, the drunks, the gunfighters, the homeless, the women, were of a different breed.

Call it the Civil War or the unCivil War; refer to it as the War Between the States. Euphemistically say the Late Unpleasantness. The armed conflict was over, but the memories festered. Three years had passed but Claw Kiley knew he was being evaluated by a man who had served in the Confederate army; knew he had sat down and sipped beer with a woman who had not supported the side for which he would have given his life. Had just shot a boy whose father or brother or uncle had died wearing the grey.

There were many, many thoughts, numerous accountings being made. All would come to play a small or a large part in Claw Kiley's life. But none of them meant more than what a nameless, faceless man at the rear of the crowd declared.

"We got ourselves a marshal!"

Ironically, the Lost Cause accepted him because he killed a man.

By being a better shot and incidentally a faster gun.

"Break it up."

Claw waved and the crowd dispersed. Only when the onlookers had retreated did he face the doctor.

"Marshal Kiley."

The physician hesitated, then made a small, low sighing noise while rubbing a hand over his short mustache, singed with white. He comprehended the enormity of the moment. The next move belonged to him.

"Buy you a beer?" No answer. "You look as though you could use one."

Young enough to believe him, the marshal made a conscious effort to alter his expression.

"Sure."

A start. One arrival, one found love, one death, one friend. One door with a lock which needed replacing.

One home.

Claw grinned.

And a free beer.

Things could be worse. Much worse. He could have been the one being carried, feet first, to the undertaker's.

He would hate to have missed his free beer.

Just as he knew how to take good advice, Claw knew when to acquiesce.

The three of them, the lawman, the physician and the saloon girl who had come out to watch, walked to the Lowdown. Claw held the door open while Cougar entered. Then, as his surrogate parents taught, motioned the doctor to go next. Respect played a very large part of Claw's life. Respect of women; respect of one's elders. Respect for the law. Citizens respecting him. He could not, would not, ask for what he did not give.

Doctor Ward understood respect. He passed through the doors, then selected a table and crossed to it. Cougar, getting the beers at the bar, watched as the lawman hesitated, then made a move to assist. She knew he would. She could not have explained why, just that he would.

That damned word, again. Gentleman.

Cougar was glad she had looked it up. It was good to be sure of things when the rest of her world had tipped upside down.

She shook Claw off, so he went to the table, drew back a chair and sat. The moment she arrived, he stood and pulled back a third chair for her. He wanted there to be no hesitation, no cause to second guess his invitation. She belonged to the group as much as he, or the doctor. He knew what it felt like to be the outsider, the one not invited to join.

Being a boy was not so very different from being a woman.

If the doctor minded the lawman's invitation to the saloon girl, he gave no indication. In fact, Claw sensed a familiarity about their relationship, hard put to express. No matter. It would work itself out. Being new, everything looked strange.

A toast seemed in order; an introduction, perhaps, or an acknowledgement of a new beginning. Neither the doctor nor the marshal seemed capable of initiating the act, so Cougar took it upon herself. Lifting her mug, she stared at the tall man.

"Here's to the new marshal."

Neither profound nor poetic, it served its purpose. With an unexpressed sensation of relief, Claw picked up his glass, tipped it to her and drank. The doctor did the same.

"Folks call me Fiz. Fiz Ward. Short for *Physician*. Or Doctor Ward, if they're in pain or can't pay." He stared down at his distorted reflection in the glass and chuckled to himself.

Cougar caught Claw's eyes and raised an eyebrow, as if to say, *He does that a lot.*

"Claudius Kiley. Friends call me Claw. Unless they break the law. Then," he finished, winking at Cougar, "they don't call me anything. They're too busy running the other way."

The unexpected humor caused Fiz to look up with renewed interest. "The last time I heard a man laugh in Hellhole was when a lady's skirts got caught in the wheels of the stage coach and it drove off, dragging her with it."

The older man, whom Claw guessed to be in his early fifties, repeated the gesture he had made in the street by running the fingers of his left hand across his mustache. Another habit. He made it a point to learn men's habits. It helped judge their tempers.

"You two know each other, I presume?" Fiz directed at Cougar. He purposely put the sentence in the form of a question although clearly he had already made up his mind.

"He came by earlier to see Bix," Cougar casually explained. Claw could not be sure whether Fiz detected the lie or not. He decided that if the physician had not, he would have supplied his own interpretation anyway.

"You tell him how the last marshal got paid two dollars a week to let Bix keep the Lowdown open late?"

"Seems like everyone knows the marshal was bribed," Claw said with a touch of awe.

"Not everyone," Fiz supplied. "Only the important ones. The *astute* ones."

If he wanted to test the depth of Claw Kiley's education, he misspent the use of a ten dollar word. Claw gave no indication whether or not he understood, leaving it up to Fiz to draw his own conclusions.

"Nothing gets by Fiz," Cougar helped.

"I'll keep that in mind."

"You going to take the two dollars?"

"No."

"Going to let him stay open late?"

"Yup."

"Thought as much."

"Why?"

The doctor did not answer the question. He changed the subject. "You're pretty good with a gun."

"Always have been."

"Make a living with it?"

"Outside the law, you mean?" Fiz shrugged. "No. I've been a lawman all my life. Raised by men who wore the star."

"Where were you born?"

"Never asked."

"What year?"

"A year considerably later than the one you were born in."

He meant to warn Fiz Ward his questions were out of line. It succeeded.

"There'll be a lot of gunfighters drawn to Hellhole to test you. Not must else to do in this part of the world. You know that."

"I know that."

"I saw what you did -- trying to talk that boy out of drawing on you. Why'd you bother?"

"It works about once every dozen times."

"Why do you care? He was nothing but riffraff."

"I don't believe that. Neither do you," the marshal added, rocking back in his chair. "Now, Miss Cougar, she probably has more of a right to that judgment than either of us."

She straightened at the sound of her name and nodded in a dazed sort of amazement.

"No argument. Every hide skinner with a dollar in his pocket thinks he's better'n me."

"Well, he's not."

Doctor Ward made the pronouncement. Cougar did not seem surprised, although she appreciated the effort. For the first time in his life, Claw felt jealousy stirring. Deep inside, in places he never knew existed. His cheeks tinged with red and he kicked the leg of the table to hide his discomfiture.

It fooled no one.

"I suppose the undertaker'll be glad to have a quick draw for a marshal. It's good for business."

"Yours, too."

"Not if you shoot them all the way you did that boy."

"Well, you get low on finances, let me know. I'll see what I can do. Wing 'em in the arm, or put a bullet through their shooting hand."

Again, he caught the doctor off guard.

"Ask 'em first if they have any money, will ya? I'm so sick of treating men with gunshot wounds who don't have a dime to their name, I could --"

What Fiz could do was lost, as he drowned his word in beer. Claw could not be certain he did that out of deference for the lady or because he could not think of an appropriate way to finish the sentence. He decided on the latter.

Fiz swallowed and wiped his mouth.

"Heard your office needs a new lock."

"News travels fast," came the disgruntled reply.

"Why didn't you open the door with a key?"

"Didn't have one."

"Why didn't you have one?"

"I heard the late marshal's effects were in the doctor's office. Didn't want to bother you."

"I don't know why not. Everyone else does."

"Want to return it to me?"

"Don't have it."

"How 'bout another beer?" Cougar asked Claw. He swung the mug handle to his left hand, raised the glass and took a swallow. On impulse, he downed the entire contents, replaced the glass on the table, then burped. That social *faux pas* somewhat dampened his feat of drinking the beer without taking a breath.

Fiz stared a moment, shook his head and turned to Cougar.

"No, thanks. I've got work to do."

He stood and had almost gotten away before being summarily summoned back.

"You didn't pay for the beers," Claw reminded him. "I wouldn't want Mr. Bradley to hold that omission against Miss Bradburn."

Fiz's eyes widened to a degree the new marshal would not have guessed. He did not lose the expression while withdrawing a small farmer's purse and counting out the change. Dropping three five-cent pieces on the table, he started away once more. When he saw Claw stand, however, he dragged his feet to see what would happen.

Claw reached into his leather vest pocket, drew out a nickel and added it to the pile. Annoyed, Fiz stepped back.

"What's that for?" he demanded. "I left enough."

"A tip for the lady."

"You can afford to be generous, can you? When you're not even going to take bribes? How do you expect to live?"

Claw had his answer ready.

"Oh, if I take bribes, Doctor, they'll be considerably more than two dollars a week."

Fiz stated a moment in stunned silence then abruptly turned away and walked stiff-legged to the doors. Without bothering to say good-bye, he slipped through and disappeared.

Fiz Ward had bought the first round, but Claw Kiley had won it.

CHAPTER 6

Conflicting thoughts nagged at the back of Claw's mind. With a disgruntled kick at a dried pile of horse manure, not as dehydrated inside as out, the new marshal stained his boots. A muffled exclamation of annoyance followed the discovery.

He did not know what to do about boys, drifters and gunfighters flocking to Hellhole when they heard a new marshal had taken up permanent abode. Normally, a reputation served to frighten riff-raff away. His status as a gunfighter changed that. Instead of repelling, it drew the undesirables. Time after time, he would be forced to prove himself.

It created a circus atmosphere. Until he got unlucky or a stray bullet struck one of the innocent bystanders. Then, there would be an accounting.

In the entire scenario, only one positive presented itself: he had never heard of any Boot Hill running out of land.

On a smaller scale, the condition of the jail and the broken lock needed tending. He could not put either off forever, but the prospect of such work presented more irritation than he could rightfully face. He therefore determined to tackle the bank. From the perspective of a robber. That should not prove difficult. Between the law and the lawless, only a thin line separated the two. Both factions had a tendency to think along the same lines. The difference came in execution.

And paydays.

Walking with a purpose, he calculated it took exactly one minute and ten seconds to reach the bank. Seventy seconds, total. He made a bet with himself that he could run it in twenty. Add the sound of gunfire to the equation and he figured he could shorten it by half.

Claw did not suppose it would take him long to put his bet to the test.

Recently constructed, the Bank of Kansas, Hellhole division, presented an imposing structure. In a town thrown up around saloons, whorehouses and the road out of town, it represented permanence. No one, from the well-to-do lawyer passing through on his way to more lucrative prospects further west, to the illiterate drunk, who could decipher the word "whisky" on a bottle and discourse learnedly on the qualities of aged bourbon, could mistake it for anything but a house of money.

Not to be confused with a house of cards, a house of ill repute, or a house of the dead.

Convenient, if prospective investors wanted to locate the nearest branch of a financial institution without asking directions; less than useful for the concealment of a money vault from those who could not read.

Prominently situated outside the main door stood a hitching rail. It gave Claw the queasy impression more than one getaway horse had temporarily been secured there. He determined to have it moved. No sense hanging a sign outside the bank advertising its availability to be robbed.

Four windows faced the street, protected by oiled shades, pulled half way down. Usually an optimist, Claw would have considered the shades half way up; but on consideration, and in lieu of the fact there were no bars on the windows, they were decidedly half way down.

Anyone with half his wits could figure out that if a thief were unable to pick the lock on the door, he could break the glass with the butt of his pistol and slip inside as easy as pie.

Easier.

Claw wondered about the credentials of the bank president, and if he had ever given a thought to the security of the money deposited with him for safekeeping.

There was one foolproof way to determine that fact. Let the bank be robbed. If the president squawked louder than the rest, then he had put his own money where his mouth was. If he were as silent as the grave, he sent his salary to Topeka.

Or kept it in a lady's hat box in the wardrobe of his bedroom.

Unless he were unmarried, in which case he kept it under his mattress. Absolutely the first place anyone would think to look for hidden treasure.

The second being in a lady's hat box.

If Claw Kiley had not been a lawman, he could have earned quite a fortune for himself as an outlaw.

Being a practical man, he kept his options open.

Particularly after having met the doctor. Robbers had far longer life spans than did marshals.

They could pay for their medical care.

Walking the circumference of the bank property, Claw counted six windows on either side, none at the rear. Adding those twelve to the four at the front, that made a staggering sixteen ways to illegally enter the bank. Not including the front door and the one out back, which, incidentally, he found unlocked.

Claw cursed.

He would wager a month's salary the bank president sent his savings to Topeka. Or Wichita. Possibly even as far away as New York. No one, but no one, with an eye for larceny, would want to keep his money in a bank with eighteen entrances.

The stockholders might as well hang out a sign that read, "Money for the Taking." Or "Robbery in Progress. Please Wait."

Claw would have made a very polite thief.

Entering through the rear, the marshal found himself in an empty room. Beyond lay a corridor. Following it, he passed several offices, all of which had their doors open. None of the men inside looked up as his shadow flitted by. In the last chamber to his right, which was, in reverse, the first anyone came upon by entering from the front, he discovered the money room.

The safe, or more correctly, the vault, stood seven feet high and five feet across. Access to it for the curious, the depositors and those who slipped in uninvited, was denied by a combination lock, guarded by one huge, multi-spoked wheel. Had he found such a device situated at the helm of a ship, Claw might have had confidence in the vessel. Discovered at the door of a vault, it looked no more efficacious than ribbons on a woman's bonnet in a wind storm.

Claw's fingers itched to try a combination, any series of random numbers, to see if he could open it. The idea so tempted him, he forbore for fear of discovering he could. The possession of that fact would send him on a homicidal mission to the residence of the bank president, where he would gun him down in cold blood for irresponsible behavior.

Being hired to uphold the peace, rather than keep the undertaker happy, he did not go closer to the safe than required to pass by and enter the main counting room. The sight of four clerks, backs to him, presented a tempting picture.

One comment, "This is a stick up," would send them all scurrying. He did not pronounce it for the same reason he had not tried the safe. It would be more trouble than it was worth trying to return the money the clerks threw at him when he explained his was only funning.

Paperwork being the bane of officials of all kinds.

He decided to cut to the quick.

"My name is Claw Kiley. I'm the new marshal in Hellhole. Where is the bank president?"

At the unexpectedness of his pronouncement, the four clerks jumped, writhed on their stools, then stared at him as though he were posing naked, clad only in a gun belt.

He repeated the question, abbreviating it somewhat for the sake of terseness.

"Where is the bank president?"

"He's at home," came the answer he knew he would get. The clerk did not have to add, *Sewing his money into a quilt.* Claw could envision that without aid.

"Why is he at home at three o'clock in the afternoon?"

The clerk blinked six times. Perhaps he communicated in code and someone had failed to initiate the new lawman on its meaning. He tried again.

Patience being a virtue.

"Why is he at home at three o'clock in the afternoon?"

"He always goes home after lunch."

His patience wore thin.

"Why?"

More eye blinks.

Making it hard to be the new boy on the block.

"Why?"

"Because that's what he does."

It did not take a genius to guess more bank robberies were committed after lunch than before. No doubt the officer wished to die in his sleep, being rocked to his eternal reward by the rolling and shifting of the money he had stashed in his bed.

"What's his name?"

"Mr. Bodkin Herbert."

It was as well Claw had never read Shakespeare or he might have guffawed at the line, "... when he himself might his quietus make with a bare *bodkin."*

A "bare Bodkin" would also explain why the man retired early. To bed. If he were married, that is.

Otherwise, he would be breaking the law.

Patience was a virtue and Claw's had run out. No one ever required lawman to be virtuous.

That remained the realm of bankers.

Those who went home at noon.

A marshal's job description demanded no more than the ability to differentiate between morality and sin. And the skill to enforce such a distinction. Not even a Federal man in Hays expected a lawman to arrest himself.

That would be asking too much of anyone.

Especially a man who counted his life expectancy in hours.

"Are you aware the back door is unlocked?"

Two blinks and an eye twitch. Claw interpreted that as a *Yes, sir.*

Being polite never cost anyone anything; something to note when standing in a bank. Naked. With only a gun belt.

"Where does Mr. Herbert live?"

"On Side Street. Number One. The big house. The one with the barred windows."

That figured.

"Thank you."

The clerk said no more, prompting Claw to finish the sentence for him.

"You're welcome, Marshal Kiley."

Number One, Side Street, was indeed a large house, constructed of wood and freshly painted. A black metal fence protected it from neighbors. No hitching rails were in sight. A ship's bell, suitable for the vessel Claw imagined the huge vault wheel capable of navigating, hung from a lamp post. Ignoring the implied method of summoning the inhabitants, he leapt the barrier, stomping heavily on the inlaid stonework comprising the sidewalk.

Trying the knob of the front door, he found it locked and had a mind to order the vault brought to Mr. Herbert's house for "safe" keeping.

He knocked. Twice, then once lightly. In code. He must have guessed correctly, for a middle aged man with thinning hair answered the summons. His expression conveyed wariness and annoyance.

"I didn't hear the bell."

I didn't ring it."

"You're supposed to."

Kiley shouldered his way through the opening. "I didn't want to be ignored." The man frowned. "Are you Mr. Herbert?"

"Who's asking?"

A Northerner by birth, a man with a nose for profit by avocation. Had this been Georgia, Mr. Herbert would have been called a carpetbagger.

Residing in Kansas, he earned the right to be styled an entrepreneur.

"Claw Kiley, United States marshal."

"Has there been trouble at the bank?"

The apprehension somewhat consoled the marshal. From it he inferred Herbert must be a shareholder, at least.

"Trouble *with* the bank."

"I don't understand."

"I found the back door unlocked. None of the windows were barred. There's a hitching post outside which makes it too convenient for robbers."

"What is it you want, and why couldn't it wait until banking hours tomorrow?"

Claw stepped over the threshold, forcing Mr. Herbert back. "Because it is 'banking hours' today and what I have to say cannot wait." Some sort of lamp with colored glass stood on a highly polished three-legged table, tempting Claw to knock it over. "Are you listening?"

Shifting his eyes toward the delicate, imported Hepplewhite side table, the banker shrugged.

"I want the back door kept locked at all times. I want bars put on all the windows. There are sixteen of them. I want the hitching rail removed. I want a --"

"Just a minute!" Herbert exploded. "What gives you the right to tell me anything? You can't order me around as though I were some sort of deputy at your beck and call."

"I don't have a deputy and if I did, he would be a man I trusted."

"What's that supposed to mean?"

Claw blinked. In code.

"And I want a night watchman hired from sundown to sun up."

"Protecting the bank is supposed to be your job." Herbert swung his arms the way a bird ruffled its feathers.

"It is, Mr. Herbert. But providing a safe repository for depositor's money is your job. One you have not lived up to." Claw moved into the parlor. The banker did not invite to sit.

"How dare you?"

"The bank has been robbed -- how many times?"

"It's not my fault this is a godforsaken, lawless land."

Claw noted an Afghan on the rocking chair. That raised the stock on hat boxes.

"I can't speak for God, but I can assure you, there is law here. And the law is ordering you to make significant improvements to your business or suffer the consequences."

"What consequences?"

"Defending it by yourself, at bank expense."

"You can't refuse to protect my bank!" More than hysteria, the voice rang with righteous indignation. He stomped his foot. Claw noted his shoes were hand-stitched. He remembered the ill-fitting brogans he had been issued during the War. Confederate soldiers had worn newspaper.

"Can't I?"

"No."

"Don't do as I say and find out."

"I'll report you, you -- you -- young pup."

Those were not Mr. Herbert's words of choice, only the ones he settled for out of propriety and a latent fear that other, more descriptive ones might cause the boy standing before him to give him a fist in the jaw.

Mr. Herbert was closer to the truth than he anticipated, although the term "young pup" hardly settled on the marshal any better than the ones left unspoken.

"Report me. Be my guest."

"You'll lose your job."

For the first time, Claw grinned. His teeth were white and evenly spaced and the upturned accent of his lips gave added sparkle to his blue eyes.

"Lose my job, Mr. Herbert? I don't think so. Not when I report to your stockholders and their officers the condition in which I found the bank."

"Condition?" There were traces of quavering fear. While a herd of marauding bandits might not strike terror into Mr. Herbert's heart, the threat of words spoken to businessmen like himself were terrifying.

Proving the tongue to be mightier than the pistol.

"What you're asking will cost... money."

"Oh, no, Mr. Herbert." Claw's smile widened and the banker's eyes upturned hopefully, thinking the marshal had discovered a way around his dilemma. Cruel, his disappointment, when Claw pursued another tact entirely. "I am not asking. I am demanding."

"What gives you the right to demand anything of me?"

"My life gets put on the line every time your bank is robbed. I treasure it more than I do your money."

"But -- you're the marshal. It's your job."

The smile faded from Claw's face. No one ever need remind him of responsibility. A dangerous glint in his eyes, not unlike the flash of sunlight off a blued-steel gun barrel, warned the banker to back off.

"Order bars for the windows. Today. Hire a night guard. And remove the hitching rail. I won't tell you twice. Do we understand each other?"

This time, Claw did not blink. His eyes would not have closed if a snow storm suddenly blew up in his face.

"We understand each other."

"Sir."

If the banker had been a Southerner, Claw might not have amended the end of the man's sentence. Not only would it have further strained their relationship, Herbert would have mistaken it for a sectional slap in the face by a triumphant enemy. Being a Northerner gave Claw the liberty, and he took it.

"I will do as you -- request. Sir."

The effort cost the businessman and he would not forget it. *Be damned,* Herbert thought, *if I put up a black memorial wreath when the bastard is shot in the line of duty.* He would not tax the shareholders with that added burden. Not after they had to approve the funds for bars on the windows and a night watchman.

He would petition the town council to reimburse him the expense of removing the hitching rail.

Being, after all, a civic improvement.

CHAPTER 7

The words "young pup" did not sit well with the new marshal. They reoccurred frequently in his thoughts, occasionally taking on another speaker's voice, sometimes reforming into the more insidious warning, *I'll report you* and *You'll lose your job*.

He had not intended to make an enemy of Bodkin Herbert. His reaction at finding the bank unprotected had irked his temper; caused him to speak harshly. But not out of line. While he might have couched his orders in a more congenial way, the terms were not open to discussion. Herbert might be able to calculate percentages in his head and he undoubtedly had an eye for judging the worth of an applicant seeking to borrow money, but the blatant disregard for safety traced his roots back to New York or Boston or Philadelphia. The greatest threat he encountered in any of those cities came from his own accounting clerks.

Embezzlement was a crime but one which did not generally involve bloodshed. A thief could ruin a man by stealing his life's savings or destroy a business by rending it bankrupt, but those were paper tragedies. In St. Louis or Kansas City or Wichita, men stole with the help of repeating rifles and blazing pistols.

If Herbert failed to adjust to his new reality, he needed to pack his bags and go home, leaving the directorship to a younger, more savvy individual. One who understood the dangers of violence from outside sources, instead of he who audited his books for arithmetic mistakes or hounded farmers for mortgage payments at the height of a drought.

Claw Kiley had ten dollars minus the cost of a stage ticket to his name and he knew little of money. He had never complained about poor wages or of going to bed hungry. He respected men for the worth of their word and the strength of their convictions.

He had not meant to make an enemy of Herbert but he had. And perhaps the first of the accusations had been true: he was a young pup. But he had grown up fast; something the banker failed to appreciate. He would try harder in future. The rest depended on the other party.

He would see who lasted longer in Hellhole, Kansas.

One hand on his gun, the other swinging at his side, Claw roamed the back alleys and dead ends. To the uninitiated, his demeanor reeked of sulk; the irritation of a man put down by his better seeking some confrontation upon which to vent his anger. Such a watcher would have been surprised, therefore, to observe the marshal take the time to straighten a house of crates, inadvertently knocked over by a drunk, crawling out to seek the last drops in a whisky bottle tossed away by a careless vendor or a cow hand on his way back to a herd. Or to hear him speak kindly to any of the numerous stray dogs which shared the dank passageways with their discarded human counterparts.

Escaped from confinement, lost on a hunting trip or born of a litter crossed between an abandoned pet and a wolf, the canine population came near equaling that of Hellhole's more respectable citizens. Most were solitary, although when they saw advantage, roamed in packs. All were starving; ribs protruding through taut hides, patches of scarred skin revealed under tangles of mangy hair. Unwanted, tolerated and feared, the haunted curs represented another dangerous element in the environs of Hellhole.

If given the chance, they would steal a picnic basket, ravage a hen house or attack an unwary child. While none of their faces would ever appear on a wanted poster and few achieved the penny-pamphlet status of a rattler or a scorpion, wild dogs, the byproduct of man's indifference, assumed their place as undesirables.

On a scale of one-to-ten, Kiley rated them a six. Two notches below Bodkin Herbert and his ilk.

Aware that his appearance in their back alley den caused their mouths to salivate, Claw paused to address a pack of ten or more.

"Sorry, boys," he apologized, adopting the universally accepted nomenclature to encompass animals and nondescript groups of townspeople of both genders. "I'd make a mighty poor meal."

Apparently one-sided, several curs rejected his opinion. Tails wagging from interest rather than friendliness, they crept forward, teeth bared. Amid the low grumble of warning and the low, nearly unperceivable sound of a thousand fleas jumping, one dared snap at the heels of his boot. It slunk away only after Claw threatened it with his pistol.

Dogs, he thought, *have more sense than men.*

Feeling a restlessness in his legs having more to do with oppressive thoughts than starving animals, he hurried into the light, leaving them behind. Finding little solace in the clapboard buildings and littered streets, he headed west, leaving the half-hearted remnants of human encroachment behind.

After an enforced march of twenty minutes, the silhouette of Hellhole fell off the face of the earth. Perching upon the apex of a high rock, blown clean of dust by perpetual dust storms, Claw stared into shimmering waves of heat coming off the unbroken sway of ground. Disengaging his concentration from the parched monotony of flatland, stretching off into eternity, he affixed his gaze on the telegraph poles. One after another, they held silent sentinel as Mankind's intrusion into what was called, with purposeful intent, "the Badlands."

A man could shimmy up one of those poles and cut the wire with a pair of pliers or a sharp knife, without anyone being the wiser. In under five minutes, he could render Hellhole deaf.

Repositioning himself into a crouch, the way a soldier on reconnaissance hid his presence from the enemy, Claw registered and dismissed the shadows cast by setting sun and mindless roll of dried and wasted tumbleweeds. Senses alert for danger, his mind played tricks with time, casting back the years. No longer 1868, but 1863; late spring. April. No, the second week of May. News of a great pitched battle at Chancellorsville, Virginia, ran through the soldier's grapevine "out west," where he was stationed.

The damn Rebs won a great victory! men passed to one another in tempered whispers. *Stonewall and Bobby Lee chased back our boys!*

Wonder, awe, anger, fear, speculation in those words. Richmond was the key. Without that city under Federal occupation, the war would drag on forever.

I wonder if they'll send us east followed upon the heels of *Mebbe it ain't true.* Then nothing, more telling than all the official dispatches in the world.

A week went by, ten days, before the full consensus of that opening battle of the Spring Campaign became known. The Rebels had cut the telegraph wires so no word of Jackson's wounding could get out.

Took half a dozen bullets to his left arm.

Shot in the right hand.

Late-night patrol. Mistaken for a Yank.

Ambushed by his own men.

Mosby's Rangers? Who knew? Who would ever find out? What matter?

Dead.

Taken to the capital to lie in state.

The Confederates had cut the telegraph wires to keep the tragedy from spreading through the ranks. Not to the Yankees, but from their own soldiers.

Eventually, the news spread. By word of mouth. Over repaired telegraph wires. In the newspapers.

The day Private Claudius Kiley heard the confirmed report, he knew he would be going home. Not in a week, or a month, but eventually. The beginning of the end had begun.

Going home. In 1863, he had no home.

Forcibly shifting his attention from past to present, Marshal Claw Kiley resurveyed the line, counting eight uprights before losing them over the horizon.

For as long as he lived, the sight of telegraph poles would be the harbinger of change. The bearer of tidings. The symbols of death.

An outlaw gang severing the wires could ride into Hellhole, put a gun to the marshal's head, rob the bank, despoil the citizens, then slip away, with no one outside of the permanent-transient town the wiser.

Claw Kiley had faced greater odds in his life, but never alone. He wondered if he would have the courage to do what it took to face a standing army by himself. And prayed he would never have to find out. To the god who protected loners and lemmings.

It would be as well, Claw decided, slithering down from his scout's position, to have Billy Brindle, the telegraph operator, check his connections before retiring every night. Just in case.

"Old Blue Light," the revered enemy general, had gone to his reward without ever knowing the outcome of the War. Kiley did not wish the same for himself. Nor did he want Hellhole remembered as just another lost cause.

Dismissing his gloomy ruminations, the marshal retraced his steps to town by the light of the rising moon. Half way down Main Street the path considerably brightened, aided by sporadically placed coal oil lanterns suspended by roughly-rounded wooden shafts the height on one man standing on another's shoulders. Several had blown out or burned away their fuel. Thus shadowed, they gave the appearance of telegraph poles. He questioned who maintained them, and by what authority. He would have to find out. It would not kill the town council to add twelve or twenty-four additional lamps.

Light, Jim Oates liked to say, *kept evil at bay.*

Darkness draped over the office like a shroud and long shadows played tricks with Claw's imagination as he entered the marshal's office. On impulse he thought to light a lamp, until recalling all the potable property had been removed. With a shrug toward Dr. Ward who might have been the culprit, he caustically decided that if there had been one, it would undoubtedly been dry. And if, by some fluke, oil remained in the base, the wick would have been burned to a nub. Or he would not have been able to find a Lucifer.

New to the job and already growing cynical.

Not the same thing as growing up.

On impulse, he decided to treat himself to dinner. He had not eaten a square meal in days and his stomach rebelled at the idea of coffee and hardtack. Enough of soldiering for one day.

Being Thursday, Ma Smitt would not be serving chicken pie. He would try the Regent.

Although brightly lit, few patrons lingered over their meals as the marshal entered. Surveying the eatery with the pride of new ownership, he took in the smells of roast beef, warm bread and lard-fried potatoes. Mouth watering, he selected a table by the door, determined to order everything on the menu. While it would set his meager budget back, the enjoyment of a full plate would take his mind off young pups, lost battles and potential dangers.

A chalk board posted on the rear wall announced the night's choices. Unfortunately, the slate surface had been so poorly and frequently erased, none of the items were legible. It made no difference; his nose had already broken down the various odors and translated that needful information to his brain. It would require no more than a command of *Everything* to sate his needs.

Ten minutes elapsed before the waiter, a moon-faced man wearing a greasy apron, sauntered in from the rear. He did not look around, forcing Claw to impatiently rap on the table with his knuckles. Assuming a disinterested air, he sauntered toward the newcomer. The sight of the badge caused him to nod in recognition.

"What'll it be, Sheriff?"

"Marshal."

He assumed a deadpan expression. "We don't serve that here."

"I am not a sheriff; I'm the new marshal."

He failed to appreciate the distinction. "What'll it be?"

"Roast beef, po -"

"We're out of roast beef. If you wanted roast beef, you should have come in earlier."

"Oh." Disappointment. "Fried chicken --?"

"We're all out of that, too."

"Chicken pie, then."

"Don't serve that 'less it's Monday."

A breach of etiquette. Only someone unfamiliar with the code of the west would have made such a foolish demand. His lips pursed.

"What-do-you-have?"

"Coffee."

"All right. I'll have some coffee. What else?"

"Nuthin'. We're closing for the night."

"What about some eggs?"

"Eggs gets delivered in the morning. By the egg lady."

Claw gripped the edge of the table. "Well, I didn't think they were delivered by the chickens." His stomach growled.

"You might try the Lowdown," the waiter helpfully offered. He conveyed tiredness and a desire to go home.

"The Lowdown?"

"Onest in awhiles, when business is good, they serve hard boiled eggs with the beer."

Claw rested a hand on his pistol, sighing loudly. "You would think," he tried, remembering other times, other lawmen, "that when the marshal comes in for dinner -- no matter the time -- someone would rustle him up some food."

He almost said "grub," then checked himself. Marshals said "food"; sheriff's used "grub."

Another unwritten law.

The west being full of unwritten laws.

He ought to know. He had read more than his share of them.

"Cook's gone home for the night."

"What time do you open in the morning?"

"Eight o'clock."

Claw's stomach grumbled again. He needed a beer. And half a dozen hard boiled eggs.

Maintaining a hand on his gun, he lifted himself up using his left. "See you tomorrow."

"'Night, sheriff." If relief had not outweighed sarcasm, Claw would have shot the waiter where he stood.

Emerging into the warm night air, the officer glanced around to see if anybody watched, then carefully unpinned his badge. With a deft movement, he repositioned it for more prominent display.

"Marshal," he muttered under a hungry breath, before loping down the street toward the Lowdown.

Compared to the Regent, the saloon jumped with activity. What it lacked in numbers the patrons more than made up for with enthusiasm. A dozen men of all descriptions littered the room, most smoking or chewing tobacco. As Claw made his way toward the bar, a bearded man who smelled worse than a tonsorial on payday, hawked and expectorated, missing the spittoon by a good foot. He did manage to splatter Claw's boot, however, the dark juice making an adequate companion to the stain caused by horse manure.

Not a cursing man by inclination, Claw rapidly became one by trade.

"Damn it!"

Elbowing his way to the bar, he shifted his eyes left, then right, hoping to spot the traditional cracked wooden bowl filled with eggs. He identified two, both empty.

"What'll it be?" the barkeep inquired.

"A half dozen hard boiled eggs."

Subtly not being his long suit.

He could have repeated the bartender's line in absolute synchronization, had he the slightest desire to do so.

"We're out."

"Where can I get something to eat?"

"Regent."

"It's closed for the night."

"You might try the Wolf's Pelt."

"If you like green eggs and watered whisky," joked a man to Claw's side. The marshal's lip curled and a chuckle died in the informant's throat. It did not prevent him from winking at his partner, however, as he turned away to finish his drink.

"How 'bout a beer?"

The question would not usually have solicited an immediate response, but asked in a woman's voice, his heart caught. Moving too quickly, he nearly brushed an elbow across the woman's low cut, tight-fitting dress. Pulling back as though stung, he mumbled an apology which she did not seem to hear. Or had never heard before and so dismissed as irrelevant.

The saloon girl was not his girl, and with acute disappointment, the lawman stared upward. Two more girls stood at the railing but he recognized neither. Discouraged beyond measure, he pushed off, shuffling toward the door. Without hard boiled eggs or Cougar Bradburn, the Lowdown became just another watering hole.

At the batwings he paused long enough to hold one side open for Dr. Ward, coming in off the street. Attempting to pass, the physician had other ideas and stopped him by placing a hand on his arm.

"Looking for the owner, I suppose?" Translated, he inquired whether the marshal had come to buy Miss Bradburn a drink. Claw frowned.

"I-came-to-get-something-to-eat."

"In a saloon? Why didn't you try Regent?"

"It's closed."

"Then you should have gone their earlier."

The medical man shoved by and disappeared into the crowd, having dispensed enough wisdom for one evening.

Irritated beyond measure, Claw faced the reality of retiring on an empty stomach. With a growl of frustration, he sidestepped the boardwalk and began walking. A turn around town, he determined, would tired him enough to sleep.

The hour neared midnight when his wandering feet took him once more to the Lowdown. Pausing in the shadows, he watched as the bartender ushered the last customer out by the scruff of his collar, then stepped forward, quietly assessing the technique.

"Good job. I appreciate a man who knows his work. You'll save me a few late calls."

"Will, if I can," the man grinned, extending a hand. "Name's Ryan -- Joe Ryan."

They shook. "Glad to meet you."

"Mr. Bradley says for me to tell you that if you want a nightcap to come on in and get one. At his charge."

"Oh? Is he inside?"

"Gone to bed. He'll be around in the morning. Generally makes his way down about ten."

Claw bounced on his toes. "My appointment book is filling up nicely."

"Have that drink now, Marshal?"

"No, thanks. Some other time."

When the bowl of hard boiled eggs had been restocked and a saloon girl named Cougar Bradburn joined him for a beer.

Returning to the office, Claw let himself in, then paused a moment to drink in the new sensations of home. There were many firsts in a man's life: the first time being thrown from a horse, the first time he made money from his own sweat and toil; the first time he killed a man, the first time he made love. Each held their own significance, maintained their own special memories.

Add to Claw Kiley's life experiences first place to call his own.

A beam of light, slipping in through the shadeless windows, caught a corner of the wall map hanging behind the desk, illuminating the word "territory." Specifically referencing the Cimarron and consequently not Claw's jurisdiction, the wider import spurred reflection.

Territory: a vast, virtually uncharted wilderness sporadically dotted with scrub cattle, mustangs, dry gulches, cottonwood trees, and almost as an afterthought, ranchers, homesteaders and outlaws. Paths to blaze, places to name, friends and foes yet to be made. In total, a frontier meant to be explored rather than conquered. The beginning of a journey it had taken him twenty-three years to reach.

One, he concluded with a sigh, which had been worth the cost.

His ticket had been paid in full; he owed no one in the world. Those who gave him a step up had received his grateful thanks; those who died before collecting their due received his grateful prayers.

Carefully balancing his Stetson over the wall peg by the door, he caught sight of a reflection in the glass. Something behind him; no mistake. Resting on the desk. Not a threat, nor precisely an intrusion. Less than a treasure, more than a pot of gold.

Gliding seamlessly to his left, he turned to face that which had seemingly formed by magic. Stiff-legged, muscles tensed, he approached the object from behind, arriving at his chair without drawing any conclusion as to its actual substance.

Who had brought it? Why? Who owed him? Who knew?

A man who disliked questions hanging over his head, his lips pursed, yet annoyance easily transferred into wonder. Tomorrow, he would discover the answer. Damned if he wouldn't. Tonight, however, he would sit at his desk -- the one without paper, pens or pencils -- and eat the present of hard boiled eggs spilling over the top of a cracked blue willow china bowl.

His new life had suddenly gotten better.

Finishing the last egg by popping it whole into his mouth, Claw chewed in contentment. Before swallowing, a sound arrested his attention. A drunk, singing in the street. Close at hand. He might have been right outside the office. The lyrics were from a War song. Not one in Claw's repertoire.

> Sons of the South awake to glory.
> A thousand voices bid you rise,
> Your children, wives and grand-sires hoary,
> Gaze on you now with trusting eyes;
> Gaze on you now with trusting eyes;
> Your country every strong arm calling,
> To meet the hireling Northern band
> That comes to desolate the land
> With fire and blood and scenes appalling,
> To arms, to arms, ye brave;
> Th' avenging sword unsheathe!
> March on! March on! All hearts resolved on
> victory or death.
> March on! March on! All hearts resolved on
> victory or death!

"Let it go," he mumbled aloud, a cold chill settling over his sweat-soaked chest. And then silently, *He'll finish up the last refrain and wander off. If he's unlucky enough, he'll trip over his own feet, fall into the street and be attacked by dogs.*

One more penniless patient for ol' fire-eater Fiz Ward.

Claw should not have cared, but he did. Townsmen of questionable loyalties were his responsibility. The War had ended. The nights no longer belonged to the Blue and the Grey. Citizens of Hellhole, Kansas, were all equal in the eyes of the law.

His mood turned sour as the man began pounding on the window, hate-filled nose squished against the glass. Grabbing his hat, Claw emerged, gun in hand.

"One move and you're dead," he warned, and meant it.

Surprised, the Rebel held up his hands in a gesture of conciliation. He had not been ordered to do so, and the action nearly cost him his life, for a gun dangled from his fingers.

"Drop it."

The weapon fell to earth, hammer striking the ground. A shot rang out, the bullet splintering bits of wood from the doorframe behind Claw's head. One chard crossed his cheek, drawing blood.

Seeing the lawman take aim, the former soldier cried, trying to divert the shot aimed at his heart.

"An accident, Marshal! I swear."

Claw's nerves jumped, nearly repressing the trigger without intent.

"Stand back!" he ordered. The man obeyed. "What's going on? What are you doing out here?"

"Heard there was a Federal man in town. Just wanted to --" What he wanted remained unsaid. "It were an accident," he repeated, instead. "You saw. The gun went off when I dropped it. No offense."

It would have been a lie to say, *No offense taken.*

"What's your name?"

"You ain't gonna put me in yer ledger, is you?"

"I asked you a question."

"Bentley."   Unarticulated went *Private, First Tennessee Infantry, Company F.*

"What do you do here?"

"I'm the gunsmith. Over there," he indicated by a twist of his head.

"Where do you live?"

"Got a house on No Name Street. I had too much to drink," he apologized. "Gotta watch that."

"Yeah," Claw acknowledged. "You gotta. Give me one good reason why I shouldn't lock you up for the night, Mr. Bentley."

He should have seen it coming.

"Stonewall."

The honorable enemy.

Claw bent down, retrieving the gunsmith's weapon.

"You can collect this in the morning. Now get on home."

"Yes, sir."

The man brushed a hand across his misshapen cap and backed away. With him, he took Claw's concern about curs and late-night repasts.

Holstering his gun, Kiley retreated into the confines of the Marshal's Office. About to toss the gunsmith's pistol into a drawer, the blued steel caught a glint from his desk lamp. Closer examination revealed the trigger honed down, the way a gunfighter did, to get off rapid shots.

He had counted the continuing days of his life in terms of men seeking a reputation, outlaws and natural disasters.

Now he had a new mix to the equation.

Citizens and accidents.

Not necessarily in that order.

CHAPTER 8

Stripping down to long johns, Claw hung his shirt, trousers and socks over the doorknob of the store room, then padded quietly to bed. He would have disturbed no one, had he thumped his way across the day-warmed, wooden board floor, but habit and breeding had ingrained in him a modesty of action as well as person.

A man don't need to make a lot of noise, Claudius, he heard Jack Duvall whisper. *His deeds do all the talkin' for him. Keep quiet; keep to yerself. Drawin' attention only makes you a better target. And God knows, you're a big enough target without anythin' else drawin' eyes to you.*

It's a question of respect, boy, Amos Carter once said. Amos was a "Renaissance man," a man who knew a little about everything there was to know in the world. He was also the best hand anyone ever knew at tracking, "speaking in tongues," and reading the sky.

You can't respect anything you don't understand, so you try and walk a mile in a fella's moccasins before you judge him. Learn a lesson from the Indians, Claw. They're a quiet people. They don't say a thing unless it's worth saying. They don't make loud noises because it's an affront to nature. Comprende?

Claw had started to answer when Amos put a finger to his lips, signifying silence. Claw nodded, then kissed the man's finger.

That, too, meant respect.

Amos had never lectured his young shadow on love, never used the word. When he spoke of relationships, it was dignity he mentioned.

Your family are those you hold in reverence, boy. It doesn't matter whether they're you blood kin or not. What matters is how you think of them. If you can get up in the morning without smiling when you see one of them first thing, then he's not your family. If you can go to sleep at night without thinking on her, then she's not your woman.

If you laugh at a man when he's down, that's your sin, son, not his. If you sleep with a lady and you don't kiss her before you leave her bed, you're an animal and not a man. If you take a life, you give one back. That's how nature balances itself out. Bury a man, give someone else a chance at life.

When you get older, you'll be a lawman, son. Always remember one thing: the law is not a book, it's a cloud. Come here, boy and lie down.

Amos Carter had gotten on his back, waited until the boy who might have been mistaken for his blood kin but was not, laid down beside him, then pointed to the sky.

See those clouds? What do they tell you?

That it isn't going to rain.

What else?

There had been a long pause. A man did not speak if he did not know what to say.

See how the wind is blowing those clouds, reshaping them from the image of a mustang into a fish leaping out of water?

Claw nodded, eyes wide with awe. Being eight years old, a mustang meant a pony to ride and a fish meant dinner frying in the pan.

The law is like the clouds. It's constantly moving, shifting, changing shape. But none of that means anything if the man looking up at it doesn't see that mustang turn into the fish. You understand?

Tell me.

Some men look at the law as though it's lightning; swift and deadly. They don't see the illumination, only the result. A man goes foul of lightning, he gets killed. Some men look at the law like black clouds, always ready to rain on the party. Others see the law as a rainbow, bringing civilization and the good life to those who obey it.

None of those men are right, Claw. The law's a little of everything. It's got to be alive, moving all the time, never static. Good laws are respected by good men; bad laws are respected by bad men. A lawman's got to understand the spirit of law. Not the spirit of any given law; the spirit of law as a living body.

This isn't London or Edinburgh or New York, Claw Kiley. This is the Indian territories. The law is what a lawman carries in his heart. And it better be a damned good heart. The day comes when that lawman has to enforce what's not in his heart, then that's the day he's in the wrong job.

That make it clearer for you?

Yes, sir.

The eight-year old did not understand, but his heart was good and he took Amos Carter's meaning into his head. He dreamed about the law and how a man ought to be able to see a pony turn into something for dinner.

He did not *comprende* it all, but he stored the words away for a future time, when they would come back to him in a dream. Or in a marshal's office.

One being the same as the other.

Claw woke at the crack of dawn, not from choice but necessity. The first bright, cheerful rays of the sun streamed in through the windows. By themselves, they might not have disturbed the peaceful slumber of the marshal. Combined with the whispered conversations outside the window, sleep fled.

Bringing his vision to "bare" on the naked glass, Claw identified three men staring at him. Apparently they had no shame, for the state of the marshal's undress did not phase them in the least. One pointed to his exposed torso. Without much trouble, their words were audible.

"Ain't them the longest legs you ever saw?"

"I tolt you he was a big'in."

"Must be seven feet tall; taller, even!"

And Claw realized, to his chagrin, he had become the center attraction of the Hellhole Peep Show.

"Move along!" he yelled. The men stared in astonishment, it being commonly held, even in the wilderness of Kansas, that bears, lions, tigers and giants did not speak.

The Cardiff Giant, for whom Claw might have been nicknamed, had that silent beast's presence been known, never spoke a word. Fortunately, at the present time he remained an unknown entity, slumbering peacefully under six feet of dirt in Cooperstown, New York. There was something to be said for lying undisturbed, even if it were in a "grave."

Something else again for being undiscovered.

Marshal Kiley had come to town and word had spread. The anonymity of his deputing days were over.

The men scurried away, leaving small, moist circles of vapor on the glass where their noses had pressed. Now, he would not only have to secure the windows with coverings, he would have to wash them.

Adding yet another task to his growing chore list.

Hoping out of bed, Claw stretched, worked out the kinks caused by overcrowding, then grabbed his trousers. While he had lived with lawmen all his life and had seldom been deceived into thinking them any more than mortal men, he found it politic not to announce that fact too loudly. A man caught in his undergarments gave the impression of fallibility. If too many townspeople believed that, his life would move a foot closer to Boot Hill.

Gingerly tiptoeing across the trash-strewn alley, he arrived at the outhouse. Another rude discovery awaited. The hole over which he sat was filled to gagging with night soil and had not been limed in recorded memory. Another expense.

One that could not be ignored.

On his list of needs, lime took precedence over pens, pencils, paper and a new lock.

It remained in second place behind shades. Shades for the windows. The ghosts of marshals past were supplied without expense.

After completing his business, Claw drew water from the well and filled his wash basin. Wetting a bar of lye soap, he unceremoniously rubbed it across his cheeks to soften the pale blond stubble. The blade, stropped only yesterday, held its edge for the morning's task. It was a good razor, a gift from a friend. A friend more after the fact than before, for Claw had not known him well.

They met during the War, after the first day's fighting at Shiloh. During the bloodbath, both had been separated from their regiments. Too tired to struggle back, they had curled in one another's arms for the night, praying the other's strength would sustain their own and keep the horrors at bay.

It had been a vain wish. The creaking of ambulance wheels, the shrieking of mutilated men and the agonized cries of wounded horses kept them awake. In the morning, Claw's companion, a big-eared soldier named Joe Something, from Somewhere in Indiana, had offered Private Kiley his razor and pocketknife.

I won't be needin' it, he explained in a distant, unemotional voice. In his naiveté, Claw thought the soldier meant he intended to grow a beard and accepted the gifts with less appreciation than their due. Two days later,

Claw stumbled over what was left of "Private Indiana," propped against a tree, both legs blown off.

He never had time to grow that beard.

The useful, three-bladed steel pocketknife with the initials "JG" had been lost between Shiloh and Vicksburg, but the razor had stubbornly remained attached to the boy who hardly needed it. Claw thought many times about giving it away, but as he aged and found more need of it, he retained the gift.

Odd, how memories lived and men died.

The ghost of Joe Something joined those of unknown lawmen crowding the United States Marshal's office on Main Street, Hellhole, Kansas. Joe had never thought to get to Kansas, but he was there now.

Stropped, wiped clean and set upon a shelf.

Call it a duty.

The creaking of rickety wagon wheels caught Claw Kiley's attention. With raised eyebrow and lively step, he hurried to the window and looked out. A boy with a two-wheeled cart just passed his door. Beside him walked a girl with a basket, covered with a red and white checkered cloth.

Stepping out, Claw hailed the pair with a wave and a "Howdy." The pair halted, looking eagerly at the newcomer.

Out of politeness, Claw first addressed the young woman.

"That eggs you have in the basket?"

She curtsied. "Yes, sir."

"Any not spoken for I can buy?"

"Yes, sir."

"Come by here every morning?"

She nodded but did not speak, intimidated, perhaps by the size of the man. Or by his badge, which she had little cause to respect.

"How about my buying a half dozen eggs from you every morning?"

"Cost you two bits, mister," she mumbled without expectation. When Claw reached into his vest pocket and withdrew the requisite coins, her eyes opened in distrust.

Claw had been a lawman long enough to understand.

"Take it," he said. Then, out of kindness, he handed her several more pieces of hard-earned money. "Here's a week in advance. That fair enough?"

Fair enough and then some.

Accepting the money with disbelief, she handed over six eggs, then shyly retreated. Balancing breakfast in one hand, Claw directed his attention to the milk boy.

"What about you? If I leave a pail outside my door, will you fill it half way every morning?"

"I kin do that," came the equally diffident response.

"What'll it put me back?"

"The same," he replied, ducking his head from a blow which never came.

Claw paid him a week in advance, then disappeared inside to look for a pail. There were two in the store room, one of which, after being rinsed with well water, served his needs. The boy would have filled it to the brim but Claw stopped him by gently placing a hand on the child's shoulder.

"I said half full. That's enough, son."

"Yes, sir."

Squatting beside the children, he explained, "My name is Marshal Kiley. You two stop by once a week and collect your pay. Will you remember? If I'm not inside, I'll leave your money on my desk."

"You want us to -- go inside?" Shock, tinged with suspicion. Everyone knew the door to the marshal's office only worked one way.

"That's right. Come here and I'll show you."

Holding the pail in one hand and the eggs in his other, Claw indicated they enter. When neither dared, he went ahead. They followed with trepidation.

"This is my desk. I'll leave the money there."

Purposely turning his back, he busied himself putting away his precious purchases. The children backpedaled, discovering, to their astonishment, the door did, indeed, work both ways.

Reaching the boardwalk, they disappeared for fear of being called back.

Take a life, give someone else a chance. Or, in this case, two someone elses.

The young marshal of Hellhole had offered more than money: he bestowed respect.

Call it the dignity of the law.

The egg girl and the milk boy would have said something different: admiration for the man.

In Hellhole, that amounted to the same thing.

Another beginning.

While the eggs bubbled merrily away in a pot of water over the stove, Claw made a quick trip to the dry goods store, purchasing coffee, a loaf of bread, a pound of salt-encrusted bacon and a frying pan.

When he got settled, he would add flour and baking powder to his stock of foodstuffs. With that, he could make flapjacks as well as his own sort of bread. For dinner and supper he could add beans, beef steak, potatoes and corn. A man could do well enough without having to squander his entire fortune at the Regent.

He would have to look around, see what other eateries were available. At the more reasonable ones, he would treat himself to an occasional dinner of fried chicken and peach pie. Add a few beers at the Lowdown and his corporeal wants would be satisfied.

After finishing breakfast, Claw began his rounds, taking a roundabout path to the bank. Grimly satisfied to see the railing had been removed, he headed for the livery stable when alerted by the sound of gunfire. Sprinting across two streets, he came upon the Lowdown in time to break up a fist fight.

Holding each at arm's length by the collar, he shook them in annoyance.

"What's going on?"

"Didn't know there was no law in Hellhole," the man on his left spat.

"Well, there is."

"Don't look like a marshal to me," the other complained. "Ya look like yer wearin' yer paw's badge."

Face reddening with anger, Claw released the first and grabbed the other by the plackets of his jacket.

"Want to say that again?"

Un-cowed by the action, the drifter huffed, "Yer big 'nough, but ya ain't growed in the face, if ya know what I mean."

"No, I don't. How would a day in jail convince you to hold your tongue?"

"That ought ta do 'er, Marshal, but it won't make you look no older."

Claw shook him until his teeth rattled then angrily let him go.

"You have business here?"

"Just passin' through. Lookin' fer work."

"Well, there isn't any, so keep on passing."

"You'll be here the next time we cum through, marshal?"

He spoke with enough sarcasm to prompt a raised fist. Backing off before getting himself in deeper than intended, he signaled his sparring partner and they ambled away.

Stinging from the insult, Claw intended to follow them but halted abruptly at the sound of rustling from the door. Hand up in an offensive posture, it froze in midair as he recognized his next "opponent."

"Good morning, Marshal," Cougar greeted, the glint in her eyes revealing the fact she had read his mind and stood ready to defend herself. Stamping his foot in a petulant manner, he kicked up a small cloud of dust.

Whereas eggs and milk had their price and even an insult to the town law could cost a man, the ever-present dust arose without cost.

"Morning, ma'am," he growled in a purposely deepened voice. If he could not look older, he would sound it.

"Glad to see you handled those ol' boys without any shooting."

Her forthright appraisal surprised him. "Thanks."

"Thought at least you'd have tossed them behind bars."

"Thought about it," he admitted. "But that'd be more trouble then they were worth." When she raised an eyebrow for explanation, he continued. "The cells are a stinking mess and I didn't want to hear 'em hollering about it for the next twenty-four hours. And then there's the problem of feedin' 'em. I'll have to establish an 'account' with one of the diners. I'm sure wherever I go, the 'marshal's office' will own the proprietor ten dollars in back fees."

Cougar laughed. He thought it the most beautiful sound he had ever heard.

"Besides," he added, voice regaining its natural timbre, "it would gall me to think they were eating better than me."

If they had not been standing in the street, Cougar would have fallen to the floor. As it was, her innate sense of propriety caused her to suppress the humor she so clearly saw. It would never, ever do to embarrass him in public.

"Want some breakfast?" was all she could think of to say to cover the other words crowding in on her tongue.

"No. I've eaten, thank you."

"Cup of coffee?"

"You make it?" He sounded more hopeful than he should.

"No," she drolled. "Mr. Bradley has it sent over from the Regent every morning."

Straightening his shirt, Claw peered over the double doors. "Is he up? I suppose I ought to meet him."

"Depends on what you mean by 'up.'" The double entendre caused his face to flush and he re-fixed his gaze at a distant point through the ceiling and over the top of the saloon. "He doesn't usually make an appearance before ten; most days closer to noon. It depends who he has up there with him."

Her words were carefully chosen and he took her meaning implicitly. Eyes flashing with a type of anger never before experienced, it took more effort than Claw would have imagined possible to unclench his fist.

"I'll have that coffee."

"Come on."

It was as well he understood. While lying to men was second nature to Cougar Bradburn, she did not want there to be any misunderstandings between herself and this giant. Not on that score.

Holding back one of the batwings, Claw allowed Cougar to pass before following her inside. A coffee pot sat at the far end of the bar beside several mugs, placed downward on a tray. She righted two and filled them.

"Sit?"

He nodded, obliging her by removing a pair of chairs from atop a table. The rest awaited the obligatory broom which would sweep away the previous night's accumulation of sawdust, grime, tobacco juice and trash. Underneath one table lay a playing card, which Cougar retrieved before joining him.

"Play cards?" she asked, casually tucking the ace beneath the breast line of her dress.

"No."

The answer surprised her. "No?"

"Well, I know how to play at cards, if that's what you mean. Never saw the point in gambling away what's so hard to earn."

"Men generally play cards to make money, not to lose it."

"And generally they lose it, whether they want to or not."

"You have a point."

They sipped their coffee before Claw resumed the conversation.

"You play cards?"

"I've been known to sit in on a hand or two."

"With the girls?"

"I never play with anyone who doesn't have something I want."

The words were spoken with a cold, deadly earnestness he was hard pressed to place. Awkwardly staring at his reflection in the cup, she completed the same act by absorbing his countenance first hand. When finally sure of what she wanted to say, Cougar spoke again.

"You know, I was thinking." He looked up expectantly, although for the life of him, he could not have said what, exactly, he expected. "That drifter wasn't far off the mark."

Pride compelled him to demand, "What do you mean?"

"You do look young."

"When I finish growing, I'll be taller."

"Your looks will make men want to try you, just because they think you're --" She meant to add, *wet behind the ears,* but did not. She did not have to. He made a spitting noise by forcing saliva between his two front teeth.

"They'll find out otherwise."

"Yes, they will. But I don't think you want that."

"A reputation has a way of finding a man."

She shrugged. "You can kill a few and by doin' that, scare some off. I was thinkin' of a way to maybe make a statement without all that bloodshed."

Elbows on the table, chin in his palms, he said, "I'm listening."

"There's gonna be a town --" She hesitated, searching for exactly the right word. "A town fair." Not exactly the word she sought, it conveyed near enough the idea. "Happens once a year. Families come in from the outlying farms; people get together, drink a little too much, buy and sell from booths. You know -- pickles and jams, quilts, crafts. Then there's horse racing, rope tossing. That sort of thing." He raised an eyebrow. "Be a shootin' contest, too."

"You want me to plug a few good ol' boys to prove my hand with a gun?"

He meant her to smile and she obliged. She liked this man. More than she ought. He didn't fit into her plans and she did not -- could not -- fit into his. He was a United States marshal; an important man. If he lived long enough, he would earn a name for himself that reached to the borders of the state. Maybe further. A man like that went on to run for senator. A man like that ought to marry a governor's daughter.

Cougar Bradburn never kidded herself. She saw truth in black, white and grey. On her colorless scale, he was white and she somewhere between grey and black.

White for good, black for bad. Nothing fancy.

Just the way it was.

The way it would be.

The way facts were meant to be taken. The philosophy of a woman who understood her world and accepted it.

Being blind only got a woman hurt. Hurt bad.

"Wouldn't mind a bit," she continued, referring to his offer to shot a few good old boys. "But I was thinking of somethin' different. You ought to try your hand at the shootin' contest."

"I don't like --"

"Maybe not," she interrupted. "But when you win that contest -- hands down, marshal -- you'll quiet a lot of tongues. Word travels fast in these parts. You might bring down on your head a few professionals, but you'll keep the skinners -- and the townspeople -- from questioning your right to be here. If they think you earned your badge, they'll be a lot less likely to call you out."

Still young enough to go fishing for a compliment, he asked, "You reckon I'll win?"

"Damn right I do."

He blushed. Not a trait usually associated with U.S. marshals. This one was different.

For the first time in her life, Cougar felt ashamed of who and what she was. She had no right talking to him as an equal; suggesting ways to make his job better, easier -- maybe even save his life. Saloon girls were a dime a dozen, coming and going like rain squalls. They aspired no higher than payday and usually got a lot lower than the mattress on the floor.

Her formal schooling had been conducted by women little better educated than herself. They taught from experience rather than primers, concentrating on what a "lady of commerce" needed to know: how to write her name, read the word "Saloon" stenciled on a window and add her sums in dollars and cents. She had once been caught pronouncing "Godey's Ladies Book" as "god-ies" and her training prepared her for handling men, not sewing kits or kitchen stoves. While proper females demurely allowed menfolk to open doors for them, her luck ran high if she weren't kicked through one.

Honesty. There was that trait again. Never lie to yourself. There wasn't any percentage in it.

What else she picked up along the way she had paid for. Not always in money.

"Of course, you know best," Cougar mumbled, oblivious to the fact he had stopped talking to stare at her. Disconcerted by the peculiar expression on his face, she bit her lower lip and bent over, ostensibly to straighten her dress.

Her discomfiture only heightened by discovering he had not moved when she straightened from the unnecessary task.

She was not one to blush. Brides blushed -- and apparently so did U.S. marshals. But not saloon girls. Because she could not blush, her temper rose.

"What are you staring at?"

"I was wondering what you were thinking."

"None of your business." Her tongue lashed with more venom than the situation required, but once said, she would not have retracted her statement for the world.

Who the hell is he to ask what I'm thinking? The nerve of the bastard. What does he think I'm thinking? Knit one, pearl two? He's a damn fool and I wash my hands of him.

In contrast to the bitter resolve screaming in her mind, Claw's words were spoken so softly he compelled her to dip an ear in his direction to hear. "I'm sorry. I didn't mean to pry."

Unable to reconcile the apology with her lowly station, Cougar snarled, "Well, don't do it again."

"You have my sincere promise."

Which moved "sincerity" up on her list of despised things. Right to the top.

"Say," he began, then faltered, wondering if he were about to trespass on yet another forbidden subject. When she frowned but said nothing, he summoned up his waning courage and plunged ahead, remembering and agreeing with Ol' Joe Morton's oft quoted saying, *Dealing with women is harder than talkin' a rattler out o' strikin'.* "Does a fella ask a lady to this town fair, or does he go alone?"

If Claw guessed how close he were to being "struck," he would have prepared a grave for himself beside Ol' Joe, who ironically died from a rattlesnake bite.

"I suppose if he can find a *lady* in Hellhole, he asks her."

Flat and terse, her statement inadvertently reflected the fact she misunderstood his implication. Claw grinned and straightened his head as though admiring himself in a looking glass.

"Want to go to the fair with me?"

"Me?" Incredulity. "I thought you were going to ask a *lady.*"

"I am."

Cougar blinked. For a distressing moment he believed her to be communicating in code, like the bank clerk. Fortunately, she had words to go with her eye flutters.

"I-am-not-a-lady."

Claw grimaced. "I sort of had a feeling that's what you were thinking. I don't like it."

"What makes you think I give a damn what you like and don't like?"

"I like you."

"Go to hell."

"Will you go to the fair with me?"

"Why should I, when you're making fun of me?"

"Because I'm not making fun of you, and it was your idea."

"What was my idea?"

"That I enter the shootin' contest. Is there a prize?"

He succeeded in taking her mind off less desirable and far more hurtful thoughts.

"I -- expect so."

"Good!"

"You don't even know what the prize is."

"Well, it's gotta be something, and something's better than nothing. I got a whole lot of that!"

She laughed and he laughed and they laughed together. And she forgot about how he had called her a lady and meant it. Thoughts of senate races and governor's daughters and all the low-down, sarcastic men who had come before him dissolved away. He said, *I like you.* They were the sweetest words she had ever heard.

Even if she weren't no lady.

CHAPTER 9

The scent of gun smoke stirred his blood. The sights and sounds of the Hellhole fair were exciting, but only the odor of black powder, wafting in from the shooting range, piqued Claw's interest. Whereas others enjoyed the challenge of the pie-eating contest or the display of skills with a rope and a gangly scrub steer, his mouth salivated at the chance to participate in the shooting trials.

Standing in line to buy his ticket, he knew Miss Bradburn had been right. It *was* a good idea to prove himself before the entire town, especially if the cost were no greater than the entrance fee of fifty cents.

Without anyone saying so, Claw fully comprehended the sentiments associated with his position. A high government job, no one got appointed marshal without having influence with the authorities. That, or a large expenditure, commonly known as a bribe.

In his case, "influence" had been delivered in the form of a dead man's name, an unwillingness to take "no" for an answer, six feet, seven inches of height and having fought four years for the Union. Not much to speak of, but in a town and a state and a territory of mixed sentiments, it was too much. Proving himself would take a long time. Unless he got killed in a short time. In that case, men would shake their heads and say he was just another Yankee bastard who finally got his due.

Three years too late.

Memories were longer than forgiveness.

The man selling tickets at a squat, low table, held out his hand, palm upward. Before accepting the fee, however, he demanded, "What's yer name, mister?" Claw had never been asked to identify himself before participating in a contest. It brought to mind images of shots gone wild and holes being dug in Boot Hill.

"What's it to you?" he asked, attempting to sound casual. It did not help that the "Hellhole Shooting Gallery" was sponsored by "Harker's Furniture." Jonathan Harker also served as the town's undertaker.

The man waved off the question. "Just give a name. Any name. It's a requirement."

"It's a requirement of *whom?*"

"The mayor."

"I was not aware Hellhole had a mayor."

"The major wants to know the names of all the men what's signed up for the Shootin' Contest because he don't want no trouble. If there's trouble, he'll know how to take care of it."

"So will I."

Terseness, more than avowal, finally made the ticket-seller tilt back his head. And then tilt it back further, until he came close to tipping over. Claw supposed that an hour previous, the man had participated in the "Punch Imbibing Contest."

The one sponsored by Bix Bradley, owner of the Lowdown.

A more accurate picture of the Hellhole Fair rapidly formed in the new marshal's mind.

He would not have been surprised to see a "Poisoned Chicken-Eating Contest."

Sponsored by Doctor Ward.

"You're wearin' a badge. Where'd ya git it frum?"

"The Marshal's Office. Work desk. Top drawer. Left side."

"I weren't aware Hellhole had no law."

"It's a day of amazing revelations."

The man hesitated, debating whether or not to charge the lawman an entrance fee. Rather than wait until he, or the ticket-seller or both suffered sunstroke, Claw volunteered his fifty cents.

He received a ticket without further ado and took his place in line.

Six men stood ahead of Claw, all wearing their gun belts low, like gunfighters. Each held his right hand down by the pistol, exercising his fingers with nervous energy. To a practiced eye, that gesture revealed how green and unaccustomed to quick-draw these men really were. To other green wannabe's, it was an excuse to call the man out.

In a land where men's gestures spoke louder than words, nervous habits were a shortcut to the grave.

The contest was relatively simple. Two men stepped forward and faced a makeshift wall. Ten empty bottles sat atop, separated in the middle by a space of approximately two feet. When given the order to "draw and fire," both drew their weapons and attempted to hit as many of his five bottles as he could in five seconds. The winner then reloaded and faced another challenger.

The current champion was a man called Joby Jim, "Short for Job James," he exclaimed to each challenger. They shook hands, then skittishly turned to face their real opponents, the five deceivingly easy-to-hit whisky bottles. Claw watched with undisguised curiosity as Joby Jim hitched his shoulders, flexed his fingers and fired on cue. He outdrew the boy to his right, hitting three bottles with six shots. His opponent hit one, then was credited with a second as a gust of wind came up and blew a bottle down.

While dissatisfied with his performance, the loser stepped away, temporary proud possessor of second place. Seven men of strikingly similar appearance slapped him on the back. Claw presumed them to be brothers.

Joby Jim made short order of the remaining contestants, none of whom hit more than one of the bottles. Joby averaged two.

When Claw stepped up to take his place at the firing line, Joby Jim gave him a wide grin, then narrowed his eyes and spat.

"That badge says yer the marshal," he sagely observed.

"That's right."

Whether Joby Jim could read the words "U.S. Marshal" was a moot point. The "star" Claw wore possessed a distinctive shape and aura of importance that even the most illiterate hide skinner recognized. It gave him time to step back and think twice.

"Hate to put you under, marshal."

Claw would have bet real money Joby Jim worked for Jonathan Harker in his spare time. Digging graves.

"Comes to it, we'll see."

Suffering a contagion of giddiness, Claw shook hands with Mr. James and turned to face the gallery. The slaughter of bottles occasioned no more harm to the shooter than the off-chance of being struck by a sliver of glass. It made a man think he could face a gunfighter with equal coolness and shoot him dead.

Killing bottles made a man feel special. Shooting the hell out of empty tin cans gave him the right to call himself a sharpshooter. Walking bravely to a line and drawing at a prearranged signal made the slap of flesh on leather feel like power.

If any of that were true, no man in his right mind would ever wear a badge. That honor would go to contest winners.

"Ready, fire!" shrieked a man with the stopwatch. Before his words had died, Claw fired, striking all five bottles. Dead center.

A gasp of disbelief arose from the crowd, followed by a buzz of excitement. No one in Hellhole had ever seen shootin' like that before. Here was a gunfighter who deserved the name. Here stood a man of legend.

Claw heard the whispered question repeated and answered a dozen times.

"Who is that fella?"

"The new marshal."

Miss Bradburn had been right. Five whisky bottles had given up the ghost and saved the spirits of as many men who might otherwise have challenged him.

A fair trade-off.

Next year, the Shootin' Contest would need a new sponsor.

"Yer good!" Joby Jim exclaimed. His praise reeked of sadness as well as admiration. No one liked to lose, even to a seven foot giant wearing a badge.

"Thanks."

Ordinarily, Claw would not have bothered acknowledging the man's congratulations, but he had come here for a purpose: to flaunt his skill. A word of recognition, an admission of prowess did not seem out of place.

It did no damage to his own self-image, either.

No one liked to lose. Not even a taciturn lawman.

"Next! Step right up and face the man who hit five in one blow!" hollered the official. Every man in Hellhole who had fifty cents in his pocket hurried to buy a ticket and face the new champion. The chance of a lifetime, made all the more unique because losing did not mean dying.

Claw faced and easily defeated eight challengers before a lean, sallow-skinned man with a drooping mustache and a weathered grey kepi, the brim of which was cracked and worn, moved beside him. The stranger's face was deeply etched with a raspberry-colored scar the size of a Minnie ball. His fingers were long and steady, while the backs of his hands bore the unmistakable signs of powder burns, long healed.

Claw guessed about three years healed.

"Name's Titus," the newcomer introduced. "Make my living with a gun, Mister Kiley. I win, I suggest you pack your bags and leave town by the next stage." He spoke softly, with the educated dialect of lowcountry South Carolina. It spoke of breeding and hatred inherited rather than acquired.

"I was about to say the same thing to you, Mister Titus."

They did not shake hands. No point prolonging the contest. Not when the semblance of friendship meant a sham.

Not when one of them would be leaving town by the next stage.

Or filling a pine box in Jonathan Harker's back room.

Claw saw her out of the corner of his eye, a man at her side. A short man with a greying mustache and a string tie. They stood back aways, watching the lawman with guarded eyes. Claw did not have to face them to see. Hers were curious, hesitant, uncertain. She did not know her place in the tall man's life, or even if she wanted one. She did not know if he were worth the trouble. Or if she were worth the trouble to him.

His were suspicious, slanted, mocking. *Prove yourself to me,* they said. *You are young and strong; you are tall and handsome. Prove to me you are worthy of consideration; prove you are different from all the rest. But even if you win, Federal marshal, all you have really shown is that you can handle a gun.*

The man behind the lines standing by the woman issued a one-sided challenge Claw could not win. Not here. Not in this way. *But if you lose,* those intense blue orbs said, *you give me the upper hand. A superiority. I will know a secret and hold it against you. For as long as you live.*

If Claw lost, his failure would mean more to the saloon girl and the doctor than just a lost prize. It would serve as free advertising that he would not live long enough for either of them to bother making a commitment.

It saved time.

For her, it would prevent a broken heart. For him, it would justify his naturally irascible nature.

The destruction of innocent red eye bottles had turned deadly serious.

"Ready, fire!" came the command. It was like war. Like aiming at a blindfolded man tied to a pole. An execution for treason where neither soldier had a blank in his gun, so both would be responsible for the death.

So easy to condemn a man. He who passed sentence never had to carry it out. That, they left to others. To United States marshals and embittered losers.

Claw fired and Titus fired and ten bottles gave up the ghost in three seconds flat. As flat as a stale beer.

"Set 'em up again!" someone shouted. The boy who had been hired to perform the task walked gingerly through the graveyard of broken glass to place ten more silent victims upon the makeshift wall.

The crowd swelled as word traveled faster than an artillery piece fired at close range. The man beside Claw had served in the long arm; as an officer. He bore the marks for life. And then there were the other scars. A Confederate who had fought at Franklin, or Gettysburg or Nashville and knew defeat, eaten defeat, worn defeat. He had surrendered at Durham Station or Appomattox and sworn to himself he would never lose again.

Titus, no second name given, was an expatriate who had nothing to lose.

Claw Kiley, United States marshal, had everything to lose.

No so equal a contest after all.

"Ready, fire!"

Eleven shots this time. Ten bottles felled.

The day grew hotter.

The contestants reloaded. The barrels of both guns singed the flesh. Claw's fingers burned as he shoved cold bullets into blistering gun-metal chambers. The former artillerist did not flinch. His fingertips had been calloused long ago. In the line of duty. For Country, if not for Cause. It no longer mattered.

A new War had begun.

Always a war. Men were never satisfied until they were embroiled in a fight. It was the struggle which made life sweet.

For the victor.

Claw had seen enough of war. He had returned west to put an end to armed conflict. The irony being, he would achieve his goal by fighting every day of his life. In the battle for civilization, there was no Durham Station.

This time, the man at the line with the stopwatch did not say a word. Both gunfighters readied themselves and responded simultaneously to the inner twitchings of the other. It was a shootout in every sense but where the bullets flew.

Twelve shots, eight bottles down, two left standing. One on either side.

There was a reason battles began at dawn. Men were fresh, and hope dawned with the rising sun. Darkness dispelled, soldiers were eager for the fray. They walked with a lively step, shot with a true eye. As the hours wore on, nerves became jangled and faith wavered like a decimated line. Rifles grew heavier and were fired, rather than aimed, more for the sake of effect than purpose. Getting a drink of water, stealing a nap, living to fight another day, became of paramount important.

Let the generals and the news correspondents decide who won and who lost. Pray for darkness and deaf ears, for the screams of soldiers suspended between heaven and hell would break a man's spirit faster than a screeching round shot exploding a tree three feet from where an infantryman cowered.

They reloaded and fired again and the crowd pressed in, eager to see, to condemn and to congratulate. They were the Washington civilians who came to watch the glorious Stars and Stripes scatter the enemy at Bull Run. They were the Matthew Bradys with cameras, the journalists from the *Mercury* and the *Inquirer,* the spectators from Great Britain. They were the judges, the fire eaters, the state senators and the speculators. They all had a stake in the outcome, although most of those gathered close behind Claw Kiley and the Rebel named Titus were on the wrong side.

Fighting the wrong war.

Twelve more times the pistols fired and gunsmoke filled the air, stinging the noses, leaving a grey residue on the tongues of drooping mouths. Then twelve more times again until two bottles stood stark still and upright on one side, while a lone sentry guarded the other.

Appomattox.

With shaking hands, Claw reloaded his gun, as he had been taught, then holstered it. He turned to face his opponent who was no longer his enemy.

"Be out of town by nightfall," he said.

He required no reply but the vanquished gave one.

"Yes, sir."

A last concession to honor.

Stunned silence, then a whoop of unmitigated joy shattered the moment. Cougar Bradburn, arms thrown over her head, raced to the lawman and threw them around him. Startled, then awash with pleasure, Claw Kiley engulfed her slender form and squeezed with all his remaining strength. The next time she whooped it was because he had expelled all the air from her lungs.

Unable or unwilling to fight back, Cougar grabbed Claw's hat and flung it into the crowd. Better than fireworks, her joy proved contagious and started a *melee* of cheering, until the voices of Hellhole were raised in celebration. They had known it all along. He was their marshal, wasn't he? He had come to Hellhole to protect them. Well, by George, he had.

"Three cheers for Marshal Kiley!"

"Hurrah for the marshal!"

"Shootin' champ of Hellhole!"

Some man, either the mayor or Bix Bradley, relieved no more bottles would be sacrificed, for they were worth a penny apiece when resold to the bottler, stepped up to the winner and made a low bow.

"Congratulations, sir, and on behalf of...." But his words were drowned out and no one ever heard the remainder of the speech. More importantly, they saw the orator presenting the marshal with a shiny ten dollar gold coin and a small wooden box. Not much as trophies went, but they were the first things Claw had ever won.

Not counting his job, which could fairly be said to have been earned.

"Thank you," Claw stammered, nonplused and awkward. He had expected something, but surely not this.

"Say a few words, Marshal!" The gathering picked up the sentiment and it reverberated as a chant.

"Speech! Speech!"

"Come on, Marshal. You're the winner. Say something."

Claw pursed his lips, licked them and swallowed nervously. He would rather face ten former Confederates in a shooting contest than make a speech. Jack Duvall never told him he would have to address crowds. Not in a peaceful situation, anyway.

What to say?

"May I have my hat back?"

The crowd whooped as though he had said something profound. More cheers rent the air and somebody, somewhere held up the precious hat.

"Here it is, Marshal. Pass it down, boys."

The Stetson passed from hand to hand, each taking a moment to touch the fabric, run their fingers over the crown or perhaps try it on. No one noticed who did it, but by the time the tan felt cowboy hat reached its final destination, a bright peacock feather had been firmly embedded between the ribbed ribbon hatband and the brim. Afterwards, some said it was so neat a job only a surgeon could have done it, but, of course, that was only hearsay, and those who knew the doctor could not imagine how he, of all people, would come to have a peacock feather in the first place.

Suffice to say, the purple-eyed feather became a real crowd pleaser, although only by constant pleading did the marshal agreed to wear it for a day. Placing the newly decorated hat on his head, he blushed, smiled and offered his treasure box to Miss Cougar Bradburn, saloon girl. When she demurred, he bent and whispered something in her ear.

In response to his request, she opened the box, revealing twenty-four huckleberry confections, covered in chocolate. They were only slightly squashed and those which had melted, she assured him, she would eat first. To prove her point, Cougar fingered a sticky mass of chocolate and purple, syrup-like treat, then popped it into her mouth. Her grin gave testimony that these were the best chocolates she had ever eaten.

The marshal and shootin' champion of Hellhole returned the grin and doffed his hat to the lady, the feather flashing in the afternoon sun.

Yankee Doodle Dandy had come to Hellhole.

CHAPTER 10

Hand-in-hand, they walked back to the Lowdown. Claw had never held a lady's hand for so long a time, and when it came time to release her, he found their skin had been permanently affixed by sweat. It required an obstinate tugging to free himself.

Cougar waited patiently for the blush on his cheeks to fade before speaking.

"Would you like to come up, tonight?" she asked. Not, *Would you like to come over and have a drink, tonight?* but *Would you like to come up, tonight?* Claw swayed in the breeze like a tree trunk which has been half-chopped through.

He swallowed, cleared his throat, wiped his brow, then grinned.

Nervously.

"I was thinking," he began, then cleared his throat again in an attempt to sound more worldly, if not more manly. "I was thinkin' of asking you out."

"You were?"

"Yes." Then, more firmly, "Yes!"

"Out. As in -- out? Outside?"

He wanted to take her outside? With the tumbleweeds and the snakes?

"Outside," he agreed. Perhaps her look of puzzled dismay rattled his cage. He reached into a vest pocket and held up his treasure. "Ten dollars!"

She almost said, and had to bite her tongue, *I only charge five. Will you be looking for change?* Instead, she settled for raising her red-tinged eyebrows.

"Out to eat," he elaborated.

She heaved a tremendous sigh of relief. Yankees sure had a peculiar way of expressing themselves.

That thought might have comforted Cougar had she believed that to be the real explanation. However, she had a sinking feeling it could not be that simple.

"Out to eat," she repeated.

"Sure. Where ever you'd like to go."

She was more than tempted to tell him. It had something to do with her original question.

"That would be fine."

"Shall I come over and get you?"

"I think you had better. It wouldn't look quite right, me going over to the Marshal's Office. People might get the wrong idea."

"Yes," he agreed. "They might think I arrested you."

He laughed and she gagged. Inwardly.

Cougar took a step back and suspiciously eyed him.

"What the hell is going on here?"

If he had any sense, or the least experience with women, he would have let the smile on his face fade into the sunset. He continued to grin.

"I just invited you out for supper and you just accepted."

A hand went to her hip. "How old are you?"

"Twenty-three."

"Are you sure?"

"As sure as I can be."

Had he replied with the least trace of artifice, he might have been in no condition for supper. Or that which traditionally came after, and to hell with the consequences.

"Have you ever been with a woman?"

Claw's blue eyes opened. He uncomfortably scanned the street. No one paid them the least attention.

"You can't ask me that," he finally managed.

"I just did."

"Well, yes," he whispered.

For a moment, she could not be certain he acknowledged the fact she had posed a question, or actually answered it. She hoped for the best and opted for the latter. "Did you know what you were doing?"

If possible, his eyes opened wider.

"I'll -- I'll tell you later," he stammered. Afraid the walls might betray his confession, he backed off then mumbled, "I'll come 'round at seven. Is that all right?"

"To take me to supper." He nodded. "That will be fine. Do you want me to dress?"

It was mean, it was unfair, it was utterly, totally irresistible. For a man of Claw's great experience, he should have no trouble divining her meaning.

"Yes!" Near a shout. Cougar demurely nodded.

"I shall be dressed and ready by seven o'clock."

Claw walked away, thanking God she had thought to ask.

Business at the Lowdown routinely picked up around four in the afternoon and reached its peak by eight. One of the girls worked the floor from noon until four, when a second joined her. By seven o'clock, all three of the girls currently employed at the Lowdown were present, taking turns serving customers or helping behind the bar. Bix Bradley, the owner, generally made his appearance at five and stayed until closing. He did not work, *per say*, but spent his time chatting with the customers or occasionally playing poker for the House.

A good card player, he seldom had a losing night. When he won a particularly large pot or when it appeared his luck ran too well, he bowed out and let someone else take his place, never losing sight of the fact his income and the good will of the townspeople were inextricably tied together. Send too many men home with their pockets empty or their brains sodden, and he placed himself in jeopardy.

Bix had returned early from the fair. He stood at the end of the bar going over his account book when Cougar entered. Her appearance occasioned no more than a second look from him and he was therefore surprised when she approached.

"I'd like the evening off. I can work 'til six-thirty, if you like," she added, to soften the request.

"Why? Not feeling well?" His voice held an edge. "Fiz Ward was here ten minutes ago looking for you."

"It's nothing like that," she assured him. He raised an eyebrow, then shrugged.

"Do what you want. That the new marshal I saw you with just now?"

"Yeah. He invited me to supper."

"You bring him back here, don't clip him. I don't want any trouble."

Clearly, Mr. Bradley thought her sole interest in the lawman lay in his salary and whatever else filled his trousers.

"I won't."

"What's he like?"

"He'll be in to see you."

"Figured he would. Tell him to come 'round tomorrow."

"What time?"

"Some time after noon."

He saw no sense disrupting his schedule to meet with the new marshal.

"I'll tell him."

She started to move away. Bradley watched her with dull, interested eyes.

"He can do better, you know."

"Thanks a lot." She did not need the reminder.

"Work until six-thirty."

They were cruel jabs and she understood them as such. Cougar had never liked Bix Bradley but that dislike had been no more than a passing irritation. As men went, he was no better than most and worse than some. As an employer, he was cheap, dirty and occasionally demanding.

Adding cruelty to the mix made him drop like a rock in her estimation.

She would have liked the extra time to prepare herself, to make herself pretty. Work the rouge in a little more, try on that special dress. The one she had been saving. Spend some time washing her arms, cleaning under her nails. Check herself out in the mirror. Ask the other girls for their opinion. Working until six-thirty would ensure she had time for none of that.

"All right."

She had no choice and he knew it. He could replace her with a snap of his fingers. Keeping her in her place just made things easier.

If Bix Bradley had seriously considered the notion Miss Bradburn was more than a passing fancy of Marshal Kiley's, he might have reconsidered. In that case, she could be a tool -- a weapon to use against the lawman.

Treat me well and I'll take care of her. Do wrong by me and I'll make her life hell.

But the idea was unthinkable. Unrealistic. An affront to the proper social order.

Cougar went upstairs and changed into her working dress. It was low cut and tight. The kind of outfit a girl used to lure men into dropping an extra fifty cents or a dollar between her breasts. For the first time in her life, such clothes were a humiliation.

Had she the breeding of a proper woman, she might have cried. Because she did not, she merely let the hurt harden her heart.

That made her regret the fact she had accepted the supper invitation.

Making her way downstairs, Cougar resolved to cancel the date. What was the point? She did not feel not hungry, anyway.

Approaching a dirty, smelly, repulsive-looking cowboy at the bar, she placed a bare arm around his shoulder.

"How we doin' tonight?" she purred. He beamed and straightened his collar. It never hurt to feel superior to someone.

Even if it were only a "painted pony."

Marshal Kiley arrived promptly at 7:00. Cougar was still downstairs. She had not gone up at six-thirty to get ready. She had not worked in the rouge, washed her arms or tried on her fancy dress. She had not even noted the passage of time. She had been busy pouring drinks down drunks' throats. For her trouble, she had earned fifteen cents.

Cougar did not see him come in, but felt his presence as though a bugler had played revile. He stopped just past the swinging doors and looked upward, where he presumed her to be waiting. She could feel his disappointment at not seeing her.

Damn the bastard.

She felt his eyes shift, scan the downstairs. She made no attempt to hide. There was nowhere to go. She laughed loudly at an unspoken joke, slapping a pimply-faced clerk on the back as though he had said something funny. He grinned and laughed with her.

Or was that *at* her?

Did it matter?

She laughed so hard she did not hear him come up behind her. He walked on cats paws. He did not touch her as another man might, he merely stood grave and silent, waiting to catch her eye. She purposely averted her head. His weight shifted from one leg to the other.

What are you waiting for? What is it you don't get? If Claw heard her silent questions, he gave no indication. *Am I going to have to hit you over the head?*

"Miss Bradburn?"

By not going away, he forced her to turn. And address his damned salutation. Her eyes flashed, filling her heart with gall. *Mister, I'm gonna tell you off, read you the riot act. I've already invited you upstairs once; you think I'm gonna beg? I don't need to be softened up by a meal. It won't work. All you have to do is cross my palm with a coin --.*

And then she saw his face. His eyes sparkled with inner light. He had shaved and smelled mildly of soap and scrubbing. He wore a corduroy jacket and held his hat in his hands. He had removed the feather.

"Am I early?"

Three words, conveying respect, hope and tenderness; descriptions far removed from her reality.

Stinging phrases sat on the tip of her tongue. For the last half hour, she had rehearsed them all.

She spoke none of them.

"No. You're right on time."

His relief appeared so palpable, she hated herself.

"Just give me a minute go upstairs and change."

Change into what? she demanded of herself as she sipped away. *Change into a lady? Change into the governor's daughter?* She did not even know the name of the governor, much less if he had a daughter.

Her new dress hung in the wardrobe where she left it. On close inspection, it looked cheap, gaudy and revealing. It looked like a saloon girl's costume, which it was. Not at all the kind of dress a woman wore when being escorted out by a gentleman.

But then, who said Claw Kiley was a gentleman? He was a gunfighter with a badge. No more than that.

The association reassured her. Slipping the new dress over her shoulders, she even paused to admire herself in a floor-length mirror some nameless woman who had come and gone before her, had placed by the bed.

With red hair, smattering of freckles, beauty mark on her cheek and bright blue eyes, Cougar Bradburn knew she was pretty. Not the most beautiful woman in the world, perhaps, but passable. For Hellhole, a knockout. She shouldn't have to worry. He was handsome and she pretty. She was tall and he, taller. His shyness matched her brassiness.

She had seen relationships start with less.

By the time Cougar skipped down the stairs, her good spirits had been restored. Allowing him to slip an arm through hers, she whispered, "It's going to be a good evening, after all." Being a gentleman, he did not inquire about the *after all.*

They almost made it to the batwings before a chair went crashing through the plate glass mirror Bix Bradley had mounted behind the bar. She heard Bix curse and she felt Claw pull away. With an impatient tug of her own, Cougar caught his attention.

"You're off duty," she warned. His formal invitation and his arm through hers conferred on Cougar the power to speak. With another man, she would have let it go, but the feel of his body next to hers made the argument worth fighting. He frowned, without comprehension.

"Fight," he muttered and left her at the door.

Had it been in her power to blast him to hell, Claw Kiley would have been no more than a fading memory by morning.

The marshal reached the fracas in three long strides. Grabbing one man by the shirt, he yanked him away from the opponent he was attempting to strangle and sent him flying. The cowboy hit the bar hard, groaned and lay still. The man with red welts around his throat revived enough to rear back his right hand, ball it into a fist and force that weapon squarely into the nose of the lawman who had just saved his life.

Blood spurted everywhere. From the stairs, one of the Lowdown girls named Julie screamed. Neither scared nor shocked at the sight of blood, she screamed because practical experience had taught her that men's thirst increased when they thought a woman frightened.

Wiping his bleeding nose on the back of his hand, Claw briefly stared at the red stain of mortality, then turned his attention back to the fighter. Angrily gritting his teeth, he landed a fist on the drunk's jaw and had the satisfaction of feeling the hinge snap with a resounding crack.

"All right. Let's go," he growled, hauling the man with the broken jaw to his feet. Making no resistance, Claw dragged him to the bar, where he collected the first combatant. "Get up!" The man did as he was ordered, receiving for his trouble Claw's other hand around his neck. "You're both going to jail."

"They owe me for damages, Marshal!" Bix Bradley called as Kiley and his prisoners moved toward the doors. "Check their pockets before you let them go."

"They'll be over in the morning to work it off," Claw promised, then unceremoniously shoved the two men through the swinging doors. His date for the evening might have opened them for him, but she did not.

A lady did not open a door for a gentleman. Or a marshal.

Claw half pushed, half shoved the drunks across the street. Kicking open the door to his office with a fluid motion which bespoke long practice, he guided them through the outer area into the back. The first he deposited in the cell to his left, the second he heaved into the center.

Grabbing the keys, he locked both doors, thus securing his first visitors to Hellhole.

"I'm hurt," one groaned.

"You'll get over it."

"I'm hurtin' bad. My jaw. I need the doc."

"Not nearly as bad as he needs his sleep. You can see him in the morning. Before I bring you back to the Lowdown to work off your debt."

"I gotta be away in the mornin', Marshal."

"Too bad."

Claw slammed the separating door, nearly closing it on the slight frame of Fiz Ward. Realizing his mistake, Claw grunted an apology. The doctor distrustfully sidled away.

A momentary standoff ensued before the physician spoke.

"Nice of you to protect my rest."

"There's nothing wrong with him."

"State of Kansas usually pays me some for looking in on the prisoners."

Claw could not be sure if the doctor were complaining or merely stating a fact. He decided he did care.

"If they're both alive in the morning and still in pain, I'll call you."

Ward hesitated, then rubbed his mustache with the pointer finger of his right hand.

"That's a bit of a cavalier attitude, isn't it?" he asked, turning away.

"What about his nose?"

Fiz stopped in his tracks and looked sharply toward the door. Cougar Bradburn stood there, eyes slanted, mouth tight. Fiz shrugged, but made a casual assessment of the marshal's face.

"I suppose it can wait until morning. I've got some sleep to catch up on."

With that, he brushed past and left.

"I'm sorry," Claw apologized. She misunderstood and made a low laughing noise in the back of her throat.

"He's always like that."

"For the trouble, I mean."

"Oh. Me, too."

She would have left, but he stopped her with a wave.

"If you'll wait a minute, I'll wash up. We can still go out, can't we?"

"I didn't think you'd want to. What, with prisoners to watch."

"They're not goin' anywhere."

"What if they have friends?"

"I saved a cell for them."

She smiled in spite of herself.

"All right. I'm in no hurry."

Claw removed his jacket, rolled up his sleeves and washed his face in the shaving basin he had foresightedly filled for next morning's shave. He made a face at the sight of his bloody nose in his pocket mirror, then cupped water in his hands and splashed away the blood. When he finished, only slight swelling and a red welt remained.

"Good as new," he tried with a smile. She did not return it.

"Are any of us ever as good as new?"

A quietly poignant question and he considered thoughtfully before answering.

"Maybe you don't want to go out." She frowned. "With me, I mean."

"Maybe I don't. Maybe I've seen the way it's gonna be."

"Yes, ma'am. The way it has to be. Doesn't mean you have to starve to death."

"Doesn't it?" He scowled. "The Regent is closed for the night."

Not what she meant, just how she chose to end the thought. Cougar gave him enough credit to divine her true meaning.

Give a man enough rope, he always hanged himself.

"Is there any other place we can go? To eat," he amended so quickly she almost lost her appetite.

"There's Ma Smitt's. It's not far." The effort cost.

"I saw the place when I was making rounds. Will she serve us if it isn't Monday?"

He finally succeeded in pleasing her. "If she won't, you can threaten to arrest her."

"On what grounds?"

"Prostitution."

Her answer, spoken in deadpan, caused him to do a double-take. He guffawed, sending a spray of spittle in all directions. This time, she laughed with him.

"I'm ready if you are."

"I'm ready."

He extended his arm and they began the journey of a thousand miles with the second of their single steps.

CHAPTER 11

Ma Smitt was just pulling down the shades when she heard the bell tinkle. Without looking up, she called, "Closed."

"We'd appreciate it if you could make an exception, Mrs. Smitt."

She did not recognize the male voice.

"Nothing fancy. We'll just stay long enough to eat whatever leftovers you have."

She recognized the female voice and started to indicate the door when she beheld a giant of a man standing beside a young woman. The man wore a badge. She covered her momentary shock by wiping her hands on her apron.

"Good evening, sir. I heard Hellhole had a new marshal, but no one told me what to expect. It gives a widow-woman comfort to have a man like you around."

Cougar felt the muscles in her abdomen tightening, but the smile on her face would have pleased a trail boss with a payroll in his pocket.

"Good evening, Ma," she greeted, purposely adopting the housekeeper's familiar name as revenge for the heave-ho she would have gotten. "I told Marshal Kiley you wouldn't mind staying open until he's had his dinner."

"We were going to the Regent, but there was some trouble in the Lowdown and I got held up," he added.

"I hope, Marshal, that by 'held up,' you mean 'detained,' rather than 'robbed'. I cannot imagine anyone having the courage to hold a gun on you."

She meant to flatter and succeeded.

"It's been known to happen," he humbly admitted. "But if you don't mind us putting you out, I'd be greatly obliged."

"Not at all. Sit down and let me stoke the fire. It will just take me a moment to put a fresh pot of coffee on."

"I'd watch out for her," Cougar whispered as the matronly woman disappeared. "She's been a 'widow-woman' for as long as anyone hereabouts can remember. Frankly, no one ever knew her when there was a 'Pa Smitt.' Some say she never was married."

He took the statement for a joke and laughed.

Whether Cougar meant it that way or not was problematic.

"I have some calf's liver left over from supper," Ma sang. "Or would you prefer beef stew."

Claw and Cougar exchanged glances.

No contest.

"We'll have the calf's liver," Claw called back.

A momentary banging of pots and pans preceded the scent of brewing coffee. The two just opened their mouths to begin a conversation when Ma joined them. She smiled sweetly.

"I'll have you fed in no time at all, Marshal. Where have you been taking your meals, if I may be so bold."

"Rustled up my 'grub' in the office," he admitted, then winked at Cougar. "'Grub' is an interesting word, ma'am," he teased.

"Is it?"

"There's 'grub' as in food, and there's 'grub,' as in little white worms."

"The 'interesting part' comes when the little white worms make grub out of us," Miss Bradburn dryly retorted.

"And where are you putting up?" Ma asked in a loud, preemptive voice, effectively preventing Claw from pursuing the subject.

"I'm staying in the Marshal's office."

"If you're looking for a nice quiet room, simple meals and good, Christian companionship, I can put you up here," the widow pursued. "Having you around would make me feel so much better. And my customers, too. I could offer you a very fair price."

"I better stay where I am," Claw confessed, feeling Cougar's eyes bore a hole through his skull. "Besides, I don't think your lodgers would appreciate being roused out of bed every time I got called late at night."

He managed to placate Ma, although she appeared deeply disappointed.

"Well, you keep it in mind," she urged. "And don't mind about a late hour if you come in tired and hungry. As long as you see my shades pulled up, just knock on the door and come on in. I'll fix you something."

Cougar seized that moment to have a coughing fit.

"Water," she managed to articulate between breaths. The housekeeper hurried after a glass. The moment she disappeared, Cougar recovered.

"She made you quite an officer, Mr. Kiley. Don't see how such a respectable gent could have turned her down. Good food, good Christian companionship, soft bed --"

"Be quiet!" he hissed, deeply mortified.

"Get those offers a lot, do you?"

"No!"

"Just because she's old enough to be your mother doesn't mean she don't have desires, Marshal. A man could do a lot worse than a marryin' up wid that widder-woman."

"Quiet!"

"She's put the mark on you. You better watch out. Next thing you know, she'll be leaving fresh baked bread and cookies on your desk."

He looked up sharply, eyes as intense, if not as knowing, as hers.

"I prefer hard boiled eggs."

Cougar blinked once then began coughing as Ma Smitt providentially returned with a glass of water in one hand and a coffee pot in the other.

"Here, Miss Bradburn," she said, placing the glass beside the young woman. Then, to the marshal, she added, "I'll be right back."

She proved as good as her word. Soon, coffee cups were filled to the brim with hot beverage and dinner served. Alongside the liver were generous portions of boiled potatoes and thick slices of bread. A plate with butter, melted from the heat of the day, completed the feast

"Anything else?"

"This looks fine."

Ma retired to a stool in the corner and went about some knitting. The two diners conspiratorially lowered their voices.

"She's chaperoning us," Cougar explained.

"Why?"

"This is a respectable house."

"She doesn't think --?"

It was Claw's turn to choke. Cougar watched unsympathetically as he washed down his interrogative with boiling coffee.

"Of course she 'thinks,'" Cougar pursued when he managed to breathe again, and consequently listen again. Then, more directly, "What do *you* think?"

"I think I'm hungry."

"So am I."

The double entendre was lost on her dinner partner.

"Do you like fish, Marshal?" came a voice from the corner.

"Yes, ma'am."

"Once a week or so Fiz Ward brings me what he catches. I clean it and fry some up for him and take the rest as payment."

"For services rendered," Cougar whispered. Claw coughed again.

Obviously, a miasma contaminated the air.

"You want I should call you when I get some catfish? Tastes mighty good fried up in corn meal."

"Doctor have that much time to go fishing, does he?"

"He's always being called off to some farm house or the other. I expect he tarries a bit on the way back."

Claw raised an eyebrow, tipped his head in Ma's direction and looked at Cougar.

"Does she have eyes for the doctor, too?"

"If she does, she sleeps lonesome. From what I hear, he's busy... elsewhere."

Claw laughed. Cougar wondered if it were for the right reason.

"You hear a lot, I expect."

"Oh, not much gets by me."

"'bout that I figured."

She had been right. He had laughed for the wrong reason.

"So," he said, digging into his liver. "Tell about yourself; your father."

"I never knew him."

He had not expected that reply and started down at his plate.

"I'm sorry."

"Why? I'm not."

"I never knew my folks, either. It leaves a hole."

She bit the inside of her lip and did not release it until she tasted blood.

"What about your mother?" he pursued. For a man of few words, he talked a lot. Too much.

"Never knew her, either. Least ways, not that she admitted to."

"What do you mean?"

She wondered if he were taking a survey.

"I mean, I grew up around a lot of working women. Any one of them might have been my mother. But if one was, she never admitted it."

As clear as ice. And just as cold.

Claw shivered.

"How is it you ended up in Hellhole?"

"I was looking for something better than I had. I ran out of money, so here's where I stopped. I'll be movin' on again soon," she added from pride. And perversity.

"Where you be going?"

"San Francisco. Ever been there?"

"No. Heard some about it."

"Or, I might go to Saint Louie. Ever been there?"

"No. Is it nice?"

"It's all right. It's on the Mississippi. I miss the river. Ever been on a riverboat?"

"Been on boats and pontoons, some. In the War. But I've never even seen a riverboat. Big, aren't they?"

She nodded, remembering. "And then some. The fancy ones have private state rooms. Ever seen a flush commode?"

"I don't even know what that means," he confessed, putting down his fork to stare at her with interest. "Tell me."

"It's sort of an outhouse without bein' dug in the ground," she confessed with a light smile. "On a riverboat, the head is situated on the upper deck. Once you've done your business, you pull a rope and river water comes up and washes away the crap. That's why they call it 'crap,' you know," she shyly added. "Because the flush commode was invented by a man named Crapper."

"Do tell."

Claw folded his hands and leaned across the table, clearly impressed.

"You know a lot. I admire that."

"I don't know much," she flustered, feeling foolish and wondering why she had said what she did. It had been her intention to impress him and now that she had, she did not know how to handle the compliment. "Not as much as you."

"I wish I knew more. You go to school?"

"I read some books. Not much. I wasn't interested then."

"And now?"

"Are you ready for some pie, Marshal?" Ma called. Her continued refused to include Miss Bradburn in her questions was not lost on him. He turned in the chair and addressed her.

"Yes. I think Miss Bradburn and I would like some pie."

The woman set her knitting down on the stool and retired to the kitchen. She returned in a moment.

"I hope you like peach pie. Not from fresh," she added. "We don't see too many peaches here in Hellhole. I made it from preserves. Canned peaches."

"Sounds good."

Ma brought the pie plate to the plate. One large piece remained.

"If I had known you were coming, I would have left more."

"There's plenty." Claw licked stray bits of liver and potatoes from his knife, then divided the piece exactly in half. "More than enough for the two of us."

His declaration emboldened Cougar and she placidly raised her eyes.

"We could use more coffee. Unless you're going to save it for morning."

"Oh, no, I never do that!"

The implied insult sent Ma Smitt scurrying to the kitchen.

"You eat the pie, Claw. I want you to have it."

"Well," he drawled, picking his teeth with the sharp point of the knife, "If'n I had one o' them flush commodes you was a tellin' me aboot, I might feel more com-fer-a-table eatin' it all. But seein' as all I got is one of them old-fashioned shit houses -- and none too clean at that -- I reckon I'll settle fer splittin' what's here wid you-all."

"That bein' the case, Giant, I'll accept yer generosity."

"I was hopin' you'd see it my way, ma'am."

He had the pie dished out by the time Ma returned. She filled both cups, then returned to her stool. They consumed the rest of the meal in blessed silence.

When the last of the crust had been soaked in the dregs of his coffee, Claw sighed contentedly and hooked his thumbs around his belt.

"I'm full," he declared. As well for him he did not say, "I'm satisfied."

"Me, too," Cougar agreed.

He stood, made a small motion for Cougar to wait, then crossed behind her and gently pulled back the chair. She allowed him this small courtesy, feeling like a grand lady.

Manners were a concept entirely unknown to the gentleman of the west. Ranking only above "respect" on a very long list of unknowns.

"Thank you."

"My pleasure."

Oddly, she believed him and she did not believe easily.

"How much do I own you, Mrs. Smitt?" Claw asked.

"Call me Ma. Everyone does. The supper 'ill cost two dollars."

Exactly two hundred cents more than it would have cost if he came alone.

He handed her the ten dollar prize coin and she demurely turned her back while making change. Handling money was not a lady-like occupation and she did not wish to tarnish her image.

"There you are, sir. Eight dollars change. And come again. Come on Sunday when I make fried chicken."

"I'll remember that," he promised. "Good night." He might have added, *And thank you,* but did not. His omission was noted and duly appreciated by one of the two women.

Whether Ma marked it or not remained a mystery.

He and she walked into the warm night air, one pair of hands created from two sets. They were young, they were excited and they were scared. The world had suddenly taken on an entirely new meaning, and the road already blazed now seemed untrodden and foreign.

The man and woman were no longer strangers but not yet lovers. Gone, their identities of lawman and saloon girl, temporarily snatched from them by the impish fingers of the Man in the Moon. A crescent tonight, his object lay in hiding as much as he revealed.

Darkness blanketed the street, lit only by celestial bodies and sporadic candles left to sputter out of their own accord. Unlike previous nights, the lamp-lighter had failed to make his rounds, rending useless the glass globes. Blackness exacerbated the couple's status as outcasts: one lacked respectability, the other tenure. Neither noticed.

Caring would dawn anew beside the sun. Tonight, they needed no more company nor any acceptance greater that that achieved by their sympathetic hearts.

Claw squeezed Cougar's hand and she responded by resting her head on his arm.

"If you give me five minutes, I'll slip into the Lowdown and find us a room," she whispered. No need existed for her to lower her voice, for only her intended could hear her. Caution stemmed from instinct, the rule of self-preservation. A lover's quest for privacy.

He hesitated, then pointed down the street.

"Will you come to the Marshal's Office? We can be alone there without alerting the town gossips. I'll put a sheet over the front window."

Choosing "sheet" proved his intentions were directed in the right direction.

"Just this once. I can't keep slipping over there."

"Why not?"

"Bix Bradley."

Two words, one name. Behind it, Cougar could have added, *He owns me, Claw. And if he knew, he'd try to own you through me. If I didn't help him, he'd throw me on the street. There aren't any other places for me to go. Drake Dixon at the Wolf's Pelt would hire me on, but I'd have my face slashed in a fortnight. That crowd is rough and they make their own rules. The other places are worse. I've come too far to start again at the bottom with the dregs.*

Claw Kiley had never officially met Bix Bradley but the slight tremor in Cougar Bradburn's hand conveyed all he needed to know.

"I don't like that man."

"It doesn't matter if you do or you don't. That's the way it is."

It never occurred to her to seek protection in marriage. That would get her fired faster than spitting in Bix's face.

No other benefits of civil union presented themselves to her.

Accepting the inevitable, they quickened pace, melding into the shadows to hide their furtive movements. A long way from where they wanted to be, they came upon their destination so quickly, neither could understand how it suddenly appeared out of nowhere.

Opening the door, Claw beckoned she pass then closed it behind him. Securing their safety by placing the back of his desk chair against the knob, he raised an eyebrow.

"I'll see to the windows."

"You'd better; you're sleeping on top."

He grunted and hurried to the task, lighting a candle stub to aid the process. When he had finished, he guided her to his bed, placing the small, doughnut-shaped holder on the floor. The flame flickered but did not extinguish. Shadows danced along the wall.

Watching quietly, as though the silhouettes belonged to two separate people, with whom they bore only a faint association, Cougar finally sat, feeling the roughness of the woolen blanket through the thin material of her dress. He joined her, resting his thigh against hers. Their exhalations, ragged and urgent, filled the chamber, while a shifting in the mattress betrayed his intent to draw near and kiss. Two pair of lips touched, briefly, a brush, no more, as delicate as bird's down, then with force, as old as nature.

Taking the initiative, Cougar slipped her hands between his vest and shirt, pushing down the leather. He swallowed, moaned softly, then assisted. The article of clothing fell to the floor, so utterly forgotten it might never have existed.

Claw's shirt followed, leaving him bare-chested. A dusting of light colored hair grew around his nipples and down his abdomen. She had not thought about what he would look like unclothed until that moment and paused to contemplate the sight. *Good,* she decided. *Exactly perfect. A nice place for a woman to rest her head when all is said and done. A place to sleep in peace.*

A night of firsts.

Repositioning herself so that he might undo the fastenings of her dress, she waited for him to avail himself. Failing to acknowledge her gift, she reached behind and flipped them open. Tugging down the tightly fitted fabric, she removed it to her waist then stooped into the undulating arc of candle light to catch his response. She expected lust and received, instead, eyes, both wondrous and grateful. A smattering of doubt, like gentle rain, washed over her flesh, causing her to doubt his whispered confession of experience.

"Claw."

His head jerked up and he grinned, a foolish, innocent expression.

"Cougar."

If he had said, *I love you,* it could not have held more meaning.

"Help me."

She stood, placing his hands on her hips. He swayed slightly as she guided his fingers. With a tug and a sensuous gyration of her hips, the dress fell away, leaving her clad in naught but cotton drawers. As a bit of wick flared, his mouth formed into a round "O."

If she had been with anyone else, the lady would have laughed.

"Claw."

"Cougar."

As well he knew with whom he sat, if not what lay ahead.

"Take them off," she requested.

"How?"

"I thought you said --"

"I have," he rapidly confirmed. Too quickly. His eyebrows knit. Her heart beat harder.

"You mean, she undressed herself?"

"She was a squaw; an Indian woman. She wasn't wearing --" His words trailed off. She finished the sentence.

"-- anything underneath?" He nodded. "You lay with an Indian?"

A nearly inaudible, "Yes."

"What were you doing with an Indian?"

"Spending the winter with her tribe. The Chief gave her to me...."

"Oh, dear God. And she was your first? The -- only women you've ever been with?"

He sighed and glanced away. A glow seemed to form around his head which she could not easily account for, inasmuch as the candle cast its light away from him.

"I tried later -- in a saloon. The fellows sent me up." He swallowed in soft puzzlement. "I -- I didn't want it to be like that."

"Sweet Jesus." Half in prayer, half in gratitude.

"That's why... I didn't want to go to the Lowdown."

He spoke so quietly she had to place an ear to his face to hear him.

"Claw --"

The sound of his name finally touched his consciousness. Or perhaps her tone struck that which he had sought and never heard. He groaned, this time loudly and with intent.

"Pull down my undergarments."

"Yes, ma'am."

Guileless. Innocent. Eager.

The man who deserved a lady, a blushing bride, a governor's daughter, had eyes only for her.

In her innocence, she did not understand.

He pulled down her clothing and she stood naked beside him. Placing her hands on the back of his head, Cougar pulled it to her abdomen. He kissed the smooth skin, then raised a trembling hand, wrapping it around her buttocks. The touch inflamed.

Hardly daring to release her, Claw stood and unbuttoned the fly of his trousers, impatiently yanking them to his ankles. Awkwardly attempting to shed this outer skin, the cuffs snared over his boot heels. She watched in wordless excitement as he kicked, using his right foot to pull off the left boot, then reversed the process until his feet were free. Socks followed, then mercifully, the trousers.

Her fingers itched.

"No, sir." He froze, fingers at the tie of his drawers. "You shall not deprive me of the pleasure." Imitating a cigar store Indian, he stood at attention as she unknotted the string, then slipped the material past his knees. "Step out," she commanded and he obeyed, remaining immobile as she completed the transformation from clothed to unclothed.

In that moment as they faced one another, a second metamorphosis occurred, creating two virgins from the man and woman of their pasts.

Love, sages observed, bestowed upon its recipients amazing powers.

Cougar opened her arms and Claw came to her, engulfed her, pressed his lips to hers, kissed her. They were young and vital, and as they fell back against the army-issue blanket, their world became no larger than the sphere of one another's bodies.

He found her breasts, played there, lingered over the hardening nipples. He laughed as she tugged his hair and he allowed his mouth to open and suck, like a baby, but with a more worldly purpose, as it was sustenance of another sort he sought.

He moved nearer. Cougar tightened her grip on his biceps, felt the muscle, ran her hands down his back, then between his legs. He jerked, mumbled an unintelligible protest, then protested no longer as he worked his hips, listening to the instructional music from her soul as it guided him.

Claw tightened his muscles, strained, then slipped easily between her legs. He pressed his face to her breastbone, arched his back, wondrous, wondering, heaving then pulling back and repeating the process until his body released the restraint of newness. He loved her and she loved him and they were joined and bound and married in an act far exceeding that of any physical pleasure.

"Cougar, Cougar," he intoned, the sound of her name sweet on his tongue.

"Shhh," she laughed, holding him tight, keeping him close. She had never laughed before, never felt the freedom, never the desire. In this new beginning they forged, coupled in one another's arms, they shared a need, a want, a craving, then parted for breath and began again in a world without end.

They slept, then woke and kissed, the touch of warm, pliable, wet lips reminding them of other things. They grappled, drew together, mated and released, to rest and play again. Insatiable, the force within them bonded until they were no longer two but one. And as dawn rose over the lip of the eastern horizon and time restarted, they nuzzled noses and dozed.

Soon after, too soon after, Cougar awoke to tousle his unruly hair. He copied suit, holding a strand of her long locks between his fingers.

"Red," he breathed.

"Red," she countered, rubbing his face with the back of her hand.

It seemed the funniest thing either of them had ever heard and they laughed, the melodious tones of their shared emotion ringing like church bells, welcoming the day, inviting the start of a new life.

Their joy echoed off the walls of the Marshal's Office, slipped beneath the doors and escaped through the barred windows of the jail cells where two men lay asleep, impervious to the life they had missed.

"Outhouse," the marshal finally grumbled in stifled protest, stretching his long legs over the side of the bunk and landing them squarely on his boots. He tripped as he stood, and Cougar laughed loud at the sight of his more prominent pair of unclothed cheeks.

He hissed, pulled on his trousers, failed utterly in his feeble attempt to button them, then hobbled away, trusting to the outside shadows to hide his sad and obvious condition.

She followed his progress with a woman's right of ownership, then continued to laugh as she dressed, remembering that a sheet made a poor curtain and curious eyes would appreciate the show they provided if she was not gone when he returned.

It felt good to laugh. She had almost forgotten how. And never, ever, had she laughed before noon.

Call it an occupational hazard.

Miss Cougar Bradburn skipped away and disappeared, laughter emblazoned in her soul.

In stark contrast, at a place called Abilene or the Cimarron, Ada Duvall, widow of Marshal Jack Duvall, wept. She had awaken from a nightmare about a laughing woman and a lawman.

Call it an occupational hazard.

CHAPTER 12

"Hey!" the man named Smith grumbled from behind the jail bars. "I'm hurt."

"That so?" Claw inquired with all the interest of a drunk staring at the bottom of an empty bottle.

"Yeah. I need to see the doc."

"He was up early and rode out of town in his buggy. I expect he has law-abiding citizens to take care of this morning."

Claw inserted the key into the lock and turned it. He motioned the prisoner out with a curt nod of his head.

"When's breakfast?" the brawler asked to delay his removal from the cell.

"I don't feed prisoners early."

"Where are you takin' us?"

"If it were up to me, I'd string you up," Claw said with a straight face. When the man did not see the joke, the marshal smiled for him. "But it isn't. That's why we have something called law. Ever heard of it?"

"Some, mebbe," the man acknowledged, glad, for the first time in his life, there existed some obscure concept called "law" which prevented maverick lawmen from hanging a man on a whim.

"Come on!" Claw urged the second prisoner. When Bailey did not stir, he unlocked the door, took one long stride inside and grabbed the sleeper by his collar. "Up and at 'em!"

"What the hell?"

"Not even close. You've got work to do."

"Work?" he asked as though the word held no meaning, which it probably did not.

"Work. At the Lowdown."

"I know a redhead there I'd like to do some work with," he chuckled. His mirth died an ugly death. Claw hoisted him up in one fluid motion and gave him a knee to the groin. He buckled over, hands to his injured organ, then dry retched, face red from pain. The first prisoner stared in fright.

"Bejesus Christ," he swore.

"Now you know why I don't feed prisoners early," Claw nonchalantly explained. "It would have been a waste of good food."

The man dully nodded and took a step away from the tall man with the badge.

"Let's go."

"I cain't even breathe!"

"If you can breathe enough to talk, you're healthy enough to work off your debt to the Lowdown. Move it."

Still in a crouch, Bailey baby-stepped out of the cell, hands rubbing his sore spot. He grunted and groaned all the way across the street. No one paid him the slightest heed.

"Morning!" Claw sang as he directed his charges to wait. "Bix Bradley! Bix!"

After an interminable wait, footsteps were heard shuffling across the floor before the door at the end of the hall burst open. Bix Bradley made an appearance, trousers drooping, suspenders hanging past his knees.

"Who calls Mr. Bradley at this hour?" he demanded, peering through half-slit eyes into the main room below.

"Marshal Kiley. I've brought these two scalawags to work off their damages."

"At this hour?"

"Yup. I need 'em back by noon, so if you have work for 'em to do, say so now. If not, they're coming back with me."

Both prisoners gave a start, glaring at Bix with a sort of twisted pleading. Better to remain in a hell you know, than return to the Marshal's Office and a hell you don't.

"We kin wash bottles," the crouched man volunteered.

"Yeah," said the second, rubbing the tender flesh around his neck that he felt the marshal sizing up for a noose. "We kin wash bottles."

"All right," grumbled the late riser. "And stick around, Mr. Kiley. I'll have a word with you."

"I don't know as you have much to say to Mister Kiley,'" Claw flippantly replied. "If it's Marshal Kiley you need, I'll stick around."

Bradley found new wakefulness and tossed his head back. Nearly bald on top, he wore his hair long in back to cover the deficiency. Claw supposed it made him feel like a gunfighter; or a yellow-jacketed hero. Writers from Back East always portrayed Western men with long hair, as though they were part Injun, part grizzly bear.

The saloon keeper hoisted the cotton braces over his shoulders, tucked the long material of his nightshirt into his trousers, then turned and spoke to someone in his room. The words were loud, the voice cruel.

"I'm done for now, Red. Stay where you are and get some sleep. I'll see you at four."

He slammed the door and walked down the hall with an assumed jauntiness meant for the marshal.

Bix Bradley was a gambling man. He was also a man who knew the score and did not mind capitalizing on another man's weakness. He meant to assert his place, not only as one of the wealthiest and influential men in Hellhole, but also as a man who made the rules, not followed them. Claw Kiley had come into his place of business and disturbed him. He did not like that. Nor did he appreciate the virtue of a man who reputedly could not be bribed.

Bix Bradley was playing poker with Claw Kiley. He knew now what he held in his hand: the queen of hearts. He did not understand its full value, or even why it held value. But as he had learned early, one man's garbage was another man's gold.

Claw waited for the owner to arrive at the bottom of the stairs before turning the prisoners loose.

"They're all yours." His voice reflected tension. Bradley presumed he played to a pair of deuces.

"Nice to finally meet you, Marshal." Kiley turned without speaking, finding his stomach working backwards. Bix raised the stakes. He thought he knew what a marshal was worth. "Wait a minute!" he summoned. Claw turned without the ability to draw.

"What is it?"

"What if they're not done by noon?"

"Clean your own piss pots."

Bradley grinned. His teeth were as crooked as his smile.

"What do I do with them at twelve?"

"I'll be back to get them."

"What are you gonna do with them?"

"Seems to me that's my business." Claw took a step away, then suddenly remembered something. "They haven't eaten. Feed 'em breakfast."

"Why should I do that?"

"Because I said so."

"And who the devil are you to give me orders?"

"I'm the man you call to save your saloon from being torn to bits, first time a war party of hiders hits Hellhole."

"Think you'll be here that long, Marshal?"

"Think you'll be?"

Bradley opened his mouth, but too late. The tall, youthful looking lawman had left. Bix spat into the sawdust, then rubbed the spittle into the floor as though the gesture would salve his wound.

Claw Kiley was a better poker player than he gave him credit for, and Bix Bradley had never issued credit in his life.

"Son of a bitch!"

His queen of hearts had not given him a winning hand.

He might have known.

One man's garbage was another man's garbage, after all.

It did not stand as the biggest bluff Claw Kiley ever played in his life, but it had been the most important.

"Git to work," Bradley grumbled. Clean his own piss pots. That would be the day.

Promptly at noon Claw Kiley appeared to collect his charges. Both were sitting on the floor, up to their elbows in cold water.

"Let's go," he directed.

"Are you gonna set us free?"

"Nope."

"What you gonna do with us? It was only a fight, Marshal. An' I gotta leave Hellhole on the next stage."

"Good thing for you it doesn't leave until four. Get up and come with me."

The prisoners rose, wiped water-pruned hands across their trousers, then dutifully followed Claw. Their progress across the street was momentarily delayed as the four-up drove past on its way out of town. The man with an urgent need to depart said nothing. He guessed the answer.

I said the next stage doesn't leave until four. The "next" one does -- four o'clock tomorrow.

"Over there." Claw indicated the alley to the right of his office. The jail bunks had been stripped bare and set out in a row. Chamber pots and blankets were piled on top beside two irregularly shaped, off-brown sponges and a large wooden bucket.

"Ain't we done enough scrubbing fer one day?" Bailey whined.

"It's either this or you both wait for the circuit judge to hear your case. I expect he'll arrive on the next stage."

"Next stage" in this case referring to September. Or October.

Pulling up a chair, Claw sat down to oversee the operation. While he had no particular interest whether the spittoons and beer mugs in the saloon were clean, it did matter a great deal that his own property shined with spit and polish.

"The water's hot!" Smith complained, holding out his reddened hands for the marshal's inspection.

"Is that so? It was boiling a moment ago."

"And you let me stick my fingers in?"

"I'm drummin' up business for the doctor. State of Kansas pays him something fer lookin' in on the prisoners. I'd hate to think he didn't earn his money."

The two men went to work without further argument.

By midafternoon, the bunks had been scrubbed and set out to dry, the pots cleaned inside and out, the linen and mattresses beaten with a stick and stretched out on a hemp line, like prisoners, to freshen in the wind.

"All right," Claw declared. "You've paid your debt to society. If I see either of you in Hellhole again, you had better mind your manners."

"Yes, sir," they grumbled in unison and traipsed off, cleaner and wiser men than they had been a day ago.

Kiley prepared his own meal, then went to work on the inside of the cells with a will. He scrubbed the walls and the bars on the windows, all of which suffered from prolonged exposure to the elements of wind, rain and tobacco juice. Completing that onerous task, he dropped to hands and knees to scour the floor.

Halting only after it became too dark to work, Claw rinsed his hands in the last of the hot water, then stretched his aching muscles and buckled on his gun belt. He left the office and fell into a natural rhythm of walking. No matter the curious stares he received, Claw had come to stay and the townspeople would either accept his presence in Hellhole or move on.

Compromise, Jim Oates had once declared, *is sometimes a one-way street.*

Doctor Ward's buggy rounded a corner and moved slowly in his direction. Seeing the marshal, he drew up and motioned him over. Claw obliged, tipping his hat in a natural, spontaneous gesture of respect.

"I heard what you've been up to," Fiz began. It was difficult to tell whether he meant his statement to be taken as a compliment or the reverse.

"Hadn't planned on making a secret of it."

"Good idea to make the prisoners work. I approve. State of Kansas has enough expenses without kowtowing to law breakers."

"Like paying the town doctor to see to their hurts?"

Fiz squinted up at the tall man in what could not have been mistaken as a friendly look. "That prisoner had a broken jaw. Did you know that?"

"Didn't stop him from talking."

"He must have been in terrible pain."

"You set it for him, did you?"

"I did not. Haven't seen him since last night. I supposed you ran him out of town."

"How is it your concern for his welfare comes out only after I've 'run him out of town'?"

"I didn't say I had concern for his welfare. I said he had a broken jaw."

Claw nodded. "Just wanted to clarify it in my mind."

"Stay away from Cougar Bradburn."

The abrupt change in subject started Claw so much he nearly tripped over his own feet.

"How's that again?" His voice held an edge not there the moment before.

"You heard me. You may or may not have a broken nose but there's nothing wrong with your ears, big man."

"The name's Claw Kiley. Marshal Kiley. Claw to friends. I'd like to get off on the right footing with you, Doctor Ward, but you're making it awful hard."

"Marshal Kiley," the doctor repeated, speaking through clenched teeth, "Did you take my meaning?"

"I did not."

"That man she works for -- Bix Bradley. You had a run-in with him this morning."

"We had words," came the guarded admission.

"He's dangerous."

"I'm not afraid of him."

"It's not you I'm worried about, you jackass. It's Cougar -- Miss Bradburn. He can make her life pretty... uncomfortable."

Claw gripped the wheel of the buggy. "Say what you mean."

Fiz reigned in the skittish horse, using the action as an excuse to contemplate how best to phrase his thoughts.

"You kept her out late last night."

"That would seem to be by business."

"Are you wet behind the ears, boy? Bix Bradley is an important man in Hellhole. His opinion sways a lot of people. He can pretty much do as he likes here."

"He'll find things different --"

Fiz cut him off with a snarl.

"It's not you I'm worried about. Cougar Bradburn works for Bix Bradley. You might say he owns her."

"The hell he does."

"The hell he does," Fiz repeated, placing emphasis on "does," rather than "hell," which was how Kiley expressed it. "Bix Bradley fires Cougar, there's no place in Hellhole she can get work. No -- clean place. Do I have to explain?"

Claw swallowed the lump in his throat and shook his head.

"No, sir."

"Well, I'm glad of that. Without a job, without friends -- how can she support herself?" Ward rapidly added before he could be interrupted. "Without a man who cares to make an honest woman out of her," he pointedly continued, "she's in trouble. I can loan her some money but she's too proud to take it. So where does that leave her? Trading her body to Jake, the stage driver, for a lift out of town? How far do you think he'll take her before he dumps her by the side of the road, or abandons her at some godforsaken way station?"

"I'm sorry," Claw whispered, face red from shame. "What do you want me to do?"

"I've already told you. Stay away from her. Don't make trouble. Bix worked her over pretty well this morning."

Removing his hat, Claw wiped his brow.

"Why?"

"Because you played games with him. And won, from what I heard. It was an expensive win -- Marshal."

"I never meant for that to happen."

"Didn't you?"

"No. I swear."

"Then you're more naive than I figured. Or just plain stupid. You saw that man; talked with him. What was your opinion?"

"That he was used to getting his own way and that maybe someone ought to put him in his place."

"I wouldn't disagree. He's a good example of the kind of filth that fills hide towns like Hellhole; the kind of man who wants everything and who'll move Perdition and high water to get it. You might have been the man to 'put him in his place.' I don't know. But that changed when you took Miss Bradburn out. Bix's not a fool. You left your calling card on her. You gave him an edge and he took it."

"I'll rub the bastard's face in the dirt," Claw vowed with the sincerity of youth and the confusion of a stinging rebuke.

"Is that what you came to Hellhole for? To take the law into your own hands? That's what he's waiting for. Don't you see?"

The answer was long in coming.

"No."

Heartbreak, conveyed in a single syllable.

"It may not be too late. Leave her alone and Bradley will think you don't care." He raised a hand to silence any protest. "So, he beat her. She's had beatings before. I dare say she'll have beatings again. That's the nature of her business. She'll recover. This time. But next time it will be worse. And each time after that you best Bradley, he'll take it out on her. Her only chance is if he thinks he's made a mistake; that you don't really give a damn.

"He's challenging you, Marshal. You've put yourself up against him and she's caught in the middle. The only way she's going to get out from between you two is if you lower her status. Put her back where you found her."

"In a room upstairs handling six or seven dirty men a night?"

This time, it was Fiz's turn to let the conversation run down into silence. When he finally did speak, his voice had softened, inflecting it with puzzlement.

"Isn't that exactly what you sent her back to?"

Not puzzlement but shame. A shared responsibility.

"I -- I didn't think of it like that."

"Neither did I. Until this moment. Maybe that's what's wrong with us men of the west. We see something that's wild and free and think it's our right to take. It isn't, you know."

He did not wait for Claw to answer, which suited the marshal, for he could not have given one. Ward briefly consulted the sky, then slapped the reins over the rump of his horse. The buggy lurched forward leaving the marshal alone on the street.

More alone than he had ever been in his life.

That evening, Claw Kiley went to the Lowdown and ordered a beer. He took it to a table and sat down by Lilly, one of Bix's other girls which he kept, like hard boiled eggs, for the convenience of his customers. Cougar came down late, saw him occupied and shunned his company. The make-up she wore poorly disguised a black and purple outline under her left eye.

He left after ordering a second beer and paying for Lilly's whisky. She downed her drink in a single swallow then brought the two untouched beers to the bar, where they were placed on a tray and resold. For her trouble she earned a five cents commission and Miss Bradburn's antipathy.

Claw hurried across the street and entered the Marshal's Office, no longer savoring the feel of his town.

Hellhole had altered. But that was nothing compared to how his own self-worth had changed.

Live a little, grow a little, Jack Duvall once said.

He neglected to add, *Live a little, die a little.*

CHAPTER 13

Claw awoke from a dream. He did not remember what he had been dreaming, but it left behind an unpleasant residue. Something about... Something about *something,* but he could not put his finger on it. His failure to recall the images and sounds annoyed him mightily.

Blackness lay heavily upon the pre-dawn heat. Rising with a half audible curse, Kiley fumbled for his boots, forcing leather over bare toes. They would have gone on easier over socks, but he did not plan on wearing them long. A short trip to the outhouse, then back to grab another hour's sleep before starting the new day.

In any case, his socks suffered from acute *rigor mortis* and he did not relish the idea of putting them on. His shirts, too, needed attention. Short of giving his wardrobe a proper burial, he supposed he would have to wash them.

None of his father figures ever said life would be easy.

Shuffling out through the back door, he made his way to the privy when a low, nearly inaudible cry caught his ear. He stopped and cocked an ear yet heard nothing. He had almost convinced himself he imagined the sound when it repeated. A sad, plaintive plea. Annoyed at being unarmed, Claw drifted toward the alley. As he turned the corner, the petitioner came into view.

It was a cat, or, more properly, a kitten, for it was cloaked in baby fur, its small, stubby tail ending in a sharp point. That point proved nothing like the tips its claws and Claw exhaled a sharp "Ouch!" when he tried to pick it up. He dropped it with alacrity and paused to examine eight needle-point punctures in his hands before attempting a different approach.

"Pretty feisty, aren't you?" The kitten's ears moved from an upright position to one directly parallel to its slanted eyes. He stooped lower but kept his distance. "Where's your mother, little fella? You can't be out here all by yourself."

Those words echoed softly in his mind and the six-foot-seven-inch marshal shuddered, remembering a time, long past, when a kindly man had said them to him. He had no more words then, than the kitten did now.

It created a tie between them.

"Come here, kitty. Kitty, kitty, kitty."

Another familiar association, this time of more recent memory. The shock of hearing his own voice repeat the word, so close in relation to "cougar," stirred him into action. He scooped up the animal and cradled it in his arms.

"It's all right," he purred. "I won't hurt you."

The baby's wide-eyed terror melted just as bit as Claw scratched behind its ears, then finally gave way to gentle mewing which grew louder and more demanding with each repetition.

"I bet that means you're hungry," he decided with the wisdom of maturity and the stomach of a boy.

He did not want to put the cat down for fear it would run off, so retraced his steps into the office, set it on his bunk, then went back outside to complete his original business. That done, Claw slipped back, checked to see if the kitten had stayed put, which it had, then opened the front door, discovering, to his relief, his morning pail of milk had already been delivered.

"Here, puss puss," he showed the cat. "I bet you know what this is."

Swinging the pail by its handle, he set it down on the floor, then placed his kitten beside it. The grimalkin gave one loud, demanding meow, then swished its tail, as if wondering how the giant with the kind voice had not anticipated the enormity of its problem. While the pail was easy enough for Claw to drink from, the cat could not reach the top, even by standing on two legs.

Realization came slowly to the worldly bachelor of twenty-three who had not, for the moment, remembered a time when he, too, would have needed help drinking from so formidable an object as a bucket.

"What we need is a saucer," he decided.

The cat signed in satisfaction, having made its point without too much trouble. Human beings were hard to train but if an intelligent feline put some effort into it, they were usually rewarded by some success.

Claw lit his newly filled lamp and rummaged through the store room, discovering a china saucer with the words "Devil's Hole" clearly stamped around the edge. He chuckled and brought it out. One of his predecessors had obviously forgotten to return that which he had borrowed.

Claw, too, would forget.

He did, after all, have much on his mind.

The brief sojourn from cow to stoop had not cooled the milk sufficiently to make it unpalatable to an infant, so he felt safe serving it without additional warming. Despite the written pronouncement on the plate declaring its place of origin as the local hotel, the little beast seemed not to mind and sniffed curiously at the offering. Claw encouraged it as best he could.

"Here you go. Try some of this. It's good."

He demonstrated by putting his finger into the milk then lapping it clean with his tongue.

The kitten meowed again in what might have construed as a laugh, then delicately consumed breakfast. It made no further mention of Claw's curious eating habits.

"You know," the marshal declared as his new companion finished eating and began grooming, "I could use a good mouser around here. There are enough mice in this building to keep you occupied for a long time. What do you say?" The kitten appeared to consider, but its answer was already a foregone conclusion. "I'll trade you a saucer of milk mornings and evenings and shelter from the rain in exchange for your keeping the office mouse-free. Agreed?"

The animal did not look up from its task of licking its fur. Being a marshal, it supposed he understood priorities.

"All right, boy," Claw grinned, taking silence for an affirmative. "You'll need a name. Do you have a preference?"

The kitten flicked a whisker. Claw picked it up and flipped it over, rubbing its belly as an excuse to determine gender. His grin turned slightly evil.

"You're a wild thing, *girl*. Like someone I know. What do you say I call you Cougar? Miss Cougar. They're fearful dangerous hunters. A man'd think twice before tangling with a cougar."

The kitten stretched out a paw and bit between its claws. Claw nodded in sympathy for his own plight. "I know what you're thinking. And you're right. *She* may not appreciate it. But on the other hand...." His voice trailed off. "Maybe she'll understand... what I'm trying to tell her."

This time, Miss Cougar looked up and blinked. She conveyed the wisdom of Bast in her stare. Human beings were always apologizing for something. He nodded in relief.

"Good." Then, with an impish expression, he held out his socks. "You don't do wash, do you? Clothing, I mean."

It was as well the marshal asked the feline rather than the female or he would have found his socks stuffed down his throat.

Such being the inexperience of youth.

Miss Bradburn would have called it something else.

And the last laugh would have been hers.

Feeling better, Claw made breakfast, then gathered up his laundry and washed his entire wardrobe save for the trousers and drawers he had on. Hanging the clothes outside on the line left over from "cleaning day," he declared himself well satisfied.

Hellhole was beginning to feel more like home again.

He would make it up to her; speak the first chance he got. Make her see.

His heart felt lighter. Miss Cougar and Miss Cougar. A man could never have too much of a good thing.

Such being the innocence of youth.

The wind dried his shirt and Claw dressed, enjoying the feel of the rough, clean cloth on arms and chest. His socks, slightly thicker and of wool, were still damp when he put them on. He supposed they would dry as well on his feet as on the line.

It was a few minutes past 9 A.M., if Claw's internal clock ran accurately, when the first shots rang out. He heard two in rapid succession, then another. A fourth came ten or fifteen seconds after the first three. No one, not even a relative newcomer to Hellhole, could mistake the origin of the gunfire. It came from the bank.

Claw raced out the door and down the street before the echoes died. His right hand slipped around the handle of his gun, un-holstering the weapon and gripping it so that it melded to his body, becoming an extension of his arm. He glided like a wolf, in the long, easy strides of one which will travel a long distance without tiring. He could have covered a quarter mile without becoming winded, but it was the exhilaration of the hunt, rather than physical conditioning, which sustained him. He was a man in his element.

The robbers were just emerging from the bank as the marshal came into view. He saw them, counted them, registered their faces in his memory then fired his pistol. He harbored no other consideration than the fact these men were thieves; no judgment of their worth as human beings, no thought to take them alive. They were lawbreakers and he, the law keeper. They had staked their lives for a sack full of gold; he had staked his on a badge.

He did not consider the odds. They were against him, four to one. Had there been a dozen men, he would not have faltered. It was not in his nature. He would not have known how.

Not at twenty-three years of age. Nor at forty-three years of age. As a lawman, he could not be expected to live that long.

Struck by his bullet, one of the bandits screamed and clutched his stomach. Long, protracted and agonized, it escaped into the atmosphere to guide his spirit.

"Hold it right there!" Claw warned. He did not expect them to heed. An obligation, no more.

A shot exploded and an angry bee buzzed by Claw's ear. He jerked his head away, too late if the "bee" had been better aimed.

Too late by a long shot.

He fired again, this time at an outlaw attempting to mount his horse. The projectile went wide but frightened the animal. It reared, bucked then sidestepped, causing the man to lose his balance. He cursed and went down, catching the end of his spur in the stirrup.

Panicked, the horse dragging the thief with it as it bolted down First Street. The second of the four also let out a scream, but more of pain than immortality and Claw ignored it when he saw the robber's pistol lying in the street where it had fallen.

The riderless horse crossed in front of Kiley, blocking his view. This allowed the remaining two a chance to shift behind cover while he remained unprotected. When they fired, he felt the bee sting, rather than whiz past.

One bullet struck Claw in the left arm. He experienced a momentary searing pain, then his fingers went dead. Instinctively ducking away, he felt unbalanced, lopsided. He tripped, stumbled and put his good hand down to block his fall. Thus bent, the next round went over his body. Had he been standing, they would have exploded in his chest.

"Get the man with the money! For God's sake, shoot the one with the money!"

Herbert's voice. Claw would have recognized it anywhere. The man with the barred windows on his personal residence, the short working hours and the high-pitched voice, indicating fear. Not for his own life; not for the well-being of the marshal. He feared losing his investor's money and consequently their good will. To say nothing about their future business.

Claw righted himself, tightened the grip on his pistol and fired as one of the two remaining outlaws went for his horse. He aimed for the broad expanse between shoulders and thighs. The shot went high but not wild, striking the robber in the head. Blood, bone and brains exploded to high heaven. The sack of money he carried dropped faster than his soul, spilling paper money and bright, shiny gold coins onto the street.

Herbert screamed again, this time in warning. His enemies had changed from thieves to the townspeople gathered to watch. Seeing currency explode from the burlap bag, they began a free-for-all, each reaching out and grabbing that which did not belong to them.

"Marshal! Do your duty!" the banker ordered. Destiny intervened to spare his life as the final robber made a break on foot. Claw took deliberate aim, then called one final time.

Not being a man to repeat himself.

"Hold it!"

The robber spun around and fired. His shot went low, plowing a furrow six inches deep at the marshal's feet. He might have tried again, but with the angel of the Lord beckoning its finger, and the vision of his partners fallen before him, he heaved his hand-gun into the street.

"Don't shoot!" he shouted, hands raised. Fortunately for him, actions spoke louder than words, for his plea lost itself in the din of Hellhole's citizens scrambling after loose bills and rolling coins.

Claw reluctantly held up, but not before sating the residue violence stirred in his own blood. Redirecting a piercing glare at the townspeople, he discharged his pistol at a ten dollar gold piece two inches from the fingers of its rescuer. Striking the coin at the edge, it skittered off down the street, scaring the heebie-jeebies out of the shopkeeper. He jumped back, eyes flashing with anger.

"What the hell are you shooting at me for?" For his trouble, the barrel of Claw's pistol leveled at his navel.

"Anyone who touches that money is as guilty as the bank robbers. Stand back."

A sobbing Bodkin Herbert ran into the street and began picking up the coins, chasing wildly after paper which had been kicked up by the wind, blasts of gunfire and the heavy breathing of those left alive.

"Help me, help me!" he pleaded to the Law.

"Pick it up yourself," he received for reply. Claw's left arm throbbed in tempo with his racing heartbeat, sending waves of agony through jangled nerves. The one thing he did not feel was sympathy.

Assuring himself no one would either interfere or aid the banker, he crossed the street, motioning with his gun to the lone standing outlaw.

"Let's go." Deep, throaty, authoritative, the command conveyed anger and pain. He did not expect to be disobeyed, but neither would he have regretted shooting the bastard in cold blood.

The authorities in Hays would never question a terse report, *Four men attempted to rob bank. All killed as they attempted a getaway.*

Raise a few eyebrows, perhaps, but no questions.

Not in Kansas. Not in 1868.

Some things were better left alone.

Far distant from courts, lawyers, legal briefs and judges, dispensing justice resided within the sole discretion of the Badge. His interpretation of law set the tone for his territory. Too much interference from Federal politicians and pencil-pushers would likely get them booted out of office.

And as any stumping official knew, a quick resolution saved the State the cost of a hanging.

As though privy to the swirling thoughts, the remaining thief reiterated, "Don't shoot. I'm unarmed."

Claw motioned with his gun. "Move." Then, to the crowd, "All right. Break it up. There's nothing more to see."

Men who had stuffed paper or coins into their pockets had already gone. Those lingering for a look at the aftermath of slaughter shrugged and shuffled off. They had seen blood and bone and brains before. The difference being, it had usually belonged to the lawman.

Dr. Ward' slight frame hurried against the tide, moving through the crowd with urgency. In his hand he carried a small black medical bag. Claw shook him off.

"You're wounded."

"Yeah."

"Let me take a look at it."

"Not here."

Not where the townspeople could have a better look at his mortality.

"I'll come to your office."

Claw turned pain-filled eyes to the doctor and made a curt nod, effectively transmitting his gratitude. Assuming a new although not unaccustomed authority, Fiz spun around and waved his arms at the few remaining citizens.

"All right you good for nothing's. Who's going to take the bodies to the undertaker's? You? What about you?"

His questions succeeded better that the marshal's growled warning to clear the street.

"I'll help, Fiz," came one soft, respectful reply. Claw did not recognize the voice and turned to have a better view of the speaker. He appeared to be an elderly man, perhaps sixty, but his looks were deceiving. He might have been fifty, possibly younger. Hard to tell with a black, battered hat pulled low over his face and hands displaying the unmistakable tremble of a chronic drunk. Something about him captured the imagination, however. A sense of dignity in denigration, perhaps. Claw liked him immediately; felt a kinship. In another lifetime, this little man might have been a lawyer. Or a lawman.

"All right, Frankie," Fiz acknowledged without due appreciation. "Go up to my office and get the rubber tarpaulin under the table. Bring it down and put what you can of *that* in there," he directed, indicating the decapitated body. You," he ordered another. "Go get Jonathan Harker.

Have him come with a wagon or a litter and take the other carrion off. 'Bout time he worked for his money."

Fiz heard Claw snort but did not bother to reply. His feathers ruffled, however, the physician gave an annoyed scowl to the robber who had gotten tangled in the stirrup and dragged down the street.

"Get up! That is, if you want that leg treated. If not, you can lie there 'till Doomsday, for all I care."

"My leg's busted, doc," he whined. He pleaded to a deaf jury.

"You don't expect me to carry you, do you?"

Ward expressed a callousness endemic to the West. The wounded man could expect no more and in a town other than Hellhole, he would have received far less.

Dragging himself to a water trough, he hoisted himself to a standing position. Contrary to expectations, the doctor joined him and indicated he put his arm around his shoulder. The man did so and together they moved like a crippled, three-legged bug toward the surgeon's office.

"His bark is worse than his bite."

A woman's voice. Claw turned slowly, more readily identifying this speaker. The red-haired woman with the black eye. His heart gave a jump.

"You're wounded," she said. The statement reflected no more than an unemotional observation. He glanced down at his torn, blood-stained shirt and nodded.

"Fiz'll stop by when he's through with that one," he mumbled, finding his lips more numb than his fingers. She shook her head.

"He'll get him upstairs, give him some laudanum then come by the Marshal's Office. Can I help?"

Claw shook his head.

"Not unless I deputize you."

He had not expected her to grin but she did.

"Lilly said you got drunk last night on two beers."

His mouth fell open and he started to protest before realizing her intent.

"Yes, ma'am. I was pretty awful."

"Not so awful. Not from what I saw. Lilly -- she makes things up sometimes."

"I'll remember that."

She was telling him she understood. Letting him know how things were. Making it clear her night with him had been worth the price she ultimately paid. He gratefully bobbed his head.

"Buy a lady a beer later?"

By using a common expression he gave it a larger meaning.

"Tomorrow night... maybe. When you're feeling better. Giant."

"Yes, ma'am."

He watched her walk away, appreciated the way her hips swayed, tasted the lingering scent of perfume on his lips. For a man with a bullet graze on his arm, he had better things to contemplate. Prisoners to incarcerate. The dead to bury. Yet, just as it had two nights ago, his own world suddenly shrunk until it was just large enough to fit two -- comfortably.

"You know," he called. She stopped and turned, a puzzled expression on her beautiful face. The twinkle in his eye caught her, made her pause. One thing she was learning about this marshal -- he was unpredictable -- in a predictable sort of way.

"What is it I know -- or don't know?"

"I ought to tell you something. Just in case you come by the Marshal's Office -- on official business, of course."

She could tell by the way he grinned she was not going to like his "You know.'"

"Of course," she guardedly responded.

"I've got a bunk mate."

"Oh?"

The boyish expression prolonged his life. Momentarily.

"That's right. Want to know her name?"

"Not especially."

"She's warm and obedient and a good worker."

"And just exactly what 'work' does she do for you, Marshal?" Her teeth were clenched, obscuring her words, but not their intent.

"She's about the purdiest gal you'd ever want to meet. She purrs things in my ear."

"She does, does she?"

Perhaps Lilly had not exaggerated as much as Cougar thought.

"That's right."

"What does she say?"

"Oh, all sorts of things. And she's cheap to keep."

"Good for her."

"Don't you want to know her name?" he baited her again.

"Any particular reason I should?"

He's a bastard; I knew right off he was a bastard. Men are just no good. And he's a man. Two men.

"She has a name like yours. Same family."

"Is-that-a-fact?"

"Yup. You should see her claws." He whistled.

"If she hasn't clawed your eyes out, yet, she hadn't gone far enough."

"Miss Cougar. That's what I call her, because that's what she is."

"What is she?" Hurt.

What she is, Cougar knew, *is a whore.*

"A cat. A kitten, actually, but a real little heller. Someone abandoned her out back of the office. I found her this morning and took her in. We made an agreement. She'd keep the office free from mice and I'd let her stay indoors and give her some milk mornings and evenings."

Miss Cougar, saloon girl, had been had.

"You tell her, the day she catches that big vermin in the Marshal's Office to let me know. I'll pin a badge on her."

He blushed. She laughed.

What was the expression? She stared at him with cat's eyes then flicked her tongue.

Even Steven.

Or, in the language of the card sharper, they had played to a draw.

An appropriate expression for a marshal, as well.

CHAPTER 14

Claw sat at his desk, face buried in a stack of wanted posters. He held one in particular, staring at it with a thoughtful expression, as the door opened and Doctor Ward entered, black bag in hand.

Fiz was seldom seen without his medical kit and it was whispered behind his back that he hid a bottle of whisky in it. Others avowed there were bunches of past due bills which he could whip out at a moment's notice and serve on late paying customers. One patient, who may or may not have had his wits about him, swore ol' Fiz kept a pistol under the bandages and strange-looking instruments.

Whatever the reason, the case was his constant companion, reflecting the passage of time as it aged with its owner. Besides a weather-beaten appearance, its edges were frayed, the sides dented and the brass closure worn shiny from constant use. While no one but Fiz had ever lifted it, general assumption held that it hefted at about the weight of an amputated leg.

"What have you got there?" Fiz inquired, setting the bag down on the mountain of wanted posters.

Claw tipped his hand and Fiz read the wording, upside down.

"Mike Stoelting. Pretty ugly cuss. Is he one of the ones you have in jail, or is he waiting to make his last and most rewarding trip up to Boot Hill?"

Claw waved a hand to indicate Stoelting now called the Hellhole jail "home."

"According to this poster, he's one of Herm Heller's gang."

"Herm Heller?" Fiz rubbed his mustache in contemplation, then shook his head. "I didn't see Heller. He wasn't one of the dead."

"He's not in jail, either."

"Not like Herm's boys to pull a job without him."

"No. It's not."

"How do you figure it?"

"I don't. Unless these *hombres* broke loose from the gang. Set out on their own."

"A rival gang? Not likely. Who's the other one?"

"Don't have paper on him; least none I've found. Might be his face is in one of those," he added, indicating the stack buried under Fiz's bag.

"Who else runs with the Heller gang?" Without waiting for an answer, Fiz supplied the names. "There's Adam Lyle and Zeke Duke. And old Hannibal Cobb is still alive, if I remember correctly. He and Herm were always close."

"Know a lot about outlaw gangs, do you?"

Fiz snorted and busied himself opening the case.

"I read all the crime magazines that come out of New York and Philadelphia."

"Why?"

"I found that if I leave a few out in my waiting room -- especially the ones with the graphic depictions of hangings or bloody murders on the cover -- it makes my patients more inclined to pay up -- without question."

It was Claw's turn to snort. He had never been in the physician's waiting room and now felt a strong inclination to avoid it -- dead or alive.

"I don't doubt it. Ever spend time reading medical journals?"

"Now, why would I want to do that?" Fiz easily inquired as he crossed to Claw's left side and indicated he remove his shirt. The marshal unbuttoned it with less enthusiasm that he might have done before Fiz's confession.

"You the only doctor in town?"

He tried to make voice speculative, rather than accusatory.

"Why do you ask? Think you need a second opinion?"

"No."

He responded too quickly, overplaying the reassurance.

"Good thing for you. There was another doctor in Hellhole once. Few years ago."

"What happened to him?"

"He died."

"Of what?"

"Heart aneurysm."

"Come to you for treatment, did he?"

"Matter of fact, he did. I always said Hellhole was too small for two physicians."

Claw grimaced. Fortunately, he inadvertently synchronized it with the moment Fiz cut a hanging piece of white and deadened flesh from his arm.

Proving they both had good timing.

"You'll live," the man of Maimonides declared. "The bullet only grazed your arm. No damage to the muscle. Could have been a lot worse."

"Yeah. I could have followed that other doctor."

Fiz did not look up. He removed a bottle of alcohol from his bag, drenched a rag and set it against the now bleeding wound. Claw clamped his teeth, breathed deeply through his nose, then slowly exhaled.

"What's that for?"

"Hurt some, does it?"

"Some."

"I'm going to put a bandage on your arm, and I don't want you picking on it. Understand?" Claw nodded. "You come up to my office tomorrow, say about noon time, no later, and let me take a look at it. Will you do that?"

"What for? It's only a scratch."

"I said graze -- not scratch. It's deep enough. But that's not what worries me."

"Bleeding?"

"Infection."

"That whisky ought to keep infection away."

"This is not whisky. Certainly not anything you could buy at the Lowdown or the Wolf's Pelt. Not that watered-down swill. This is medicinal alcohol." He finished cleaning the wound, then placed a cotton pad against it and proceeded to wrap cloth ties around Claw's arm to hold it in place. "If this slips down -- in the night or when you get dressed in the morning, pull it back up. And come and see me tomorrow. I mean it."

Claw heard the concern and frowned. Having learned he could not get a straight answer to a question, he attempted a slight subterfuge.

"I might be busy tomorrow. I'll come up in a week or so."

Fiz looked up sharply. "You want to lose that arm?"

"No."

"Then you do as I say."

"Not unless you tell me why."

Fiz scowled, turned his back and dug into his medical kit, producing a spent bullet.

"You know what this is?"

"I know it wasn't fired by one of those bank robbers. It's from a rifle."

"A Spencer carbine, to be exact. I keep it as a reminder. Take a closer look." Doctor Ward held the bullet out for Marshal Kiley's inspection. "Right there, at the end. Where a cross has been cut into it."

"I see it." Claw felt his flesh tingle and the muscles in his stomach tightened. "Where'd you get it?"

"From the same bunch who had this in his six-shooter."

He displayed another bullet, this one spent. It had the same cross carved into its end.

"The Heller gang?"

"Yeah. About six months ago they hit a bank in Spearville. Mortally wounded a teller and shot the sheriff. I was called down there. Couldn't do anything for the teller but ease his pain and write a letter back east for him. The sheriff -- name was Tim Gagney -- was shot in the leg. Nothing much. I dug the bullet out. Told him to stay off his feet for a week or so. Didn't think anything more about it. Went back to Hellhole. Next morning, I was awaken by a banging on my door. It was the deputy. He said Tim was in a bad way and I had to come quick."

Ward fingered the bullet the way a cautious man handled a rattler. "I was surprised; didn't see any reason Tim should have taken a turn for the worse. But I went back to Spearville and found him burning with fever. Real high. I did what I could. Stayed a week. Ended up amputating the leg."

He paused, licked his lips then scuffed his foot against the floor. "I waited too long. I should have performed the operation as soon as I made the diagnosis. He begged me not to. Shouldn't have listened. Last time I do that. Damned fool."

Claw did not have to ask which one Fiz considered the damned fool.

"It was the bullet, you see. The sons of bitches had rolled them in dog shit; the grooves here keep in the feces. Shoot a man with a bullet like this and even a scratch can lead to infection. Saw it in the War, some; should have known better."

"One of the dead men have that bullet in his gun?"

"He did. I went 'round to Jonathan Harker's before I came here. Just wanted to see. Heller is a mean bastard. His boys are no better."

"You think I was shot with a bullet like that?"

"Can't say. Mebbe. Mebbe not. Not all the bullets were poisoned. Hope not."

"Me, too," Claw agreed. Fiz busied himself rearranging items in his little black bag. "Comes to it, Fiz," Claw said. "I don't want my arm amputated."

"Comes to it," Fiz replied. "I won't ask." He finished his task and met Claw's eyes. "I'll look in at the prisoners, now."

Fifteen minutes ago, Claw might have replied, *I expect you know where the cells are.* Knowing, or suspecting he had been shot by a poisoned bullet, however, proved a great curb to any man's tongue.

"I'll let you in," he politely offered.

Fiz stopped in mid-motion, considered the words and the tone in which they were spoken, then abruptly nodded.

"Glad to see you have some sense. Maybe you will last." Having learned some of the doctor's ways, Claw waited, knowing more would follow. Fiz did not disappoint. "A year, anyway. Having you around that long will make it worth my while to teach you checkers."

"What makes you think I don't know how to play checkers?"

"Cougar said you don't know anything about cards."

"I never said that," he protested. "Besides, cards and checkers are different."

"I play two bits a game; loser pays up at the end of the day."

"Is that in case I don't live to pay you tomorrow?"

He finally succeeded in making Fiz smile.

"Good an answer as any."

He shuffled toward the cells, affecting an old man's walk, although this time Claw saw through the ruse. His first impression had been fifty years. That had been high. Forty seemed closer to it. That made him thirty-three when the War broke out. He wondered where Fiz had lived before that and what kind of life he led. And why his experiences on the battlefield had taken him west at the conclusion of the bloody conflict.

Questions for another day.

The doctor did not wait for the marshal to admit him into the back. He merely took the key off the peg, opened the door and went in by himself. Claw was not altogether certain he would have brazenly entered either cell without a gun in his hand. Perhaps rumors were correct: the "Surgeon and General Practitioner" did hide a gun in his bag. Or possibly he had imbibed freely of that hidden bottle of whisky before coming over.

More likely, Fiz's seeming fearlessness stemmed from the same reason Claw had spoken politely to him when informed he might have been wounded by a dirty bullet. No man wanted to die. If Doctor Ward were the only thing standing between life or a one way ticket to Boot Hill, that made his person sacrosanct.

Had he the ability to read minds, Fiz Ward would have been sardonically amused. Had he been so inclined, he could have removed his own shirt, displaying several scars which he had received in the line of duty.

Sacrosanct, he might have said, *is better applied to saloon keepers. A man may die without a doctor but he doesn't want to live without a drink.*

Claw did not know, but he would learn -- if he lived that year the doctor granted him -- that townspeople regarded the doctor as the wit of Hellhole.

Which said little or much, depending upon one's point of view.

Not caring to watch the proceedings, Claw busied himself with the wanted posters. He eventually dozed, awakened only when Ward dropped his case back on the desk.

"The other one's name is Bart Philben and he's one of Herm Heller's boys, too."

"How'd you find that out?"

"I asked him."

A considerable pause, then, "What else did he say?"

"The usual." Fiz shrugged. "Herm will never let them hang. Herm is a loyal man; he'll spring them somehow. That sort of thing." He hesitated, then added, "You've heard it all before."

"Yeah," Claw agreed. But he had never been a marshal when those statements were issued from prisoners held close confined. The threats were directed against the man in charge; not the deputy. That situation had now altered. He had become the target; the man Herm Heller and his gang would come gunning for.

A sobering thought, especially for one who did not have a bottle of whisky hidden in a desk drawer or a doctor's bag.

Disconcerted, as well, by the healer's easy camaraderie with his prisoners, Claw wondered, not without some hesitation, which color uniform Herm Heller wore during the Late Unpleasantness.

He would have bet his next month's salary it was grey.

"Philben didn't happen to say where 'Herm' was, did he?"

"Matter of fact he did. Last he saw him -- which was two days ago -- Herm had a camp on the boundary of Masson County."

"Which side?"

Asked in so sharp a manner, Fiz scowled and may have misinterpreted the question.

The answer he gave, however, could have stood for either.

"Not your side."

Claw grunted in annoyance. He was damned sorry that other doctor had died of a heart condition.

There should have been an autopsy.

Fiz removed his pocket watch and appeared to be working out a complicated equation. Finally reaching a satisfactory conclusion, he snapped the lip closed with a definitive click.

"We'll call it two hours."

"We'll call what two hours?"

"The time I spent with those prisoners. And an hour repairing your hide. That makes three hours."

"I can add."

"Glad to hear it. You send a telegram to Hays informing them you have two prisoners to pick up and add that Doctor Ward spent three hours tending to State business."

"You haven't been here thirty minutes." Fiz stared up at him, blue eyes bland and expressionless. Claw would not have bet his thoughts were as placid as his expression. "You always pad your bill to Hays?"

"Never."

"Never?"

"You're going to do it for me."

"The hell I will."

Fiz shrugged as though the matter were of no consequence.

"Come see me tomorrow."

While not spoken as a threat, it could have been taken that way.

"The hell I will," Claw repeated, standing dutifully in preparation for the doctor's departure.

"Suit yourself."

Ward picked up his bag, which appeared to have grown heavier, rather than lighter, after the dispensation of his healing arts, and started for the door.

"Noon," he said and let himself out.

Leaving Claw speechless. And having no one to complain to, had he a mind.

The lawman bounced slightly on the balls of his feet.

Who does that old man think he is? This is the Marshal's Office; I'm in charge here, not some old sawbones who fought on the Losing Side. The hell I will pad his bill. And I don't believe a damn word he said. 'Camp on the boundary of Masson County.' Not likely 'ol' Bart' would have offered that tidbit of information. I'll see to it, myself.

Claw marched in proper military fashion to the door, took the keys from the peg where that "damn doctor" had replaced them, and entered the jail block. Both prisoners were snoring. Not a natural slumber, but a drug-induced type, from laudanum.

They would sleep the night through.

The doctor had not seen fit to leave a dose or two for the lawman. No doubt he thought Claw ought to stay awake guarding them.

"The hell I will."

Before finishing the exclamation, a sudden, deep-set weariness assailed him. Returning the keys to the peg, he crossed to his bunk and slumped down. It required nearly all his remaining strength kick off his boots before sleep overwhelmed him. He dropped heavily, head landing squarely on the pillow.

Doing any Rebel *sodger* proud.

Later that afternoon, he went to the Telegraph Office and sent his message to Hays.

"Attempted robbery of the Hellhole bank. Two men killed, two taken prisoner. All four members of the Herm Heller gang. Heller is reputed to be in the area. Doctor Ward treated both prisoners and myself for wounds."

That ought to be good enough, he decided. More than fair. Let Hays figure out how long "treating wounds" took. If they erred on the side of the physician, that wasn't his affair. And if they erred on the side of fiscal responsibility, that wasn't his affair, either.

Let Doctor "Fiz" Ward take it up with Hays, if he dared.

Claw would like to see how far he got.

CHAPTER 15

"The wound looks clean," Fiz pronounced. Claw thought he detected a note of sadness in the physician's voice. Clearly, Hays would pay him more for treating a "serious injury."

Nor did Claw doubt that in the case of his own demise, Ward would send the telegram to the authorities himself, demanding payment and incidentally mentioning the fact Hellhole would need another marshal.

"How much do I owe you?"

Being uncertain whether the state would adequately compensate the doctor, he did not want to be beholding. Treating prisoners was one thing: tending him another. While he did not think the physician would purposely withhold any life-saving measures, there was always the question of pain.

Holding credentials as a Rebel surgeon, Kiley knew Ward understood how to work while a patient screamed.

He did not fancy being the one under the surgeon's knife while Fiz took a journey down memory lane.

Ward looked up sharply, scrutinized the tall man, then carefully removed his wire-rimmed glasses, tucking them away inside a cheap metal case he always carried in the upper outside pocket of his suit jacket.

"Your life. What's it worth to you?"

"You're never going to win any personality contests around Hellhole, you know."

The answer was so spontaneous and so sincere, Fiz laughed.

Of the two, if was a toss-up who was more surprised.

With a jerk of the thumb, the doctor dismissed the lawman.

"Off you go. Don't make it a habit of coming up here. Wounded," he added under his breath, and for the first time, the youth got a glimpse of the other's loneliness. The secret touched a nerve.

"Fiz," he began, then hesitated.

Fiz turned his back on Claw and busied himself washing his hands in a basin of water which always sat on the counter. He continued to mumble, ostensibly to himself.

"Do you know that hand washing is a lost art? They don't even teach the importance of cleanliness in medical school. I've seen doctors go from house to house, treating everything from blood poisoning to delivering babies and never wash their hands. Incredible."

"I found a checkers board in the office. Why don't you come over and play a few games tonight?"

Fiz ignored him. He had been caught in a vulnerable moment and did his best to cover the fact.

"I saw what you did in the cells. Washed them out, by God. It's a wonder the walls didn't dissolve. The only thing holding them up was dirt."

Claw replaced the hat on his head and slipped away.

Lesson learned.

Invitation accepted.

He finished rounds early and stopped by the undertaker's. Seeing no one in front, the sound of hammering prompted him to stick his head round back. With the ear of experience, he divined the purpose and steeled himself for the sight of two corpses laid out on a table awaiting the completion of their final resting place. Great his relief to discover the work area devoid of bodies.

"Hallo," he called in a friendlier voice than might otherwise have been the case. Harker looked up from his work and nodded in recognition.

"Mornin', Marshal. There's coffee on the stove. Pour yourself a cup."

"No, thanks." Taking meals in an outer office while prisoners banged on cell bars, calling out disparaging comments on his ancestry was one thing: permitting any sustenance to pass his lips in a house of the dead constituted another, entirely.

The coffin maker's disapproving stare made him regret the rash decision and he wordlessly changed his mind, selecting a heavy white mug from a mismatched set. The boldly emblazoned "Rycroft's Quality Embalming, Wichita, Kansas" did not improve his desire for a taste of the brew.

Appeased by the acceptance, Jonathan Harker banged in a final nail, then dropped the hammer onto a bench. The sudden silence proved disconcerting.

"What can I do for you? Looking for something for yourself?" Kiley choked while swallowing and coughed.

"The men brought over yesterday --"

"Oh, they're gone."

"Gone?" Visions of Herm Heller making a late night withdrawal chilled his blood.

"Gone to their reward."

"I know they were dead --"

"Buried. First thing this morning. Took 'em up in my wagon and had 'em planted. It's the heat, you know. Can't leave customers lyin' around. Draws the flies."

A fact he had not before considered.

"Who performed the service?"

"I did. Two pine coffins at five dollars, each --"

"Read the words," Claw clarified.

"No charge for that."

"*You* read the Service of the Dead?"

"Generally do in cases like these."

"What about a preacher?"

He might have been asking why one of Harker's mugs read "Devil's Hole."

"Get one of them through here about as often as the circuit judge. In case anyone needs marryin'. You fixin' to get hitched, Marshal?"

"The next time he comes through, I'll make arrangements. A man of the cloth ought to say a few words up there on Boot Hill. A man may be an outlaw but he deserves the right to have a proper burial."

"Can't say anything's righter than a pine box. Now, if he were payin' for it himself, I'd suggest a denser wood -- maple makes a fine coffin. They come standard with brass handles. Silver ones look fancier. Don't have much call for gold; have to special order them from St. Louie." Claw clenched the mug, waiting for Harker to ask his preference. When he did not, a pall seemed to lift from the room. "If you've come to see about the bill, I'll fill out the form and have it to you directly. Just sign it and forward on, if you don't mind."

The statement reinforced Claw's awareness of his true self-worth to the businessmen of Hellhole.

"It'll say 'Ten dollars for two pine boxes'?"

"That's it. Plus a dollar each for the grave diggers. That's twelve dollars, total."

"Thank you. I can add."

"Was expectin' another corpse but the doc says them two you got over at the jail will live."

"Too bad for business."

"Business is where you find it."

Claw replaced his mug by the stove, picturing the undertaker scouring the prairie for "customers," and recalled Fiz Ward's comments about hand washing. Or more specifically, a lack thereof.

"You get that form to me, I'll send it in at the end of the month." Hooking a thumb under his belt, he stood on tiptoe, appraising a quantity of newly-made furniture at the rear of the shop. "Actually, I'm lookin' to buy a table and chairs. Weren't any in the Marshal's Office when I took over. Don't know what happened to them, do you?"

Harker scratched his head. He seemed oblivious to a smattering of sawdust over his apron.

"You're right. Used to be a table there. Serviceable, but of no particular value. Oak. Three chairs. The one closest the door had an uneven leg." Apparently, he, too, had taken inventory. "I offered to replace the short one, but the last marshal never took me up on it. Three's an odd number, don't you think? Guess he figured it didn't matter."

"I was looking for two. And a table."

Harker perked up. "I have a very nice one -- black walnut. The wood came all the way from the Ozarks. And matching chairs; four of them. Fine enough for a dining set."

"For the Marshal's Office."

"Oh. I see. Used."

He said the word the way he might, had Claw demanded a less expensive coffin. With reluctance, touched by contempt.

I suppose I could disinter a body and re-use the burying box, Marshal, but it just isn't done. Unless the State has lowered its reimbursement again. As it is, I barely make a profit.

For a man who lived month-to-month, Claw was receiving an education in finance. One he probably could have lived -- and died -- without knowing.

"I have a table over here." Harker snaked through the narrow aisles, occasionally pausing to stare wistfully at a highboy or a wardrobe, before arriving at the rear.

"This ought to do for the Marshal's Office. Oak. Sturdy." He peered down. "Yes, it has all four legs."

"And two chairs. They don't have to match."

"You don't want three?"

"No. Two will be enough."

"Do you want to have a look at these?"

"I'll take your word on their being... serviceable. How much?"

"Three dollars for the table and a dollar apiece for the chairs. That's five dollars, total. I can let you have the third chair for fifty cents."

"No, thanks."

Claw no longer wondered why the furniture maker felt compelled to do the arithmetic for him. A man who just bought back his own property was clearly incapable of higher reasoning.

That afternoon, Claw set out the checkerboard on his new table. Not knowing which color Fiz preferred, he laid out the red markers by the least wobbly side. Red, for blood. He figured he would like that.

By midnight when the physician did not come, Claw replaced the game in its dog-eared cardboard box and went to bed.

Three days later a man presented himself at the Marshal's Office. He wore a shabby, dark blue jacket and black trousers. A misshapen blue kepi with a torn visor, nearly white from trail dust, perched on the back on his head, revealing tufts of steel-grey hair.

"Afternoon," he greeted, performing a casual salute. "I'm Gabby. Sergeant Gabby, in charge of the Kansas State Prison Wagon. You the marshal?"

"That's right," Claw agreed, standing up and moving out from behind the desk. "I'm Claw Kiley. You come for the prisoners?"

"No, sir. Didn't know you had any. I come from Garden City wid a mean pair me an' my partner picked up. Takin' 'em as far as Kinsley, where another team'll cart 'em on to Hays. But I run into trouble; wagon broke down about three miles outside of Hellhole. I brung the wheel in wid me. Need to git it fixed befer I go back."

"There's a blacksmithy across the street and down the way a bit. I'll take you there."

"No sense you bothering, sir. Shouldn't take too long. Trouble is, I left Private Miller back at the wagon guardin' them two murderers. They're dangerous, Marshal, an' I'm a bit worried. Miller's a good man, but young. Know what I mean? He ain't got a lot of experience. I'm a worrier, Marshal. Not fer myself, mind, but for the boy. He's my responsibility: him and cartin' then two carrion to Kinsley."

"I wondered about that; you being here for my prisoners. I just sent the telegram yesterday. Care to take 'em off my hands?"

"Cain't do 'er, sir. Like to oblige, but I'm afraid if I put yers in wid mine, they'd kill one another befer I got another fifty miles. Not that I mind so much as I got my orders. Bring 'em in alive."

He wrung his hands, then removed his cap, twisting it awkwardly in a gesture which readily explained why the brim had partially torn from the front. Waiting until he felt the other's stare, he offered an apologetic shrug.

"I'm used to seein' a 'U.S.' here." He indicated where the initials had once been affixed. "Cain't git used to bein' widout. Looks sorta naked, don't it?" Claw nodded, responding to the military demeanor, the sense of orderliness and dedication. "I shoulda stayed in the army, but they drummed us out. Been workin' this route now a year, year an' a half. You new here, Marshal?"

"That's right."

"Then I 'spect we'll be seein' a lot of one another. Good Lord willin', sir."

Perching on the edge of the desk, Claw asked, "What can I do for you?"

"I dunno. I was thinkin' o' askin' you to wait on the wheel an' bring it out to me, so's I can git back. I'm not sayin' there's trouble, mind. Them murderers is shackled in the wagon pretty good. It's jest that I'm a worrier."

He sighed heavily. His face was red from the exertion of riding and his lips were cracked from sun and prairie grime.

"Why don't you bring the wheel over to the smithy and rest awhile? Get a beer at the Lowdown. I'll ride out and look in on Miller."

The guard hesitated, then shook his leg. He nervously licked his lips, then stepped back, running his eyes over the marshal, judging whether to allow him the responsibility. When he made up his mind, he grinned.

"Infantry, sir? Kansas regiment? I served under General U.S. Grant. Got sent down to Louisiana; fought at New Orleans. Don't care what innybody says. When we secured the Mississippi, that were the beginnin' of the end. Know why?"

"Tell me," Claw encouraged, matching the former soldier's grin.

"Beef cattle, that's why. Lotta men's think I'm crazy to say that, but when the Rebs couldn't git their herds from Texas across the Mississip', that starved 'em. Didn't have no leather, either. Funny thing to think on, isn't it? Not havin' inny leather for harness or boots. An army ain't an army if it ain't fed an' it cain't move its caissons or its ammo wagons. That's how I learned never to take innythin' fer granted."

"You're right about that, Sergeant."

"Then I accept yer offer an' thank you, kindly. Be my pleasure to buy you a drink when we git the prison wagon safe to Hellhole."

"You've got a deal. Where'd you say you left the prisoners?"

"Three miles outside o' town -- that way," he indicated. "You oughtn't to have any trouble followin' my tracks. I left a clear trail. And Marshal -- I owe you."

Claw buckled on his gun belt, clamped on his Stetson and the two men walked outside together.

"Don't say I sent you, sir," Gabby pleaded as they walked toward the livery. "Don't want it to look like I don't trust Miller. Fact is, I do. Jest say you was passin' by an' saw the wagon. That way, there won't be no hurt feelin's."

Claw basked in the sergeant's trust. Considering that Miller's age likely approximated his own, having his experience acknowledged instilled a sense of worth. He also responded to the camaraderie of one Union soldier to another. There were few in Hellhole who would have appreciated the story about possession of the Mississippi River and how that contributed to the Confederate defeat.

He had not come to battle citizens but to protect them, yet they had become part of his problem. Working on the same side as someone else reminded him how good it felt to fight with, rather than against, an enemy.

If he had not made a friend, then, at least, he had shared a past. Sooner or later, he would bring them both together.

Call it Reconstruction.

CHAPTER 16

Regretting the fact he had not yet bought a horse, he quickly arranged to rent one from Canker, the stableman. Paying up front, he made sure Gabby would have no trouble getting the wheel re-rimmed, then headed west, the sun to his back.

As promised, Kiley had no trouble picking up the guard's trail. Enjoying the new found freedom of riding, he made good time, taking advantage of the dry wind to evaporate his sweat. Unfamiliar with the specifics of the countryside, he noted the landmarks; high rocks, stands of long wood, the wild grasses, some clumps reaching as high as his horse's knee, other areas swept clean of vegetation.

"A patchwork quilt," Ada Duvall had once described such a scene. Swatches of blue-flowering stalks, green fields, yellowing heads of languidly waving weeds. At the rim of the horizon he noted willow trees. Their presence indicated a high water table. In times of drought, men searched for cottonwoods, the frontiersman's gauge of danger. When the leaves wilted on those scraggly branches, that meant the water had gone deep underground, for they grew their roots far into the soil.

Reining in to watch a rabbit pass, he curiously observed the furtive movements. Sniffing one area, it flicked its long ears then hopped to another before stopping to eat. For a man who did not have the eyes of a jack, one spot looked the same as the other.

"The grass is always greener on the other side," Claw observed with tempered humor. "A boy with a string trap could make a meal for himself out here pretty easy."

Stroking the horse's neck, Claw stretched in the stirrups, nostrils distended. There was a sweet smell to the air, like honey. He licked his lips, savoring the taste, as if it were tangible and not ethereal. Around him, sounds filled his private acre of the Lord's unkempt Garden. The hum of insects, the chirping of sparrows, the thump of a prairie dog. Good sounds. Add to that the steady breathing of his "for-hire" horse and his own exhalations, and a man felt at home.

Pay attention to the land, Claw, for it's God's gift to His children. The land feeds us, waters us, warms us. There's some that curse the land when the snow is high, or the wind cuts through the fastenings of a jacket. That's disrespectful, boy. The land's only doing what it's gotta do; prescribed by a hand more knowin' than you and me.

The land doesn't belong to anyone, Claw. Some may hold title to portions of it, but even that passes away. The land belongs to the Most High and those who remember that can live with the hard times, knowing better ones are coming.

Nodding in reverence, Claw rode on another mile before spotting an object in stark contrast to its surroundings. A pole or a way-sign of some sort, standing four feet tall. He might have overlooked it, save for an elongated positioning of rock immediately beyond its base. Dismounting, then picking his way across the uneven ground, he identified the object of his curiosity before his shadow crossed the grave.

The upright, he supposed, had once served as a cross, although the arm had fallen away, the latigo or temporary binding of grasses used to bind it long gone. A cursory inspection did not reveal the board. Either it had washed away in a flash flood, or rotted enough to have been carted away by some animal seeking material for its burrow.

The name, if the survivors had chosen to engrave one, had vanished with the perpendicular. Only the upright remained as an anonymous reminder of a man's passing: one departed in the hope of discovering a better, more permanent world. Claw wondered if the lost soul had been a good man or a bad, and if it made any difference. Had he respected the land or cursed it? Did he perish in youth or had the ravages of age finally caught up with him in this desolate place?

It never occurred to him to question if the body, rendered to dust and fragments of tooth by the passage of time, had been a woman. The prairie was the sole domain of men. Women stayed in the homestead, raising children. Waited for their husbands to return from hunting trips, or from long, arduous days rounding up scrub cattle or tilling the fields.

Women were a striking omission in Claw Kiley's upbringing. The men who raised him were bachelors, widowers, wild loners who sowed their oats in towns like Hellhole. In his entire childhood, only one female stood out with any clarity. To Claw's unenlightened mind, Mrs. Jack Duvall was not a "woman," but a partner. Like her husband, she followed the law from town to town, drifting like a tumbleweed. No roots. No complaints. Just a job to be done.

Claw had never witnessed any tender display between husband and wife, and thus held little association between love and the fairer sex. He knew of it only from reading dog-eared pamphlets left out on tonsorial chairs and from stories told around campfires about "Back East" men who drank tea from "China," and worked in tall buildings so high a man could hardly see the roof for looking.

There had never been any issue between the Duvalls. To Claw's reckoning, that was as it should be. Partners did not raise families. They shared danger, swapped tall tales, tended one another's wounds, and moved on when the wind changed direction.

Out west, ranchers and farmers and townspeople raised children because they needed help tending the animals or plowing the fields.

Lawmen planted fairness and occasionally raised Cain.

Ada Duvall might have remarked that her husband's ward's upbringing had been sorely neglected. His opinions would not have surprised her, but would have cut her to the quick. She should have told him; taken him aside before the men of the star and the trappers and the brawlers corrupted his youthful mind. She should have explained about marriage being a partnership of a different kind. About the expectations of home and hearth.

About a time which never came when a marshal put down his badge, because he owed something to his wife.

She might even have lectured him about the women who followed their men. The women who abandoned the outpouring of their wombs in shallow graves over which they placed wooden crosses in the errant hope someone besides themselves would ever think of them again.

Ada Duvall was a strong woman but she knew her place. Claw Kiley was not her son; he was the boy who could never replace that which she had buried. To say she did not love him would be unfair, for she cherished a strong affection for the lanky, sandy-haired youth. But he belonged to Jack, and after him, to and Jim and Dan. And to the Other Jim and Amos and Ol' Joe. They reared him as a wolf cub, admitting him into their pack by instilling their restless, searching, seeking ways. It was not her lot in life to wean him from his fathers.

Of all the regrets Ada had, which were many, Claw Kiley lay somewhere in the middle. Between praising the Lord and cursing Him.

Leaving the nameless pile of rocks as he found it, Claw spurred on his horse, returning to the road carved from wear rather than design. It meandered across hills, down shallow dales, never a straight line. In the beginning, it had been a deer path, followed later by other wild creatures, those without a concept of home. It started at a place without a name, and ended in the distance, beyond where a man could see.

Nowhere to nowhere.

Dust to dust.

He made good time. In less than an hour Claw saw the prison wagon ahead of him. Hailing the guard, less he be suspicious of a stranger and take a pot shot at him, Claw had the satisfaction of seeing Miller return the greeting.

"Howdy," the youth called, coming out from the lee side of the canvas-covered conveyance, rifle slung carelessly in the crook of his arm.

"Howdy. I'm Claw Kiley, law out of Hellhole. Having a bit of trouble?"

"Yes, sir. Dang wagon busted its wheel. My sergeant went to git it fixed. You pass him?" he asked, hopeful worry in his voice.

"Seen a man like that," Claw agreed, remembering the sergeant's admonition not to hurt the boy's feelings. "Anything I can do to help?"

"Sit with me awhile?" came the soft pleading. "I don't mind being alone," Miller hastened to add, puffing out his chest to assert his worth. "It's jest that... listening to them men in the back callin' out their threats... kinda gits to ya."

Claw dismounted and held out his hand. They shook.

"I'm Miller," the private introduced. "Dave Miller. Don't mind sayin' I'm glad you come by."

"Hey, wet-behind-the ears!" called a husky voice from inside the wagon. "You talkin' to yerself again?"

"You gonna be talkin' to Saint Peter befer ya ever git us to Hays," another shouted. Crude, mean laughter followed as the prisoners shared the joke.

"We're gonna git us sprung frum here an' then we'll have a time wid you, boy."

Claw's lips pursed and he moved to the back of the wagon.

"Seems to me," he began, drawing back the flap, "that two men convicted of murder ought to have better things to think about than --"

He never finished the sentence. Before he could defend himself, a hand grabbed him by the shirt, the other pressing the cold steel of a gun barrel against his chin.

"Move back slow."

Claw did as ordered, sidestepping as the two men jumped out, the forerunner maintaining the gun at his head.

"Lookee what we got here," the escapee laughed, the sound harsh and superior. "A U-nited States marshal."

"Nice of you to pay us a visit," the other agreed, removing a pistol from a holster at his waist.

Claw's look of astonishment caused them additional merriment. He turned to Miller for an explanation, but the expression on the youth's face made it all crystal clear.

Set up.

Gabby had not ridden into Hellhole to get a wheel fixed, for the wagon sat perched, perfectly balanced on four good wheels. Something he should have spotted half a mile back.

He had been so sure of his own worth and experience, he had ignored the obvious indications of a trap. His face flushed and his fists tightened.

A fool's mistake.

An inexperienced, boy's blunder.

And he had ridden into it with his eyes open.

Jack Duvall would never forgive him.

Claw reckoned Jack would tell him so.

Soon.

The veins in his neck throbbed.

One bullet would still them forever.

"Where are the real guards?" He tried to make his voice sound deep, authoritative. He need not have bothered.

"Oh, we shot them, Marshal. Buried 'em back on the trail so the buzzard's wouldn't alert you somethin' was wrong."

"Who are you?" A question, for the sake of form. He already knew. The outlaw bowed in mock respect.

"Herm Heller. At your service, Marshal. You got two of my boys in your jail. I never leave my boys to rot. They know that. I thought we'd have more trouble," he added. "Needn't have worried, I see. They sent a whelp to do a dog's job." Claw flinched from the cruel sadism.

"That's Miller," Heller continued. "You already met him. This old scout is Hannibal Cobb. Heard the way you busted up our robbery. Didn't know there was law in Hellhole. No matter. There ain't no more."

He grinned, showing a mouthful of crooked teeth. "Gabby, he said he knew jest how to git you out here. Make an offer, then let you think it was yer own idea. That way, it'd all seen right. He's a thinker, that one."

"You can threaten me all you want, but I'll never release the prisoners."

"Don't have to. Gabby's got it worked out. By cozyin' up to you, that established his credibility. He jest goes in, unlocks the cells an' escorts them dangerous criminals right out to the prison wagon."

"You need papers -- authorization."

"Who's gonna ask to see 'em?" Cobb jeered. "The mayor?"

"Maybe."

"Don't care if he does. Them guards we waylaid were haulin' convicts. Sad to say they're standin' at the Pearly Gate right about now alongside the Federals. Hated to do it, but I ain't recruitin'."

"They had papers on 'em." Cobb flexed his fingers. "It didn't take much to make a few additions. Sergeant Gabby is 'authorized' to take 'Marshal Kiley's' prisoners on to Hays. All legal and proper."

"The mayor -- or someone else -- will make him wait for me to get back."

"We jest say," Cobb continued, "we're in a hurry. Herm leaves the papers on your desk. Simple. As easy as pie."

And so it would be. A well-executed plan.

With the emphasis on "execution."

The outlaw turned his back just long enough for Claw to make his move. With a desperation born of fear and shame, he dove at Cobb, trying to take him down, to disrupt the complacency of the gang just long enough to give him an edge, open an opportunity.

Claw succeeded in bringing Cobb to his knees but failed to use him as a shield. Heller fired his pistol, striking the lawman in the leg. He screamed from impact as the force, magnified two-thousand times by the near-deafening noise and the acrid, burning smell of gun powder, propelled him backward.

Clutching his leg only long enough to ascertain exactly where the bullet had struck, Claw pushed himself up with his arms. He threw a punch at Miller, landing a blow on his jaw. It lacked enough force to inflict damage and the murderer danced away, fists held in a defensive posture.

"Come on, Marshal," he taunted. "Let's see how big a man you really are."

Claw's eyes, already wild with pain, grew flinty blue in anger. Glancing sideways at Heller, he saw the gun leveled at him and hesitated. Heller smiled and lowered the weapon.

"Go at him," he invited.

An unequal contest from the beginning, the arena reflected the tragedy of the bullring where the lithe, well-armed matador outmatched the wounded animal. Claw fought, not from any sense of improving his fate, but from anger and pride. If he were to die, he would make them earn his death.

Such being the Law of the Plains of which he played an inextricable part. His self-worth, his identity, the badge he wore drove him to face the assassin, one-on-one. To have accepted his fate would have been easier, but the need to fight boiled in his blood.

Consequences, he had heard, were for the living.

Claw raised his hands, then feigned right. Miller countered, but Claw changed course, putting as little weight on his injured left leg as possible. Reaching out with arms longer than the youth anticipated, the bandit suddenly found himself caught in the giant's grip.

Spittle flew forth from Claw's mouth as he growled in fury, wrapping his fingers around Miller's neck and squeezing for dear life. He sensed, rather than saw, the man's face turn purple. The awareness made him drunk, incited his blood lust, drove him to near insanity. Leaving his left hand around Miller's throat, he fisted his right and smashed it into the vulnerable cartilage of the man's nose. Blood spurted from the nostrils, drenching both in sticky, warm fluid.

"Bastard!" Claw cursed. "Damn bastard. Take my words to the grave with you."

He beat the man, never releasing his grip from around the windpipe, feeling the throb of the pulse diminish, drawing strength from the other's weakness. Another moment and he had Miller on the ground, mindlessly stomping him the way a tortured bull trampled its oppressor.

Unfortunately for the crazed lawman, the outcome of the fight had been fixed from the beginning. Seeing it turn against their companion, Heller signaled Cobb to put the symbolic lance through the heart of the beast. Sneaking up behind Claw, he jammed the butt of his rifle against the back of the marshal's knee, toppling him. Down but not out, a second kick, this one to the jaw, finished the job.

Kiley's world went black. Struggling for breath, he regained semi-consciousness, swatting furiously at the stars exploding before his eyes. In his crazed state, unable to distinguish between two and three dimensions, he took everything for an enemy.

"Look at him!" Cobb leered in smug superiority. "He don't know what he's doin'! He's taking swipes at the air."

"Stand in his way and he'll remember well enough," Heller warned, raising his pistol to shadow the lawman's movements. He had seen men struggle like this before and knew their strength could be prodigious. Temporarily blinded by a blow to the head, such a man became impervious to anything. Nothing less than a fatal shot would fell him, and only then if it were directed to the skull. Shoot him in the knee, blow off an arm, gut-shot him and he would keep on coming.

The final moments were always the most dangerous.

"Son of a bitch!" Claw hollered, furious and single-minded.

"That displaced jaw didn't shut him up much, did it?" Cobb asked, distancing himself from the lawman with a dread bordering on awe.

Claw heard the voice through a haze of agony and turned in that direction. Cobb moved back faster but he miscalculated both the speed and the intent. Struck by a fist, he staggered, regained his balance then came up on Claw's blind side. A blow to the ribs sent him sprawling. As he went down, Cobb snarled his own curse, delivered another chop to the back of the head, then straddled his foe. Grabbing a handful of hair, he viciously yanked it backward.

"There isn't ever gonna be any law in these parts, Kiley," he promised. "You're a dead man."

Claw went limp, making it appear Cobb's words had been prophetic. The robber relaxed his grip, not much but enough to provide a slight edge.

Scooping up a handful of loose dirt, Claw threw it over his shoulder, striking Cobb in the face, temporarily blinding him. Taking advantage of the combatant's weakness, Claw rolled out from under him, effectively changing positions. Once on top, he used the weight of his good leg to pin Cobb's gun hand. Lacking anything more substantial, he pummeled blows with both arms.

He would kill, must kill, needed to kill. They had fooled him, mocked him, hurt him.

Gone, the veneer of civilization; dissipated into the high blue sky any concept of law. It was justice Claw sought: the justice of revenge.

His anger was older than his species; his need as primal as the struggle for survival.

It became Heller's turn. He had let his boys have their fun, but like all amusements, this had its price. Now, he would finish the job.

The question of fairness never entered the equation. Just as law and civilization had drown in a sea of blood, so, too, fairness died an inglorious death under the hot Kansas sun and the searing agony of unendurable pain. He kicked Claw's face, then drove a fist deep into his belly. As Claw retched and gagged, Heller repeated the blow.

The crazed giant staggered but refused to concede. He twitched, clutched with claw-like fingers and lunged forward. Encountering no earthly form, he dropped, face first, onto the ground. Before he had a chance to recover, another enemy, this one in the form of a rifle stock, crashed against his skull and he knew no more.

Claw awoke to the sound of a man groaning. The noise was far distant but so constant he regulated his breathing to it, so that for every pain-filled cry he took a breath. Groan, breathe, groan, breathe, groan, breathe, the pattern of evolution repeated since the dawn of life.

Born into pain to die into pain. The rhythm of life and death. The triumph of night over day, of dark over light. The struggle to persist giving way to the clutches of eternal nothingness.

"Oh, God," he heard a man plead. "Have mercy." The words were garbled, perhaps not even comprehensible. It made no difference.

Jim Bennett had lectured him once on the concept of prayer. From deep within his haze of pain, Claw remembered.

There isn't any sense in begging the Almighty, Claudius, because if there is a God of mercy, He doesn't need your prayer. And if there isn't any God of mercy, you're only wasting your breath.

Jim might have added, but had not, that a man did not beg. A man never showed pain, never admitted weakness. The credo of the West was expressed in four words: "Die like a man."

Claw had seen men beg. Good men. He had seen them plead. For some, he had even wiped tears from their faces. According to the Creed, these men were cowards, worth no more than the effort to dismiss them to hell.

Claw Kiley was not of that faith. Some would say his warped opinion resulted from a lack of formal religious upbringing. Without the Good Book as his guide, he had grown up a heathen.

Men of the West understanding that worthy tome set the guidelines for conduct.

An eye for an eye.

A life for a life.

Vengeance is mine.

Claw Kiley, the boy, had once asked the "Reverend" Bennett about the Good Book, and Jim had produced a Bible. It was a small, leather-bound copy, ten times thicker than the tracts given out at Revival Meetings. Jim had said, *I'm never without it, son.*

When Claw inquired his reasons, the man, who was neither young, nor old, but in between youth and old age, replied, *I keep in my shirt pocket. Over my heart. In case I'm shot, there's just a chance it'll stop a bullet.*

Jim Bennett had been called a cynical man by some and a wise man by others.

In his misery, Claw came to a full awareness of both perspectives.

He knew the identity of the groaning man and the realization shamed him. Not because he thought himself a coward, but for the chances he had squandered, the life he might have had. Tears came unbidden to his eyes, condemning himself to other mens' perdition. He did not care. Their hell was not his hell.

He wept because he had overlooked suffering; for the badge he had betrayed; and for the omnipotent power of the law, which had abandoned him.

For the first time in his life, he understood the hole his passing would create. Such sentiments would have wrung sobs from Ada Duvall's sunken breast.

A jolt, as one of the wagon wheels rolled into a crevice, cascaded agony through his frame. He did not remember being placed in the wagon. The fact being what it was, he accepted it without further consideration. Clamping his teeth shut to prevent a scream, Kiley made a vain attempt to right himself. Beyond the flap, he heard shouting.

"Move it, you old crowbait!"

The sound of a whip, then the conveyance lurched up, ahead, and finally out of the depression. His world straightened. The change in position did nothing to ease his pain. He would have to remember to make that comment to Fiz Ward.

Then, with the memory of the physician fresh in his mind, awareness came. They were headed for Hellhole.

Going home.

Not home, as in a town or a Marshal's Office, but to a coffin and a grave.

A hard, brutal slap to the face forced him to open his eyes. He stared at the confines of his world, no larger than a prison wagon.

He lay on the floor, hands tied behind him, legs bound together and drawn back so that he resembled a taut bow. The arrow was a symbolic one, stabbed through his heart. Being imaginary did not lessen his suffering.

"Didn't want you to miss anything, Marshal," Heller explained. He basked in his glory, his crowning achievement, the triumph of evil over good. "We're almost there. Within the hour I'll have my boys back and you'll be buzzard bait."

Heller's weight shifted as he squatted close. Prying open Claw's broken jaw, he stuffed a soiled handkerchief into his mouth. Using a leather thong, he wrapped it around the marshal's head, securing the gag in place. "Can't have you alerting anyone by that moaning of yours," he cheerfully remarked, petting Claw on the head like a good dog. "I ought to finish you now, but where's the fun in that? I want you to hear -- to know that help is only a yard away -- but that it will never come. You make a better foe, Kiley, because you know what lays in store."

Claw knew Heller had read his mind; understood about the bullring. A brute animal had no appeal; once down on its knees, no one cheered for mercy. The bull's tragic bravery meant nothing in the scheme of things. The contest was not about losers but winners.

"We're at the outskirts of town," Miller called from up front. Claw's heart sank. He hoped he had disabled the outlaw, perhaps fatally, but the sound of his voice dashed that dream. He had done nothing, then: Heller, Cobb and Miller were all on their feet and capable of doing what they threatened. They would bluff their way into having the prisoners released to their custody, drive out of town and then dispense with their hostage.

If he were even that much. Claw first believed he was being kept alive in case the men encountered trouble in Hellhole. Trussed up in the back of the wagon, he represented a bargaining tool. He now realized even that expectation was too high. Heller and his boys did not expect trouble; they did not hold him as a hostage. They were merely toying with him so he could experience one last denigration before putting a bullet between his eyes.

They had stripped him of his dignity. Now they were going to rape him with it.

Slipping away, Heller joined the others up front. The wagon crept slowly forward, inching its way down Main Street. He heard the outlaw leader call out a greeting and a muffled answer in reply. Hellhole accepted these men for what they appeared to be far more readily than they had accepted him. The realization was bitter.

When the prison conveyance came to a halt, Heller jumped down, making a point of stretching his cramped limbs. Removing his cap, he stared into the sky, smacking his lips.

"Sure could use a beer, Boss," Cobb complained in a whiny, rehearsed tone.

"We could all use a beer," Heller agreed. "But we ain't gonna get one. We got a job to do and we're gonna do it. Prison guards who get drunk end up dead."

"An admirable sentiment."

Claw froze as he placed the voice. Fiz Ward. *Oh, God,* he prayed. *Look in the wagon, Fiz. Ask who's in there and if he needs a doctor.*

"Yes, sirree bob," Heller agreed, adding a Southern slant to his otherwise regionally unidentifiable speech. "That's one thing I learned, sir. A man with two beers in his head ain't the clear-thinkin' critter he is when he's sober."

"You're right about that. Come for the prisoners?"

"Yes, sir. I'll be presentin' my papers to the law -- if there is one -- and be rollin' out of here soon's I can."

"There's law here, all right. His name's Marshal Kiley."

"Oh. Got a new marshal? Good. Always like to deal with a lawman. Makes my job a lot easier. If you'll excuse me, I'll jest go in an' see him."

"He's not there. He went out earlier." Fiz's voice reflected caution. "You didn't see him, did you?"

"Haven't seen no one, Mister --"

"Doctor Ward."

"Nice to know you, doctor. No, me and the boys didn't see no one."

Heller shrugged, glanced at the declining sun, then sniffed and wiped his nose on his shirt sleeve before turning bland eyes on the physician.

"You have call to look in on them prisoners? Hurt, are they? Need any special handlin'?"

He winked, implying a professional bond between himself and the physician.

"They're banged up some; nothing too serious."

"Good. Don't sound as though it'll prevent my taking 'em. I'll go and collect them rascals and be on my way."

Claw tried to call, made a furious attempt to propel the gag from his mouth, but failed. He groaned deep within his throat, made as loud a noise as he could, but the sound did not travel past the sides of the canvas covering.

"You better wait for Marshal Kiley to get back. You'll need him to check your authorization papers and sign a release."

Heller apologetically smiled.

"Wish I could wait, doctor. But that marshal might be gone for days; a week. You don't know why he left or when he's coming back. Sorry I don't have the leeway to wait up on him, but I don't. There's a bad one in the back of the prison wagon. He's got an appointment with the hangman in Hays an' I'd hate to bring him in late."

Heller used his hands to demonstrate. "Killed a woman, he did, doctor. Brutal. Savage. What he done to her... It makes a man's insides boil. No, sir; I cain't wait to get shed of that one. Don't hold much fer hangin' folks, but anyone'd make an exception fer that one."

Fiz nodded sympathetically then hesitated and frowned before reaching out to draw back the flap. Heller stopped him by laying an authoritative hand on his arm.

"I wouldn't do that, doctor."

"I thought I heard something."

"Most likely you did. That prisoner's an animal. We had to rough him up a bit. And as you can see," he added, stroking his chin, "he took a bit out of our hides, too. I'd like fer you to have a look at 'im, but I'm afraid I couldn't take the responsibility. Too dangerous."

"Let me be the judge of that."

"No, sir. He's bound an' gagged but that don't make me feel easy. You jest stand back, now. Private!" he called, motioning Cobb. "Stand guard outside this wagon and don't let nobody git close. You," he indicated to Miller, "follow me."

"Yes, sir."

The pair stepped up onto the boardwalk, crossed to the Marshal's Office and slipped inside. Fiz watched uneasily then shook his head. He had already taken a step away when he heard the sound again. A low noise, the kind a bound man made when raising and lowering his legs to draw attention.

The doctor's diagnosis was exactly correct. Although the wound in Claw's leg made movement excruciating, desperation forced the action. If he could not plant a shred of doubt in Ward's mind, Heller would get the prisoners and drive off with him in back. That constituted a death sentence.

Dead man told no tales.

The marshal who never returned.

Run off, they would say. Scared; shit scared.

Damn Yankee.

Claw could hear it in his mind. He easily envisioned Greg Thomas and the local man from Hays discussing the telegram they received from Hellhole.

Too young. Just a boy.

Inexperienced. I never should have trusted him.

What was that name you said? The marshal he deputied under?

Jack Duvall.

Teach you to trust the word of a dead man.

Claw could see the Federal man shrug and reach for the pile of applications.

Bring these men back. We'll send one of them in his place.

Which one?

It doesn't matter. One that won't run away. This time we won't send a boy to do a man's job. Hate to be wrong.

Too bad about Jack Duvall. They don't make lawmen like that, anymore.

Claw was not a boy and he had not run off. Greg Thomas *was* correct about Marshal Duvall, however. A lawman like him did not come down the pipe every day.

When one did, it was to follow in his footsteps.

A one-way trail leading to the grave.

CHAPTER 17

Heller emerged from the Marshal's Office holding his two prisoners at gunpoint. The outlaws appeared uncomfortable and frightened. It was clear to any onlooker they did not want to get in the prison wagon.

"Just one moment, here," Fiz began, almost too late to stop the proceedings. Placing himself between the men and the street, he addressed the officer in command. "Those papers of yours -- someone better check them."

Heller's eyes slanted as he considered the request. Had the doctor's expression conveyed anything greater than dubious suspicion he might have chosen that moment to shoot his way out of town. Sensing he still held the upper hand, the outlaw wearing a dead guard's uniform shrugged.

"Private Miller -- go back inside and bring out my commission."

"Yes, sir."

Miller saluted and did as directed, returning with a tri-folded paper. He handed it to his superior who, in turn, offered it to Fiz. Accepting it with the respect due an official document, the doctor set his black bag by his feet, then further delayed by removing his spectacles from their case, using one hand to affix the wire sides around his ears. Adjusting the lenses closer to the bridge of his nose, he carefully read the wording. Everything appeared to be in order, except the last line. He pointed out the problem to Heller.

"This requires a signature."

"Told you, sir. I can't wait. But here's an idea," he said, brightening appreciatively. "You seem to be in charge. Why don't you sign the paper?"

"I have no authorization to do that."

"You'll note it don't say the lawman in charge has to sign; jest someone who can certify I took the prisoners. I think my superiors at Hays would accept your signature, sir. And probably pay you a small stipend for your trouble," he slyly added.

Doctor Ward hesitated, clearly torn. His interest did not lie in receiving a fee, but rather in the proper chain of command. Being a man who understood authority, he simply had no right to authorize the release of any prisoners.

"Can't do it. You'll have to wait for the marshal."

"I explained why I have to move out. If you won't sign, is there anyone else in Hellhole who will?"

Heller raised his voice, scanning the small contingent of men who had gathered to watch the spectacle.

"Any of you responsible citizens care to put your name on this release? Or do you feel comfortable having these desperate bank robbers coolin' their heels in your jail until the next prison wagon comes to git 'em? Which may be," he darkly warned, "two weeks or more."

"I will." A man stepped forward, smiling easily. "I reckon I'm about as respectable a citizen as you're likely to find in Hellhole. My name is Bradley. Bix Bradley. I own the Lowdown Saloon."

"Pleased to meet you, sir," Heller greeted. The two men clasped hands. "I'm mighty glad to know there's someone here who understands the urgency of the situation."

"He's got a man due for hanging," Bradley explained, turning to Fiz. "I don't see any reason to hold him up."

"Why don't you go with him, Bix? Maybe you can get a ringside seat."

"Might just do that. I'm a man who believes in justice."

"I've heard that said about you," came the caustic rejoinder, as Fiz replaced his eye glasses in their case.

"Just step back into the Marshal's Office and I'll use his pen," Bradley invited. Only too glad to oblige, Heller accompanied him inside. In his absence, Cobb inched closer to the rear of the wagon, protecting it from unwelcome inspection.

Dr. Ward drifted away, ill at ease, though convinced the proceedings were none of his business, when Frankie MacPhearson, the town drunk, emerged from the crowd. He approached the physician, hat held piteously between two hands.

"Not now, Frankie," Fiz growled in dismissal. When the scarecrow of a man did not cringe and slink away, but rather placed a tentative hand on the doctor's arm, Ward stopped.

"Fiz... how many wheels does a wagon have?"

"Four," he snapped before realizing the seeming ridiculousness of the question. His eye twitched as he stared at the drunk. "For heaven's sake, you know a wagon has four wheels, Frankie."

"Fiz..." Frankie's voice had a whiny pitch, usually reserved for his most ardent pleading.

"What is it?"

"There's something ain't right."

Fiz dismissed the man in annoyance, then reconsidered. Grabbing him by the lapels, he guided the drunk out of ear shot.

"What do you mean, 'there's something ain't right'?"

"I saw a man with the Marshal... earlier this morning. A man in a uniform, Fiz. Just like them those men are wearing." He indicated the prison guards. Fiz did not have to look back to refresh his memory.

"Well?"

"That fellow went into the Marshal's Office, then came out with Marshal Kiley. The man in the uniform was carrying a wagon wheel. It was all bent up, like it'd come loose an' busted the rim."

Fiz's eyes narrowed. "Then what happened?"

"They walked over to the livery stable. I followed 'em," he apologized in a pathetic, lifetime habit. "The guard asked the smithy to fix the wheel. Marshal Kiley rode off." He pointed. "That way; west. Where the prison wagon come in from."

"Are you sure? How much have you had to drink today?"

"A shot at the Lowdown; an' that was breakfast. Nuthin' more."

"You're not making this up to seem important, are you?"

"I swear on my mother's grave."

Spoken with reverence, Ward had to believe the avowal.

"All right, Frankie," Fiz decided, pushing him away. "I'll handle it from here."

"Do you think the Marshal's in trouble, Fiz?"

"Yes."

"What are you going to do?"

"I don't know."

Which was the truth.

Fiz ambled back to the wagon, scrutinizing Miller's face with professional curiosity.

"That's a pretty bad bruise you've got there, son. You ought to let me take a look at it. Could be dangerous."

Cobb intervened, stepping between the two. "It ain't nothing. He can have it tended to in Hays."

"How'd it happen?" Ignoring Cobb, he directed the question to the youth.

"The prisoner," Miller began, then hesitated. His eyes shifted toward the Marshal's office. Cobb spoke for him.

"Told you we had a bad one in the wagon, Doctor. He got loose; jumped Miller, here. They had quite a tussle before I got him off."

"Roughed you up a bit, too, I see."

"Yeah. Well, he's a --" Cobb started to say, *He's a big one,* then changed his mind. "A strong one. Cain't wait to git him to Hays."

"I expect not," Fiz agreed. Pushing past Cobb, he placed himself between the guard and the wagon. "The law requires a competent surgeon to take a look at all prisoners injured while being held by the state of Kansas. I'm sure you boys wouldn't want to ignore any provisions like that."

Before either guard could stop him, Fiz grasped the canvas backing and lifted it up.

"I wouldn't do that if I were you," Cobb warned, too late. Surprisingly agile for a man who play-acted twenty years older than his actual age, Fiz sprang into the wagon, black bag in hand.

"What's going on here?" Heller demanded, rushing out from the Marshal's Office. Cobb motioned furiously with his gun hand.

"That damn doc -- he went in to check the prisoner."

"Oh, he did, did he?"

Smiling amicably at Bradley, Heller took long, casual strides toward the wagon. Motioning back his boys, he jumped inside, momentarily lost from sight.

A second later, a blast rang out. Herm Heller came flying through the opening, backwards. His life expired before he handed on the street, bits of his head blown almost as far away as Boot Hill.

A woman screamed. The horses harnessed to the prison wagon bolted and lurched forward. Cobb and Miller, realizing their only chance of escape lay in jumping the runaway and riding it out of town, broke for the conveyance. Stoelting and Philben, the two prisoners taken from the Marshal's Office attempted to follow, but the gunsmith with the honed-down trigger drew his pistol, leveling it at the outlaws. Their arms shot up in self-defense.

Inside the wagon, Fiz dropped his gun in order to grasp Claw by the head. His eyes desperately tried to penetrate the gloom.

"Are you all right?"

Claw slurred his words but the physician understood his intent. Removing a small pocketknife from his trousers, Ward cut and removed the gag with a surgeon's finesse.

"My hands!"

Fiz would not be hurried, but his deliberation in severing the bonds proved deceiving. In seconds he cut the rope behind Kiley's back. Sighing in relief, the lawman shoved out his two bound hands. Mistaking the intention, Fiz put the blade to the hemp.

"The gun," Claw hissed. "Give it to me."

Fiz did as directed, placing the smooth grips between Claw's palms. The marshal shifted position, now facing the front of the wagon. Aware the mad careening had been brought under control, that conveyed the fact a man now directed the team.

"Get down," he ordered Ward.

"I'd rather get off."

"Get behind me, then."

Fiz considered his alternatives, then gladly placed the marshal's body between himself and danger.

Claw never hesitated. Without bothering to aim through the drawn covering, he fired blind. A man screamed and tumbled from the seat. Immediately, bullets whizzed into the rear, several striking near the lawman. He did not flinch. A cannon shot could have ripped through the sides and he would not have reacted.

He fired again, then sensing he had not hit his target, inched forward. Another shot rang out as he grasped the canvas, ripping it down. Daylight flooded the interior, silhouetting the occupants.

Cobb remained on the seat. Face contorted with fury, eyes wild with hatred, he spat a vile oath and aimed his pistol. Not at the marshal, but toward the meddling doctor. If there were time for only one death, he would opt for the one who had spoiled their plans.

Fiz caught the murderer's eyes and held them without fear. *You can kill me,* his stare communicated, *but you cannot make me cower.* Fiz Ward was commonly held to be a religious man.

In the time it took the outlaw to react to the doctor's overt contempt, as great as his own hatred, Claw pointed the gun and fired. A rent, the size of a whisky bottle, appeared in Cobb's chest. He attempted to scream, but air gushed out the hole rather than his mouth. His last words were mercifully lost to humanity.

"What about the prisoners?" Claw screamed over the pummeling of horses hooves, the flapping of loose canvas and the pounding of his own heart.

"Left behind," Fiz shouted back.

Grabbing his wounded leg for support, the marshal pushed through the opening, grabbing the free-flying reins. He drew in on them, summoning strength he did not have. Somehow, the terrified animals responded.

"Whoa, whoa," Claw called, attempting to comfort himself as well as the horses. "Whoa, boy."

Pulling the wagon to a stop, he dropped the reins and sagged into the well of the seat. Fiz reached him, quickly ascertained he suffered no mortal wound, then pressed a hand to his shoulder.

"Hold on. I'll get you up to my office."

"Can't afford it," Claw muttered before passing out.

Miss Cougar Bradburn sat in the outer chamber of Doctor Ward's surgery and waited. She had been there before as a patient, but never as a visitor. On the whole, she decided she liked neither scenario.

The operating theatre, if such it could be called, also doubled as Fiz's office. Separated from the waiting room by a five-by-five foot screen decorated with a colorful Chinese motif, it rolled back when not in use, doubling the size of the room. While seated, Cougar could not see past it, but the occasional sounds of metal instruments being tossed into a bowl of tepid water proved gruesome enough. Had she been in a better mood, she might have observed that the odor of blood, alcohol and sweat were not that different than the smells permeating the Lowdown.

Her chair had been placed by a small, pot-bellied stove adjacent to the door. In winter, it provided the sole means of heat. In summer, the small fire used to heat the coffee, proved oppressive.

Fiz's roll-top desk leaned against the wall to the left of the main entrance. A clutter of papers covered the flat surface, while an assortment of pens, inks and old letters filled the pigeon holes. Atop it perched a small bronze bust of a bearded man. She had never asked his name, presuming it would mean nothing to her. Between a pair of windows to her right sat a curio cabinet, filled with nostrums and notions. In the drawers beneath were stored a quantity of bandages, varying in width from one to six inches. She had watched him roll them the way housewives made balls of yarn.

Leaning sideways, Cougar observed the profile of Claw's boots. Dusty, stained and worn unevenly at the heel, she uneasily contemplated the significance. Had he the time, the doctor would have removed them. The fact he chose to cut off the patient's trousers and leave the boots offered no reassurance.

"Open the window, will you? Then grab a towel and wipe my forehead."

Startled out of her reverie, Cougar obeyed with the alacrity of one accustomed to accepting unpleasant commands.

Pulling up the glass, she paused to watch the small breeze ripple the curtain before grabbing a white cotton towel from a pile he had placed on the sill. Clutching it in both hands for fear it might take wing and fly, she stepped behind the curtain and crossed to him. Fiz paused in his work to lift back his head. She ran the absorbent cloth over his brow, then without being told, pushed the slipping eyeglasses flush to the bridge of his nose.

"That better?"

He nodded. "Fill a glass with red eye."

This task proved more familiar and she obeyed without thinking. Questioningly extending the glass, he titled his head in that peculiar sidewards glance she knew so well and blinked.

"Drink it."

"Fiz, I don't need --"

"I don't like to drink alone."

She downed the glass in two swallows, then refilled it and brought it to his lips. He drank the whisky in one shot.

"What about him?" she inquired of the prostrate man.

"Between the three of us, he's feeling the least pain."

Cougar doubted that were true, for Claw's ashen-white features were contracted and his teeth gritted tightly shut.

"I could try to get some past his lips," she offered.

"He doesn't need any."

"Some anesthetic, then? I could pay..." she whispered, shamed for having to ask.

"Pain's the best thing in the world for him right now."

"Fiz --"

She had heard it said the doctor's sympathy was open to question, and as she stood, alone in the office with no one to whom she could appeal but the surgeon himself, she no longer doubted.

"Fiz --" she repeated in a stronger voice.

"Ask him."

She hesitated, then maneuvered her way to the patient's head. Claw's eyes were tightly shut. He did not open them as she addressed him.

"Some whisky, Claw?"

A whisper, an avowal of love; a promise she would stand up for him against any odds.

A wetness appeared at the corner of his eyes which she attributed to the agony he endured.

"No."

"Please, Claw. If you can't swallow, I'll ask him to administer some ether."

"No."

"There's no sense you suffering."

To have replied, *I am not suffering* and meant it would have earned him a place in P.T. Barnum's freak show.

"Fiz, please," Cougar begged. Claw's refusal went against rational comprehension. If she could not convince him, then her only chance at sparing him agony was to appeal to the surgeon.

Fiz did not respond. Angry, now, Cougar gripped a restraining hand on his right arm.

"You will give him something for pain. I'm not asking. I'm telling."

She asserted a right older than the healing arts. He finally understood.

Looking back at his patient, Fiz clamped a vein with his German-made instrument, then pressed a cotton pad down onto the bleeding site. When convinced he had temporarily cauterized the wound, he made a curt nod.

"Follow me."

"Whatever it is you have to say can be said in front of Claw."

"He already knows it."

If it had not been for the peculiar way in which Fiz spoke, she would not have acceded. Strangely frightened, Cougar followed him into his spare room, which also served as a recovery area. He shut the door, blocking their words from the outer chamber.

"Cougar, I know what you're thinking. But you're wrong."

"Convince me."

Her eyes were hard and uncompromising. The man she loved was suffering and she saw no good reason for it.

"Claw needs to endure this operation without laudanum or ether."

"Needs to?" Fiz nodded. He did not back away, but stared at his hands. "Tell me," she pursued.

"Those men... they did something to him. They... frightened him. Scared the tar out of him. They beat him, but they hurt him deeper than just mere physical abuse. He's been beaten before; he could have taken that. But they did --"

"Did what, Fiz?"

"I don't know. Can't say."

"Did he -- did Claw tell you this?"

"No." He shrugged, forcing himself to raise his head. Perspiration dripped down the sides of his face.

"Then, how can you be so sure?"

"I saw it. When I first stuck my head in the wagon, they had him trussed up like a turkey. They had worked him over pretty good. His jaw was out of alignment and I could smell the blood. But that wasn't what I saw in his eyes. I saw fear. They had broken him down, gotten beyond his defenses. Made him.... I don't know. I won't ask. Neither will you."

He went to the window and peered out. "Whatever they did, they stripped him of something precious. His pride, maybe. Whatever you want to call it; whatever it is that makes a man stand up to a fast gun, chase down a gang of bank robbers, put his life on the line, time after time. Lose that and he's left   with   nothing."

His hand rested on the curtain. She thought he would draw it but he did not. "At least, not enough to let a man like Claw Kiley hold down a U.S. Marshal's job. He needs that pride, that arrogance, that belief in his own invulnerability. Does that make sense?"

"I think so. They -- took that away from him?"

Fiz hesitated before facing her.

"They came close. Damned close."

"And now?"

"Now, he needs to suffer; to endure what most would call unendurable. To face pain without complaint. To find his bravery again. I wouldn't be telling you this unless I thought you'd understand. It's not an easy thing to say. It takes guts for him to do what he's doing; but he has to face his devils. By caring about him, so do you."

"And you?"

"He squirms around some; nothing an experienced surgeon --"

"That's not what I mean."

He hesitated a long time before speaking.

"Now, we both know a secret. We know Claw Kiley is vulnerable. We know he's a man, just like any other. Sometimes, it's easier not knowing," he concluded, nearly obscuring the last words by holding a hand to his mouth.

"No," she said, straightening her shoulders and staring into his shiny blue eyes. "It's never easier not knowing. I live by the truth and I'll die by it. It may not be pretty -- seldom is," she confessed. "But that's the way

I've always lived my life. I guess maybe you're right, Fiz -- I guess maybe I did think there was something special that protected lawmen. I don't know why," she grimaced in derision. "I've seen enough of them die. They're nothing special. Not really. It was just that he...."

"I know," Fiz said, revealing his own heart to this very special woman. "I thought so, too."

"You did?"

He dropped his head. "Yes. We're a pair of old fools, aren't we?"

"Make that a --" She faltered for the word.

"A triumvirate; three. That makes the three of us fools."

"What do we do about it?"

"We ignore it. We go about our business as though we didn't know."

"What about him?"

"He does the same."

"Will -- suffering the pain of the operation make him feel -- will it give him his pride back?"

"It's a start." He meant to end the conversation there, then changed his mind. She had earned his complete confidence. "Just a start."

"What happens when someone calls him out?"

"That's up to Claw."

"He'll be all right," she decided. Her faith gave Fiz hope. "This time. And the time after that. I can't say for how long. But not forever. And when that time comes, he'll either put down his gun, or he'll be killed."

"That's a reasonably fair assumption."

"Then think it," Cougar bitterly retorted. "Pretend you don't know the ending. I'll keep that to myself." Fiz inwardly shivered.

"So, now you know two secrets."

"I'm good at keeping secrets."

"Yes," he decided. "We're both pretty damn good at doing that."

"Some, she accused, "better than others."

He pressed against the wall, wishing he had his back turned.

"Maybe that's because no one ever asked."

Cougar Bradburn's shoulders sagged. A sob wrenched its way from her constricted throat. Before he could stop her, she fled.

Fiz took a deep breath then held out his hands. They were sure, steady, knowledgeable. He was too good a physician to be practicing medicine in a raw-boned hide town like Hellhole, where any man with a modicum of intelligence and a whit of courage could do what he was called upon to perform. His talent was better suited for....

He knew where and did not want to travel that road. Not with a patient on the operating table and a woman nearby. He only revisited that past when locked behind closed doors; with memories and brandy his best earthly companions.

"Damn it!"

He did not want to become involved, but a damned marshal and a saloon girl had drawn him into their lives.

He had not asked to be privy to secrets. He had enough of his own.

Returning to the surgery, he crossed, stiff-legged to his patient and removed the cotton pad. He observed some blood there, not much. He had stolen ten minutes and gotten away with it.

This time.

He comprehended what Claw was going through.

He understood Cougar's feelings, perhaps better than she did.

Pain, fear, loneliness, secrets.

The universal common denominators.

Chapter 18

"Claw'll sleep, now," Dr. Ward announced, wiping his hands on a fresh towel.

"Will he be all right?"

He nodded then rubbed his eyes. His bones ached.

"He'll be up and about in a day or so. I expect he'll limp for a week, maybe two. Then he'll be as good as new."

As good as new this time.

The waiting had begun.

"I guess I'll back to the Lowdown. It's late and Bix will be looking for me."

"You tell him if he lays a hand on you, I'll shoot the bastard myself."

"Yeah. I'll tell him." Her voice sounded dead. He knew she would not tell him.

"You might -- beg off. Say --"

Fiz let the idea die. She shrugged and disappeared. He paused to listen as she walked down the stairs. She took them one at a time, descending slowly. Yet he sensed a resolute quality which he admired.

Call it courage.

He should have called her back, made her lie down on the bed and get some sleep. Gone to Bix Bradley himself and told him she was under doctor's orders.

He should have but did not.

He made any number of excuses.

His patient needed watching.

Bix Bradley would not give a damn what orders she was under.

Bradley would take it out on her in the morning.

Cougar had already refused.

None of them held water. The real reason stood out like a sore thumb. Fiz was weary. Sick and tired of hopeless causes. He wanted to sleep and forget everything.

Shuffling to the patient, he slipped his numb fingers around the man's wrist. He took out his pocket watch and timed Claw's pulse. Rapid and regular. What he expected.

The action represented habit, no more.

He no longer wanted to be a doctor; he wanted to hide. He wanted to forget secrets.

Fiz crept down the short corridor to his own room, a small cubbyhole at the left rear of the upstairs office. He opened a drawer, took out a bottle of brandy and poured himself a drink. He swallowed it, then carefully replaced the cork. He needed to steady his nerves, not get drunk. Getting drunk was the last thing he had on his mind. Drunk men did not sleep: they dreamed the dreams of the damned.

He stretched out and closed his eyes. He would wake if Claw stirred. Such being the physician's mentality.

Call it an occupational hazard.

There were times when he had called it a curse.

He'll be all right. This time. And the time after that. I can't say for how long. But not forever.

He remembered Cougar's words.

She was a wise woman. Too wise for the likes of a hide town doctor and a lawman.

She would forgive him for not going to Bix Bradley because the thought would never occur to her.

He slept. Mercifully did not dream.

Fiz awoke with a start, not because his patient had groaned or called out, but because he had not. The silence in the office felt preternatural. Without bothering to fasten his shirt collar or put on his shoes, Fiz padded softly into the antechamber where Claw lay still. Almost dawn, he could just make out the big man's silhouette on the operating table.

"Claw?" Fiz called.

"I'm awake," came the low, pain-filled voice. If the physician had not known better, he would have guessed the owner of such a voice between eighteen to twenty years old. He started to chastise himself on the acuteness of his ear when he realized he had not been far wrong.

A twenty-three year old youth had no business being a Federal marshal in a place like Hellhole.

Yet, he had the potential to be one of the greatest men to wear a badge the west had ever seen.

That, in itself, was enough for Fiz to give Claw a piece of his mind. Without charge, something he did not often do.

"It's time for you to have a dose of laudanum."

"No."

"Have you decided to practice medicine without a license?"

Claw blew air through his nose.

"You don't have one, either."

The fact of the matter being, licensing physicians, which had been the rage in the late 1700's and early 1800's had gone completely out of style by 1868. Anyone, from a surgeon schooled in the best medical college in Philadelphia, to the itinerant branch water healer, could rightly call himself a doctor.

Dr. Ward could have argued that he did have a medical license, obtained at one of the greatest colleges in the United States. That he had studied under some of the most revered physicians of the day. Written and published medical papers under his own name. Been a doctor of prominence in his own right. Made more money in a month than Bill Bixley took in in a year. But he said nothing. That subject remained sacrosanct and private.

"You seem to know a hell of a lot for an uneducated boy," Fiz growled in annoyance.

"I am not uneducated," Claw replied with hurt pride. "Not formally educated. There's a difference."

"Yes, I know. You could write a thesis on the mechanics of pistols, hand guns and the effects a bullet has when impacting a man's chest at twelve feet."

"What's a thesis?"

Asked in so innocent a way, Fiz stopped in his tracks. He considered, then grunted and decided it best to ignore the matter entirely.

Opening the glass doors of his curio cabinet, he extracted a small bottle, wrapped in brown paper and secured by a string wound around the neck. Using his fingernail, Fiz expertly ripped the paper, bit away the white string and popped the cork, all in one fluid motion.

"Here," he said, holding the bottle up for Claw's inspection. "I'll give you a tablespoonful of this now, and a teaspoonful every time you wake for the next two days. Thereafter, you can dose yourself, until the bottle is empty."

"And then what?"

"You're on your own."

"I don't want any."

"You don't even know what it is."

"You said it was time for a dose of laudanum."

Fiz considered, then shrugged.

"That's right. I did. Must be getting soft in the head to tell you anything." He took a well-used spoon out of his military-issue metal coffee mug, wiped it with his shirt tail, then poured an ounce of the sticky brown liquid into it. "Here. Open your mouth and take this."

"I said --"

"You might as well do as you're told because I've already opened the bottle. That means I'm going to charge you for it, whether you take it or not. Suit yourself."

He went through the motions of replacing the mixture in the bottle, tipping the spoon with exaggerated carelessness when Claw spoke.

"All right. But only because I'm paying for it."

"Expect to see it on your bill."

Fiz placed the still-full spoon to Claw's lips and watched with fatherly satisfaction as the patient eagerly sucked the medicine.

"That's more like it," he decided, replacing the cork in the neck and setting the bottle aside.

"Gonna put my name on it, so you won't be able to sneak a dose of it for some other patient?"

"You're the only patient I've got right now, and I don't expect any more gun fighting until you're on your feet again."

"Why is that?"

"Who wants to bother shooting hiders or drunks when he can wait until the U.S. marshal is up and about? Besides, you make a damned good target; something I imagine you've had occasion to notice."

"A time or two," Claw agreed.

Fiz took his pulse, frowned from habit, believing it better to express displeasure and thus keep a patient compliant, then grabbed his coffee pot and opened the front door.

"I'm going downstairs to get some water. I'll be right back."

Knowing Claw could not see from the angle at which his bed was situated, Fiz did not want him to worry about being left alone. He also knew the morphine in the medication would work rapidly. If he did not make his intentions clear, Kiley would lose track of time and begin to worry at the doctor's absence.

A standing communal water pump stood by a trough two doors down from Fiz's office. He rinsed, then filled the coffee pot with cold water and returned, taking no more than five minutes to complete the task. By the time he had climbed the stairs and re-entered the office, Claw had already dosed off.

Hearing the door open, the wounded man raised his head and stared bleary-eyed at the entrance.

"Who's there?" he demanded, forgetting, for the moment, he was in the doctor's office and not his own.

"Doctor Ward. I'm going to make some coffee. Do you think your stomach can stand any?"

A long silence ensued while Claw consulted his ravaged insides.

"Yes," he finally declared. Once, he had been a soldier. Even on his deathbed, no soldier ever refused a cup of coffee. Or a smoke. It was the kind of lesson a man learned only once.

Fiz spilled some beans into his grinder and worked the handle with deliberation, grinding the coffee until it the pieces were no bigger than rough gravel. Satisfied, he measured out a generous portion, dumped them into the pot and placed it on his stove. It took only a moment longer to brush ash from the still-smoldering coals and add wood before an adequate flame generated enough heat to have the room smelling like coffee.

"Fiz, I can't stay here," Claw began while they waited for the mixture to boil.

"You're right. If you keep the coffee down, I'll let you limp into my spare room and lie down on a real bed."

"That's not what I mean."

"Two days, Marshal. Not a moment less. Better get it through your head."

"But if people know the law is laid up --"

Fiz made a low, deprecating noise as he busied himself inspecting the patient's bandages.

"For a man with a broken jaw, you sure talk a lot."

"It doesn't hurt much."

"Didn't think it did, or you'd be a lot more humble."

Claw flinched and Fiz regretted his ill-chosen word. They waited in silence after that. When the coffee finished brewing, Fiz helped Claw into a semi-sitting position before handing him a cup.

"It's hot," he warned.

Claw took a sip and nodded.

"I've tasted worse."

"I can't imagine where. It's not like you boys were deprived of any luxuries during the War."

Claw wisely let the subject drop.

When he drank all he could manage, Fiz took the cup, slipped an arm around the patient's back and helped him up.

"Careful, now. Your head'll be woozy and your legs won't hold for long. We're only going down the hall and into the room on your right. Understand?"

"Yes, sir."

Once on his feet Claw swayed unsteadily, motioning Fiz wait until the dizziness passed. On his signal and with the physician's aid, he managed to half limp, half hop into the bedroom. He stared at the Spartan room a long beat before allowing himself to be seated. The action allowed him to gather his thoughts.

"That daguerreotype you have on the wall in your office -- that you standing outside the tent?" he suddenly demanded.

"You mean the one with all the embalming equipment? Yup. That's me."

Claw chucked, despite the searing pain shooting down his leg.

"That wasn't an undertaker's tent. And there wasn't any embalming equipment. Who were you standing with?"

"What's it to you?"

"Thought I recognized the officer."

"Oh, him," Fiz agreed, placing a hand on his patient's shoulder and gently pushing him down.

"You're not going to tell me?"

"Wasn't planning on it."

"Doesn't matter. I recognized him."

"So you said. You have pretty sharp eyes."

"Oh, you know us Yankees. They say we have eyes in the back of your heads."

"They? Who's 'they'? 'We' only said that when one of you boys got your brains aired out by a Minnie ball."

Claw eased himself onto the bed and closed his eyes. Fiz frowned as the bandage on his leg showed bright red blood.

"I'll have to change that dressing after all," he decided.

He went about his task with quiet efficiency, clucking his tongue at the sight of the red and puffy stitches he had placed last evening.

"Look all right?" Claw asked.

"Mebbe."

"That's encouraging."

"Wasn't meant to be. Shut your mouth and get some sleep."

Claw obeyed as a dutiful soldier. Fiz pulled up a straight-backed chair and sat by the bedside. He had almost convinced himself the morphine put his patient to sleep when Claw spoke.

"Fiz?"

"I'm here."

"Fiz...?" Lower, more pleading. Ward took Claw's hand and held it.

"Yes, Claw?"

He could have said, *Yes, boy?* or *Yes, son?* in the same tone and been no less sincere.

"Fiz... when you first came in the prison wagon, that outlaw pointed his gun right at you and you weren't scared."

He sought understanding, an explanation Fiz did not think himself prepared to give.

"Who said I wasn't scared?"

"I could see your face. I looked into your eyes. You weren't scared."

Fiz stared down at his hands and began working on a hangnail he had meant to clip yesterday before all the excitement. It became utterly imperative to perform that operation immediately.

"Maybe I was; maybe I wasn't," he quietly admitted.

"I know when a man is scared and when he's not, Fiz. I need to know."

"You know too much, already."

"So do you."

A muscle pulled in Fiz's side. He twitched uncomfortably. When that did not ease his discomfort, he rubbed at it with his hand.

"What do you want me to say?"

"I want... I *need* to know, Fiz."

"Need to know what?"

He remained purposely obtuse because he did not want to answer Claw's question.

"*I* was scared, Fiz. More scared than I've ever been in my life. More scared than I ever thought I could be. You weren't afraid to die and I was. I need to know the reason."

The confession cost him, and Claw turned his face away in shame. Fiz put a hand on his shoulder, hesitated, then cleared his throat.

"You want to know why you were scared? I'll tell you why. You were scared because you finally have something to live for. You've worked for this, waited for an opportunity to prove yourself, hold a marshal's job in your own right. Now you have that chance. And more you didn't count on," he added. "Cougar Bradburn -- she's a good woman."

Claw closed his eyes, remembering how he felt when forced to consider the idea of impending death. He had thought of how he had failed the law -- and of her. Fiz was right. His life had changed, had taken on new meaning, assumed different values.

He slowly nodded, the pain in his leg all but forgotten as medication and profundity demanded priority.

"If that's true -- and you may be right -- then how does that explain you? Why you weren't scared."

"That's none of your business," Fiz snapped.

"Isn't it?"

"No."

"You made it mine."

"How do you see that?"

Without waiting for an answer, Fiz got up, fussed with the curtain, then retreated into his bedroom. Claw had almost given up on him when he returned, pipe in hand. He sat down again, packed the briar with tobacco, then struck a Lucifer and held it over the bowl. He did not speak again until his head and shoulders were obscured by the halo-like cloud of white-grey smoke.

"How do you see I made it your business?" he repeated.

"You saved my life."

"I've saved lots of people's lives. None of them ever said that made *me* beholding to *them.*" He puffed awhile without speaking, thinking perhaps Claw might make a comment. When he remained silent, a not unfamiliar bitterness welled up inside Fiz Ward. "I've seen more than my fair share die, too. What does that mean I owe the dead?"

"An explanation."

"Go to hell," Fiz snapped. He rested his arms on his thighs, prefatory to rising, then the energy seemed to deflate out of him and he sagged back into the chair, attempting to become more a part of the hard, insensitive wooden object than a living, breathing, feeling human being.

"I'm not going away," the marshal reaffirmed.

"You'll be dead within the year. Hardly worth wasting my time with."

"I set up the checkers board. You didn't come."

"Had no intention of coming."

"It was your idea."

"Bad idea."

The clock on the mantle in another room began to chime. Neither man counted the strokes. They were unimportant.

"You know, Fiz, I never knew my parents. I was raised by so many men -- passed around from one to another so many times I didn't know who to love. Or if I should love any of them. Cougar sort of said the same thing about herself. She and I -- we're outcasts, wandering from place to place, never knowing, really, who we are or where we're going. We both know there's something out there -- maybe a place where we can belong;

someone who will make sense out of it all. You might say, we're looking for what you found."

Fiz shuddered, then put his pipe down and raised his hands to his face. He wept, his thin frame growing visibly smaller as memories reduced him to little more than a broken heart.

"You can't know," he said, finally, without uncovering his face.

"I don't know. That's why I said I'm not going anywhere. I'm waiting for you to tell me."

"Why?"

"Because you're looking for something, too. Someone who can make sense out of it all."

"You think you can do that?"

His words were a challenge, more deadly than any gunfighter's Claw had ever faced. If he doubted his bravery a day ago, he had no qualms now.

"No, sir. Only you can do that. But if you share it, maybe you can work your way clear to understanding."

"No. I'll never be able to do that."

"Then maybe letting someone else carry the burden with you will make it lighter."

"You're a smart ass boy. How can I tell you, when you don't know what life is all about?"

"I couldn't have understood two nights ago. Maybe that's why you didn't come and play checkers with me. But I think I can understand better, now. Now that I know what coming close to losing someone I really care about means."

"You think it's that easy, do you?"

"I think I trusted you enough to let you see my shame. I don't know you very well, Fiz. We sorta got off on the wrong foot. Some of that was my fault. Some of it was yours. But I do know one thing. I'm not afraid to say I love you."

The man in the chair jerked spasmodically. His hair seemed grayer, his wrinkles deeper, more penetrating.

"I'm not a father figure; if that's what you're looking for, I'm not interested."

"I didn't say a father. I had a dozen fathers. I meant as a friend. I never had a friend."

Fiz leaned back in his chair, positioning his head so that he could stare up at the ceiling.

The room became so silent both men could hear Fiz's pocket watch ticking away the seconds. It sounded like a heartbeat.

"I was born in Baltimore," Fiz began. His voice was hard, unemotional. He told the story by rote, as though repeating it for the hundredth time had taken the edge of its poignancy. "I studied in Philadelphia; graduated at the top of my class. I could have gone anywhere and made a good living, but I went back to Maryland. No particular reason."

He cradled the cooling pipe in his hands. "I had a feel for medicine. It didn't take me long to establish a reputation. I wrote papers, had them published. Thought I might go to Europe and lecture; maybe to Edinburgh. I was ambitious, wanted to make a name for myself. Then I met her. At a party. She was the most beautiful woman I had ever seen. He name was Mary Elizabeth Connors. She was from Boston -- visiting relatives in Baltimore. We fell in love."

Outside the window a dog barked. Lonely, mournful and on edge. The kind of dog which had never sat at a campfire and wolfed down scraps from the fingers of a man.

"Falling in love was not something I planned on. I guess it never is," he sighed, pausing a moment to drop his head and stare at his patient. Claw nodded with his eyes. "All of a sudden, medicine didn't mean anything to me. All I could think about was Mary. She was the belle of every ball and I had no reason to suspect she could ever return my feelings. But she did."

He smiled and for the first time, the hard edges of his crusty image fell away.

"We were married almost before we knew what was happening. I was madly in love. But she wouldn't let me forget medicine. She said I had too much to offer the world. I believed her, because I believed everything she said. When she thought my career would be better served in Boston, we moved there. I would have gone anywhere with her.

"It was a magical time for us. I bought a house, hung up my shingle. Her parents were wealthy, influential people. Once they threw their support behind me, my practice really took off. Men from all over New England came to me for treatment. And I helped them."

His voice reflected pride, but not arrogance.

"I continued to study, wrote more medical papers. I could feel the healing in my hands. It was something powerful, wonderful, exciting. I never gave up on even the most hopeless case; no one I ever turned away. Money didn't matter, although I made plenty of that. It was -- the belief I could do anything. She gave me that. *She* believed, and I believed through her."

Through the same window, a man cursed and stomped his foot. Without seeing the dog, both men knew it slunk away, tail tucked between its legs. Teeth bared. Ears flattened.

"We talked about starting a family. She wanted children. So did I. Funny. You never think about those things and then the very thought becomes everything to you. We used to sit by the fire on those cold evenings and talk about the boys and girls we would raise. What we would name them. She thought the first boy ought to be named for me; I said the first girl would be named after her. We compromised by choosing a half dozen names. None of them were either hers or mine.

"That's the way it was. Just perfect. We worked things out between us, never had an argument. When she told me she was with child, I cried with delight. Wept like a baby, I was so happy.

"Two months later, I found a lump in her breast. Just a small node, nothing more. I didn't think too much about it. I thought it would go away. A complication of pregnancy.

"I, the great physician; the healer."

More sounds filtered in through the window. Neither heard.

"It didn't go away. It started growing and I knew what it was. I denied it, pretended not to notice. She got weaker and weaker. It was then that I gave up my practice; turned my other patients away, devoted my time and attention to her. I started researching, pouring over every medical book I could find. Wrote letters. They all came back with the same answers. Answers I didn't want to believe.

"*She* didn't believe them. She had faith. She never gave up. Not even at the very last. Not when I held her in my arms and watched her... wither away. She had every confidence I would find a cure. We were going to be parents. Nothing could get in the way of that.

"She went into labor early. The baby was stillborn. She died the next day. I buried them together."

Fiz's voice failed and tears streamed down his face. His watch kept ticking. It required the passage of many heart beats later before he continued.

"Her faith was not justified. I couldn't save her. I couldn't save the child. No one blamed me, of course. A lump in the breast is always fatal. A tragedy, people said. Poor man. They didn't know what they were talking about."

The pipe had gone cold. He felt the chill.

"I didn't work for six months after Mary died. Then one day I up and sold my practice. I didn't belong in Boston any more. I packed my bags and boarded a train. Returned to Baltimore. There was talk of war. I went to Virginia and volunteered. I thought that ought to be just about right. A man who couldn't save the woman he loved would fit in as an army surgeon."

Claw envisioned the picture on the wall and said nothing.

"I worked four long, arduous years as a Confederate officer. Saw so many men die I stopped counting. Performed more amputations than I care to say. Lost more than I saved. Those I helped went home, pitiful wrecks of men. Cripples. Others went back into the ranks to die. I was where I wanted to be, because I knew I couldn't make a difference.

"It didn't matter how many perished under my knife. Or even how many lived. I just went about my business, writing prescriptions I knew would never be filled, sawing off limbs, sending men back to be shot, or starve, or freeze to death. It was a good experience for me. It numbed the senses, that useless slaughter. Men were not men, they were nameless, faceless bodies. I immersed myself in blood the way other doctors downed themselves in alcohol."

The rattle of wagon wheels shook the building. A man-made earthquake.

"I told myself I didn't care. It got to be I could write a last letter home for some poor bastard and never shed a tear. That was what I wanted. I was making myself callous; burying my heart with all those tattered, blown-up bodies.

"I was the first one up, the first in the field, the last to go to bed at night. I operated on twenty, thirty boys a day and never complained. Jesus, they would have made me Surgeon-General if I'd have let them. No one knew why I did what I did. They thought me... dedicated.

"I fooled them all. Every last one.

"And then the War ended. Terrible thing. For all of me, it could have gone on forever. I had found my home. Right out there on the battlefield. I never flinched, never stopped, even when Grant's big guns were booming away and not even the officers would face them.

"Funny thing was, the soldiers admired me for it. That's a laugh."

He laughed bitterly. An empty, hollow sound. A death knell.

"I was the only one who didn't laugh. The only one who knew. And I hated them because they didn't understand.

"When the truce was signed, I was at a loss. Unlike those poor, wretched survivors of Lee's army, I had no home to go back to. Not unless you consider a grave a home."

He knit his hands. Hands he had washed in blood.

"I could have gone to Richmond. That's where Hunter McGuire went. He was Jackson's surgeon. I didn't want to follow him. He still believed. He wanted to make a difference. To repair the damage that had been done. To teach. All I wanted to do was keep hiding.

"So I headed west. As far west as I could go. When I ran out of railroad, I took a stage. This was where the stage line ended. Hellhole. I liked the name. Hellhole. That's what I was trying to do: bury myself in hell. So I hung up my shingle. Come to me if you dare. Come to me because you have to. I liked the irony."

Fiz stopped talking and stood up. He stared down into Claw's face.

"I don't want your friendship. I don't want your love. Do you understand, now?"

"I'm not going to die on you, Fiz."

"You made a mighty goddamned good try at it."

"You saved my life."

"I just got done telling you, that doesn't mean anything to me."

"It means something to me."

"That would seem to be your business."

The doctor turned walked away. He did not stop when Claw spoke.

"Thank you, Doctor Ward. God bless you."

He could have ignored the first part of the statement but not the second. He spun around, eyes blazing.

"God bless me? Wouldn't you say I've been 'blessed' enough?"

"I'd say you've been blessed with a love not many men on earth are ever privy to. I'd say you were blessed by every man you tried to save in that war. I'd say you were blessed by having the gift of healing."

"Not enough."

"Then I'd say you've cursed yourself enough for not being God."

"I never said I was God."

"Glad to hear it."

Fiz turned on his heels and stomped off, cursing himself, cursing Claw Kiley, cursing God.

Two of the three forgave him instantly and loved him more for it.

CHAPTER 19

She did not come to see him the three days he remained at the doctor's, and he did not question her motives. He had hoped, but hope was for children. United States marshals were grown men, feet planted firmly on the ground.

It was as well he did not try that expression on Cougar, for she would have told him exactly where *her* feet were planted, and he would not have liked the answer.

It was, therefore, not Miss Bradburn but Miss Cougar who greeted him as he limped into the office. Planted in the middle of the floor, the cat interrupted her grooming to appraise the lawman with an inquisitive stare. Beside her lay a milk pail, recently tipped. Some, but certainly not all of the contents had been lapped up by said occupant.

The cat meowed. She whisked her tail once, then stood, stretched and walked to him. Arching her back, she rubbed her cheek against his trouser legs, reasserting her claim on the large, nearly furless cat, inexplicably named "Claw."

"Glad to see someone missed me," he mused, bending down to scratch her ears. "But I hope you've done more than help yourself to my breakfast. What about the mice population of Hellhole? Have any luck reducing it?"

The question was beneath contempt. Therefore, she did not answer it.

Claw shrugged. Using the cane Fiz loaned him, he dragged his sore leg over to the desk and observed that some kind soul had thought to bring his mail over from the post office. Awkwardly lowering himself into the chair, he tipped and nearly fell over backwards as the loose springs gave way under his weight. Embarrassed to display such lack of coordination before the graceful feline, he affected a frown and picked up the stack.

The first envelope contained wanted posters. He grunted with bemused annoyance to see Herm Heller's face stare back at him from the top of the pile.

"I think I can be reasonably sure his fate in 'known,'" Claw commented, referring to the text, which advertised a $500 reward for the outlaw "dead or alive," or a $50 reward to anyone "knowing the whereabouts" of this dangerous criminal.

Behind Heller's poster were notices on Cobb, Miller, Gabby and the two prisoners who had been returned to the cells.

"A little late," he acidly remarked to the now dead faces of the Heller gang. Tempted to throw them out, he stayed his hand and separated out the four. The first men he had captured "dead or alive" in his new job, they would always evoke a special remembrance.

Some memories were better than others, but they all went into making up a life. The fact he still had a life made him unique.

A light knock on the door diverted his attention.

"Come in."

A slightly-built man wearing a black lawyer's coat and holding his battered hat in both hands stepped in.

"Good morning, Marshal," he began in a so refined and cultured a dialect Claw had trouble believing the words came out of such a lined and stubbled face, marred with deep circles under the eyes.

"Good morning, Mr. MacPhearson."

"You wanted to see me?" Frankie inquired, a tremor sneaking its way into his quaint and distinctly Northern dialect.

"Yes, sir. Won't you come in and take a seat?"

"Oh, you must not call me 'sir,'" Frankie quickly corrected, eyes widening in horror.

"Why not?"

"I should think that designation reserved for gentlemen."

Claw reacted sharply to the statement, articulated so clearly it might have been issued by a judge or a man of letters.

"What makes you think you're not a gentleman?"

"I might have been once," Frankie confessed, then grew flustered and shook his head. "It's the drink, Marshal."

"I see. Well, won't you shut the door and come in? I have something I want to say to you."

The older man hesitated, clearly torn.

"What is it you think I done?" he whispered in a lower, more pitiful and less educated voice. "It's possible I done it," he quickly added. "And I don't mean to shirk my duty, but.... Mebbe I don't remember. My mind isn't so sharp as it used to be."

"And what did it used to be?"

"I don't remember."

Which was as close to a lie as Frank MacPhearson ever told anyone in his life.

"Mr. MacPhearson --"

"Everyone calls me Frankie," he dared interrupt, then frightened by his audacity, clamped his jaws shut with a resounding clink of rotten teeth.

"Thank you," Claw acknowledged. "I shall be honored to do the same."

"No honor to it, Marshal."

"A subject -- sir -- we shall not debate. Dr. Ward told me about the conversation you had with him -- concerning the man pretending to be a prison guard, and how you asked about the wheel. He said if it had not been for you, he might never have gone back and looked in the wagon. Do you understand what that means?"

Asked kindly and meant to be rhetorical, the thin man gave it due consideration then slowly shook his head, unable to work out the puzzle.

"No, I'm afraid I don't," he sadly admitted.

"If Dr. Ward had not gone back, those robbers would have gotten out of Hellhole with their friends they were breaking out of jail. They would have killed me."

Frankie made a low, gasping sound then shuddered.

"It would have been a pity to see that happen, Marshal."

"It took courage for you to do what you did. And a keen bit of deduction."

Claw paused, trying to ascertain whether the man before him knew the meaning of the two dollar word he purposely used. Detecting a light behind the eyes, he satisfied himself he did.

"I only done what I thought was right."

"It was right, Frankie. I wanted to thank you."

The drunk grew visibly flustered and began to shake. Aware of the tremors wracking his body, Frankie took a step back and indicated the door.

"Is that all?" he began. Claw prevented him from leaving by motioning him forward. He obeyed very reluctantly.

"No, sir. That is not all. Do you see this wanted poster?"

He shoved forward the notice of Herm Heller. Frankie took a long look before giving a slight indication of recognition.

"It says here," Claw continued, "There is a five-hundred dollar reward for his capture. If it had not been for you, Heller would have gotten away. I believe you are entitled to that reward."

"Me?" came the astonished gasp. "Oh, no! I don't want that money."

"Why not?"

"I wouldn't know what to do with it."

"A man like you could use it to -- buy a fresh suit of clothes. He might spend some of it and buy himself dinners at the Regent. He might even try a shave and a bath and a haircut. It might just turn your life around."

Frankie stiffened his back, then deliberately replaced his hat before bowing.

"Good day, Marshal," he said with consummate dignity and retired.

Win one, lose one.

The books were balanced.

Claw filed the wanted posters in his desk drawer, then began his official notification to Hays. It was the first report of such an incident he had ever written as marshal and he took his time with it. An hour later, he had wasted six sheets of paper, worn down his pencil and achieved the following.

"Herm Heller and three of his men attempted to break out two gang members incarcerated in the Hellhole jail. All four died in the attempt. Two outlaws remain in my custody. Guards out of Garden City, identities unknown, along with the convict they transported, were murdered by Heller's gang. The prison horse and wagon has been recovered. Claw Kiley, U.S. Marshal."

As succinct and revealing as Mr. Frankie MacPhearson's refusal of a reward.

When the telegram from "Claw Kiley, U.S. Marshal" was received in Hays, a copy was delivered to Albert Stewart, deputy assistant to the governor of the state of Kansas. Mr. Stewart initialed the paper and placed it in the governor's "in" basket, along with the suggestion that Greg

Thomas, the man who had hired the new law officer in Hellhole, receive a personal note of congratulations on a job well done.

No other mention was given "Claw Kiley, U.S. Marshal." His name, however, was noted.

Kiley was known to be the protégée of Marshal Jack Duvall. Had Marshal Duvall been alive, he, too, would have received a hand-written note of congratulations from the governor.

Ada Duvall would have filed it for her husband. In the outhouse.

Claw Kiley did not see Bix Bradley, helpful citizen, for two weeks. During that time, when the marshal presented himself at the Lowdown for a beer or to break up a fight, the owner was noted to be busy working on his books, taking inventory or occupied elsewhere on business.

On payday, which happened to be the last day of the month, Bix did not, however, neglect to dock one saloon girl's pay for the time she missed being away from her position.

For services rendered to the owner of the saloon above and beyond the actual requirements of her job, Miss Bradburn received no compensation.

Nor had she expected any.

One played life as it came and did not complain. This being the wild west, after all, injustice played as much a part of survival as did justice.

More, in fact.

Claw stopped by the Lowdown Saloon before starting his evening rounds, hoping to catch Cougar's eye and receive a smile for his trouble. The beer hall was particularly crowded, and with a frown, he stepped through the swinging doors and looked around.

"Buy you a beer, Giant?" a familiar voice inquired. By the time he turned around, his grin spread ear-to-ear.

"Thought maybe... later?"

"Beer's all it'll be," she agreed, lowering her voice to a conspiratorial whisper. Then, louder. "Place is full up tonight."

"So I see. What's the occasion?"

"Bix Bradley got a telegram from Washington. He's been appointed deputy-lieutenant to the president."

Claw's look changed from a sunny day to an overcast sky so fast she almost did not have time to laugh at her own joke.

"I'm kidding, Claw." She reminded herself not to push him too far or too fast. He might be the marshal, but he was still a boy, after all.

A nearly innocent boy.

God be praised. She had thought God stopped making them a long time ago. It was good to know He was still on the job.

"Kidding?" he repeated, then smiled because she did.

She noted he was good at taking cues, if not making fast inferences.

"Bix's gambling for the House tonight and a pair of professional sharpers are in town. They've been at it for hours. Around here, that makes for fine entertainment, son," she concluded in a drawl.

This time he laughed on his own.

"I see." Without having to stand on tiptoe like the rest of the crowd, he started over at the poker table, took in the scene, then glanced back. "Who's winning?"

She felt tempted to say, *The one with all the money piled up in front of him,* but forbore. That would have been mean.

Mean, but tempting.

"Bix's winning right now. Fifteen minutes ago, it was the man to his left; name's Jud Fisher. The other one is called Black. Just 'Mister Black'."

"They come in here often?"

"No. Mebbe two, three times a year. I've only seen them twice, myself. They're big tippers. When they win," she needlessly added.

"What about Bix?"

The question reeked of inexperience. She had to imagine he asked it more from a lawman's perspective than a lover's.

"I've never known Bix to spent one thin dime if he doesn't have to."

"Do you expect trouble from the losers?"

Not: *Is there ever trouble from the losers,* or, *Are the gamblers bad losers?*

He did not seek past history, but rather her opinion. If he had said, *I love you,* he could not have flattered her more. A man may love a woman he does not respect, believing females do not need both affection and dignity, but a man who respects a woman is a knight in shining armor.

And just as rare.

As dragon's teeth.

"No. I don't think so. Not from Black and Jud. If Bix starts to lose big, he'll stop playing and recoup some other night when there are easier chickens to pluck. The only trouble I see is from some of the other men who may get in the game."

"Thanks for the warning. I'll stop back later and look in. On the game," he added. She nodded.

It was as well they both understood the rules.

The clock hands approached midnight when Claw returned to the Lowdown. Some of the local men had slipped away but for the most part, the crowd had stayed to watch the excitement. He guessed there were thirty or thirty-five men crowded into the saloon. The outside lights burned brightly, inviting the stray traveler to drop in for a drink or two and some high drama.

He made his way to the bar and ordered a beer. Before he could slap his nickel onto the polished mahogany, Cougar came up behind him and jostled his elbow.

"Save your money. It's on the house."

"Oh? I thought you said Bix was a tight one."

"With a dime," she reminded him. "You were putting down five cents."

He grinned and she returned it.

"Actually, Mr. Bradley looks to be the big winner tonight. He's celebrating."

"Is that good news or bad news?"

"It depends," she said, lining her words with caution.

Claw grunted, shook his leg in agitation, then repositioned his Stetson.

"I think I'll stay awhile. In case the winner needs someone to guard his money."

"Not a bad idea. There's probably close to one thousand dollars on that table."

"A thousand dollars?"

"That's what I said."

He whistled appreciatively. "This, I have to see."

Claw doubted the bank housed that much currency at any one time. He had guarded train shipments, Army payrolls and recovered money sacks from robberies, but had never actually laid his eyes on so much cold, hard cash. His interest being less professional than curious, he followed Cougar as she cleared a path for him to the table.

He would never possess that much himself, but it would be nice to think he had at least seen someone who had.

The two professional gamblers, Jud and Black were seated opposite each other. Both had removed their hats and jackets and played in shirt sleeves. Their linen was soaked with sweat and both looked in need of a shave and a good meal. Bradley still wore his coat, although lines of strain were etched beneath his eyes. When he caught sight of the marshal, he waved a friendly greeting.

"Howdy, Claw. Glad to see you."

"Claw" was not deceived. The voice reflected no warmth, no possibility of camaraderie between them. It lay within his authority to close the Lowdown and thus effectively end the game. Bradley tacitly acknowledged that fact, nothing more.

The idea tempted him. Had Bradley been losing, he would have ordered the saloon to stay open all night, but the fact he stood to win big considerably altered the circumstances.

Reading his body language, Cougar inconspicuously nudged his elbow.

"Let them keep playing." She did not have to whisper, for the players around the table were nearly shouting to each other over to be heard the din. Nothing she said to Claw could be overheard.

Ordinarily, Miss Bradburn, saloon girl, would not have had the audacity to suggest any course of action to the Law, but his earlier acknowledgement of her judgment emboldened her. Not until he nodded agreement did she realize what his refusal would have cost her, and she sucked air between her front teeth in silent acknowledgement to the gods. They were surely watching over her this evening.

"My name's Anston Jud, Marshal. Draw up a chair and join us," the card shark offered, following Bradley's line of vision. Claw demurred.

"No, thanks."

He did not want to play. He had come to watch.

There were many things to observe. What interested him most would not take place for an hour, perhaps two.

Seeing Lilly come down the stairs with two men on her arm underscored his concern.

Bradley might win the night but he was not going to buy his girl.

Not tonight.

No one deserved that kind of luck.

Call it a payback.

If this were the army, it would have been labeled, "Rank hath its privileges."

Six men sat at the table when Claw arrived. One by one the amateurs were weeded out until only the three professionals remained.

By one-thirty, Black folded. It neared two o'clock when Jud finally threw down his hand and rubbed his bloodshot eyes.

"That's it for tonight," he declared.

With sagging shoulders, the sharper gathered his few remaining dollars and swept them into his pocket. Bradley peered around the crowd, smiling broadly. As the big winner, he felt his oats.

"What? So soon? A pity, gentlemen. I was just getting started." He waved his hands in a "come on" gesture. "Who else will play? No one? Anyone?"

"Anyone?" a voice repeated. A momentary silence descended as men craned their necks to see who had the audacity to ask such a question at such a time.

Only a gambler with nothing to lose.

"Anyone," Bradley challenged. His smile broadened.

"I'll play you."

The hush deepened.

Cougar Bradburn stepped forward. She had gone upstairs some time during the past half hour and changed. She no longer wore the low-cut saloon girl attire but had exchanged it for more conservative dress.

Claw had inspired her.

Call it a craving for dignity.

If a woman could be asked her opinion, she had a right to take a gamble with Fate.

Ordinarily, Bradley would not allow a woman to play cards in the Lowdown. Men did not like to sit opposite females. Gambling remained a male domain. A man's reputation, his very life and death, were often staked on the pasteboards. Men squirmed, sweated, cursed, prattled and prayed to gods only another of his kind could understand. Men staked their own dignity on the cards. They did not want to lose to a woman.

Tonight was different. Bix had garnered a fortune and savored his power.

"One rule," Cougar said. Bradley raised an eyebrow. "No one can raise the other more than twenty-five dollars at any one time. Until the last hand of the night. And," she added. "We play for table stakes."

There was no point playing if he won every hand by out-betting her. Less purpose leading him down the Primrose Path, to have one of his friends keep adding money to his reserve of cash.

"Do you have a stake?"

Bradley's voice dripped with innuendo and dirty knowledge. He looked at Claw. The marshal swallowed the sudden lump in his throat. He had just been rendered helpless.

"I have."

Cougar did not look at Claw. She could not afford the emotional drain. Not now. He would have to take care of himself.

Call it an occupational hazard.

She opened a small leather poke, the kind prospectors used, and dumped a handful of coins onto the table. It was not a fortune, but all she had.

That and the unspoken treasure which would be paid in something far more precious than gold, if she were the loser.

It was the kind of courage which chilled the blood of a knight errant.

CHAPTER 20

"Sit down." Bradley invited. His blood ran hot. This was the kind of game at which he excelled.

Cougar accepted the offer, paused to survey the onlookers, then promptly put them out of her mind. From this moment until the end of the game, they would cease to exist for her.

"Deal?" Bradley asked. She smiled and nodded agreeably. It was an affable smile; a woman's smile. It was meant to disarm Bradley, and as far as it went, her tactic succeeded. He slid the deck across the table. She rested her hands, palms downward and winked. Suggestive and coy.

"Let's start out on an even footing, Bix. How about you being a big man and calling for a new deck?"

Bradley returned the wink and gestured. The bartender handed him a pack. Without breaking the seal he tossed them to Cougar. They landed a foot in front of her fingers. She made no move to retrieve them.

In the interests of speeding the game along, Bix corrected his trajectory and placed the cards by her fingertips. Satisfied, Cougar took the deck, broke the glued paper tab and removed the pasteboards.

Separating the two jokers from the top, Cougar caressed them with her fingers, then made an exaggerated show of ripping the cards in half. When Bix reacted as though she were tearing a limb from his body, she arched an eyebrow by way of explanation. He made no further comment, audible or physical.

Riffling the cards, Cougar familiarized herself with the texture, the feel, the sensation of each individual placing piece. When finally satisfied, she placed them dead center and allowed him to cut. He did so and she dealt out ten, five for her, an equal number for her opponent.

They played draw poker, opening with five dollars. Bix asked for three cards. She took none. Bradley folded. She raked in her winnings and passed the cards to him.

Taking his time, Bix shuffled the cards for a full minute before dealing. Both placed five dollars in the pot and looked at their hands. Bradley took one card and she asked for two. They bet again, each using the lull it took the other to separate two dollars from their pile to study the other.

The game of chance took on a heightened significance. They were no longer employer and employee but two equals, two enemies. For Bradley, it constituted a step down. For Cougar, it represented an elevation into the clouds.

If only it did not rain on her parade.

When Bix called her, she revealed two pair, tens and fours. He held three sevens and took the pot, grinning smugly behind what had once been his superior position. Unruffled, Cougar took back the cards and they played a third hand. He won.

After winning two consecutive rounds, Bix became careless. He bet higher amounts; she met him at each turn. When the pile of coins and paper situated between them reached forty dollars, Cougar called. The saloon keeper had been bluffing. She took in the money. He stomped his foot and motioned the bartender bring a bottle. Joe Ryan placed it by his right hand and he poured himself a drink.

Only after downing the first shot in one gulp did he think to offer her any. She politely refused.

"I've been drinking, one-on-one with the customers all evening," she confessed in a slightly inebriated voice. "I think I had better not push my luck."

He laughed at her slurred speech and the choice of words.

"Lady luck is what this game is all about." She shrugged, as though the concept were new to her.

"I'll keep that in mind."

Her deal. She shuffled, then dealt the cards. He opened for ten dollars. She met him.

"I'll take one," he announced with bravado. She looked worried as she slid him the card, face down.

"Dealer takes four."

No wonder she's worried, the crowd whispered, some to onlookers standing beside them, others quietly, to themselves.

Bix looked at his card, stroked his chin in a purposely obscene manner, then raised his eyes without lifting his head. He stared at her across the table.

"I'll bet twenty," he decided. She bit her lip, struggled with the enormity of the sum, rechecked her cards.

"All right," came the reluctant acknowledgement. "I'll meet your twenty and raise you five."

He had already counted his coins by the time she pushed her money into the figurative collection plate.

"I'll meet your five," he said with aplomb, "and raise you another twenty."

She appeared as though she were going to cry. She made a point of counting her remaining stake, then sighed. A deep exhalation of breath, from the heart.

Some of the men standing behind her crudely imagined the sigh coming from a point somewhat above the heart.

"I'll match your twenty and raise you fifty," she said.

The room grew as quiet as though thunder had crackled and the Lord asked each man if he could swim.

Bradley's eyes opened in black astonishment. He checked his hand again, then frowned. His foot shook under the table. He made a motion and the bartender, who stood by his side, poured the master another drink. Bradley sipped the amber liquid. Apparently he did not find the answer he sought in the bottom of the glass, for he muttered an inaudible curse and made a chopping motion with his hand.

"Take the damn pot." As Cougar's hands enveloped the money, Bradley had a change of heart. He reached out and stopped her. "On second thought, I'll raise you --"

"I don't think so."

The voice of authority. Bix jerked around and stared at Claw Kiley's benign countenance.

"I said, 'I'll raise her --'"

"And I said, 'I don't think so.'"

"This is my table, Marshal Kiley, and my saloon. I set the rules here."

The lawman repeated the same sentence a third time. He did not propose to do it a fourth.

"I don't think so."

"Are you telling me how to run my business?"

"I'm just enforcing the law, Bix." He sounded calm, almost uninterested. "In checkers, when a player takes his hand off his marker, he's made his move and he lives with it." The alternative, he implied, hooking his fingers under his gun belt, was that he also died with it. "In poker, when a man says he's folded, he does just that."

Miss Bradburn drew the money to her side and replaced the loose cards in the deck. She did not look up as much as to acknowledge this was not her fight. Bradley hesitated, then shrugged.

"Have it your own way, Marshal. I'll have my way later."

He almost made Claw a liar.

I don't think so.

"Your deal, I believe, Bix."

Bradley snarled as his eyes hardened. Leaning across the table, he accepted the deck.

"You know what I mean... Cougar."

Her face assumed a look of puzzlement.

"I'm afraid I have no idea what you're talking about. I wasn't listening to your conversation with the Marshal." Emphasis on the word "marshal," with a capital "M."

Bix shuffled the deck and dealt the hand. Without looking at his cards, he shoved fifty dollars into the pot to open. She promptly folded. He swore and she retrieved the pasteboards.

Cougar won the next three hands. On the fourth, Bix raised her one hundred dollars, only to be reminded of their original agreement that he could not raise more than twenty-five. Furious, he threw down his cards. One landed face up, effectively ending the hand by his own carelessness. She took his money and added it to her growing pile.

When she dealt the next round, she opened for twenty-five. He bet with her, meeting, then raising the maximum each time. When the pot contained over three hundred dollars, she called.

"Three of a kind," he announced.

"Show the cards."

He did so, spreading them out, one by one. He held three queens, an eight and a ten. Just as he reached for the pot, Cougar stopped him.

"I have a flush. That beats three of a kind." If looks could kill, the game would have ended right there.

Cougar dipped her cards, revealing a sequence of two, three, four, five and six of spades.

Bradley slumped in his chair. If Jonathan Harker had been present, he might have had reason to employ another type of "spade."

Play resumed. Bix won the next hand, played carelessly and lost the following.

"Fresh deck!" he called. Ryan brought him another pack of playing cards. Lilly confiscated the used deck. When no one of significance watched, she casually tossed it through the grill of the large cast iron stove at the rear of the room.

One of the locals, staring cross-eyed at his watch, called out, "Five o'clock." What importance the hour had to the rest of the congregation remained obscure, but he grinned sleepily and stomped his foot.

"This is one night my misses won't thrash me fer stayin' out late. I reckon she's rockin' up a storm in that chair o' hers right now, wonderin' about the outcome. If I wandered in widout knowin', *then* I'd git it, sure!"

A twittering of amusement swept the onlookers. Many, if not all, were thinking the same thing.

Finding his situation less humorous, Bradley played out the current hand, lost and flung his cards on the table. Bleakly observing the considerable money Miss Bradburn, card sharper, had piled up in front of her, he gritted his teeth, making a grating sound audible at the rear of the room. His good mood had been dispelled hours ago. Rather than anticipate a good night and a triumphant march to the bank in the morning, he stared failure in the face.

Nothing in life had prepared him to expect Defeat coming at him with red hair and varnished nails.

Forfeiting a king's ransom to Jud and Black was one thing. Losing to an upstart saloon girl another thing, entirely. Without ever laying it on the table, he had staked his manhood on the outcome and stood in danger of losing it.

He weighed that against her life, which he was not above taking.

"It's getting about time to wrap this up," Claw suddenly announced. He had been so quiet, his presence had almost been forgotten.

Almost.

Cougar turned her head, the better to see the tall man with hollow, black circles beneath his eyes. A woman might think a man cared about her, looking that way. For the first time all night, she smiled.

"One last hand," she pleaded.

Something in her tone conveyed a message he could not decipher. He could not go by the words: they were spoken for the audience. Did she mean for him to call the game "against her will," thus ensuring her a victory? Or to permit one final game?

Why is it, he wondered, not for the first time, *everyone in Hellhole speaks in code?*

She might as well have tapped her message out in Morse. Or blinked her eyes.

He had little time to make a decision. Before he did, Bradley interrupted.

"Marshal Kiley. I have lost a considerable amount of money. One last hand." Claw narrowed his eyes.

That made it clear.

"No. I don't think so. Let's break it up." He turned to the crowd. "Time to go home, boys. Finish your drinks and be off. No more entertainment, tonight."

Cougar sighed and began stacking her coins into even piles, as much as to say, *That's fine with me.* Bradley squirmed in his chair then reached out and arrested her by putting a hand on hers.

"Just a minute," he demanded. Then, to the lawman. "Marshal, I have asked for one more game."

"Take your hand off the lady." Not a request. Bradley removed his hand. "Apologize to Miss Bradburn."

Bix swallowed his pride. For the sake of that much money, he would have eaten worse.

Which would be nothing compared to what he would make Cougar Bradburn absorb.

"I beg your pardon, Miss. One more game?"

She critically eyed his stake.

"I have a little less than fifteen hundred dollars here. You don't have twenty-five. That means you can't meet me. What's the point?"

She drove her point home with deadly accuracy, yet her voice remained as calm as though she were questioning a preacher over his Sunday sermon.

One in which he had discoursed upon the differences between heaven and hell.

Both Cougar Bradburn and Bix Bradley stood on the brink of Limbo. One would fall down, the other fly up, for who did not know the common expression, "Being broke is hell?"

"I have... the Lowdown." She gave no reply. "The saloon," he clarified, thinking perhaps she had not taken his meaning.

"The Lowdown?"

"It's worth three thousand dollars. I'll stake my ownership of the saloon against everything you have on the table."

If Claw had drunk one beer, he would have vomited it over his boots. The skin on the back of his hands and neck sent a prickly sensation through his body, as though he had received a jolt from a galvanic battery. He twitched uncomfortably.

"We did say we were playing for table stakes," she thoughtfully considered. "I suppose it could be said I brought my body to the table and you brought the Lowdown, inasmuch as this table is part of the saloon." She caught Claw's eyes once more. "What would be the position of the law on such a bet? Legal?"

He could not have told her his own name with any certainty.

"Legal."

His right hand rested on his gun. Not a casual gesture. If Bradley won, he would find some excuse for arresting the bastard.

"Legal," Cougar repeated. Then, more forcefully, "There will be no need for gunplay, Marshal. As long as Bix and I both understand what we are betting. I have no qualms with the terms."

She conveyed to him that she would pay the price. He shook his head.

"Cougar --". She anticipated him but not in the manner he expected.

"Yes, Claw. I think I would like a drink. Thank you."

He waked, stiff legged, to the bar, poured a glass of whisky and returned with it. His face was long, tired, unendurably sad. Cougar went to accept the shot glass, did not get a good grip and dropped it. She immediately bent down to pick it up.

Mortified, Claw apologized. "I'm sorry. I'll get another."

She waited for him to return, accepted the second shot and downed it like a man dying of thirst in the desert.

"Dutch courage?" Bix asked, a superior edge to his voice. She shrugged. "My deal."

"Wait a minute. You dealt the last hand."

"Ladies first. Are you forgetting your manners, Mr. Bradley?"

He took a deep breath, then waved his arm.

"Stand back, everyone. Give us some room."

No one moved an inch. If he thought the law would enforce his order, he was sadly mistaken.

Cougar riffled the cards, offered him the opportunity to cut. He did so, making sure he did not do so evenly. She smiled beguilingly.

"One hand," she said. "Since we have already set the stakes, I see no need of any further betting. Agreed?"

"Agreed."

She flipped out ten cards, alternately setting one before him, the other in front of her. When they were dealt, each player looked at what had been issued.

Sweat lined Bradley's brow. He paused to wipe it away with a linen handkerchief.

"Two cards."

Cougar gave him the requisite number, off the top.

"Dealer takes one."

She took one card, looked at it, then rested it back on the green-felt table, face down.

"I'm calling you, Bix."

Had she a gun and were he a gunfighter, she could not have challenged in more deadly tones.

The hush in the room deepened. Previously slack limbs tensed. Men leaned forward. For the first time in hours, a sneer curled around Bradley's wan lips. He nodded familiarly to one of the men. A gesture of superiority; of ownership, as much as to imply, *You'll still be coming to me tomorrow for that drink. And the night after that. I know your weakness but I don't have any of my own.*

Smug, superior, once more in charge, he spread his cards across the green felt.

"Three of a kind. The king of diamonds, the king of spades, the king of clubs. And a six of hearts and the deuce of clubs," he added as a calculated afterthought. Although anticipated by his demeanor, gasps and intakes of breath made the rounds of the spectators. Several men cleared their throats. One coughed and blew his nose. No one applauded, although they might have. Out of fear, perhaps, or the re-establishment of the proper order.

"Beat that, *Miss* Bradburn," Bix continued with sarcasm. Patently, he did not expect to call her "Miss Bradburn" again anytime soon.

"Three pair," she thoughtfully acknowledged. "That's a winning hand if ever I saw one."

Bradley actually beamed at the confession, acknowledging her submission with a bow of his head. She waited until he reached out for her money before continuing.

"Unfortunately, it doesn't beat a full house."

She turned her cards over, one-by-one. Jack. Jack. Jack. Queen. Queen.

"Jacks and queens," she announced, stating the obvious with all the pride of her kind. A pride only recently discovered.

"Read 'em and weep," one of the townsmen observed with piety.

Bradley did indeed read them. And came close to weeping. His jaw dropped open and he stopped breathing. Fortunately, the town doctor stood in the crowd. Unfortunately, had Bix dropped on the spot, he would have been trampled by the onrush to congratulate the winner and been beyond help by the time said physician could reach him.

"I don't be-lieve it," he hissed.

Speaking in monosyllables, none of the uneducated in Hellhole had trouble interpreting his sentence.

Bradley looked up at Kiley. Man to man. One last appeal. All the kinship, bribery, avarice and begging the man possessed reflected in his orbs.

The Marshal had eyes only for the lady.

"It appears Miss Bradburn has won."

A man in the back of the room let out a whoop. Another took it up and soon the entire saloon was awash with heartfelt cheers. Balled-up hands rent the air, feet stomped and hats were tossed, like confetti.

A changing of the guard.

The King is dead!

Long live the Queen!

Men who had previously rooted for Bradley dismissed him with a cry of wonder. Those in Hellhole understood what it meant to support the winning side.

To the victor belongs the spoils.

The town had lost one respectable citizen and gained another.

If money could be said to grant respectability.

It's a hell of a good start, the new owner of the Lowdown would agree.

Lips moving without sound, Bradley gaped at the merrymakers, acutely aware he had lost his identity. Those who tipped their hats to him a day ago now equated him to the lowest drifter, the dirtiest hider. Gone, his veneer of power, his sheen of importance. He no longer owned the Lowdown Saloon. He was, therefore, an itinerant.

And the west already had enough of them to go around.

Cougar pushed back from her chair, turning to accept the congratulations of her new friends. Cynicism aside, she greeted those who had refused her a tip six hours previous, and who now wanted to wrap his arms around her waist and spin her in a victory dance.

Time for that, later. Never, ever, did she forget the game still in progress, the face she must assume which went far deeper than rouge and powder applied before a cracked mirror.

"Drinks on the House!" she called to give herself breathing room. Waiting until the universal exodus drew men toward the bar, Cougar demurely took her winning hand and those played by Bradley and added them to the deck. Shuffling the pack once for luck, she discretely passed them to Lilly. They joined the other deck she had burned earlier in the evening.

Gambler's creed: never leave evidence, incriminating or otherwise.

A wise card sharper lived to play another day.

Sometimes, one even went on to own a saloon.

Assuming her rightful place behind the bar, Cougar poured drinks with the bartender until the six o'clock bell of the early morning milk wagon drifted in through the batwing doors. Suddenly, everyone remembered he or she had not gone to bed and the new day had already begun. Cougar caught Claw's eye and this time he had no trouble reading her intentions.

"That's enough, boys! I'm sure the new owner of the Lowdown will continue the celebrating this evening, so I want you all to go home and get some sleep so you can be back here tonight."

The marshal's words were the occasion of one last round of cheers, then the men piled out through the swinging doors, each praying for a bit of *Miss* Cougar's luck to rub off on them. They would need it.

None more so than the married men.

The bachelors' primary trouble would come when they awoke with a staggering headache from drinking too much and shouting too loudly.

Only Doctor Ward seemed pleased. He would do a good business in nostrums and notions and sundry powders of mysterious composition.

Cash on the barrel head.

Excuses for the spouse two dollars extra; five dollars if his wife believed it.

"Drop it!"

She thought he had gone, but the familiar voice, deepened by the warning conveyed in the tone, alerted Cougar that Claw had stayed behind. Turning quickly, she observed him standing in the entranceway, pistol drawn.

She could not see the object of his ire, but another voice, familiar in a different way, told its own story.

"I'm only taking what's mine, Marshal."

"There is nothing in this saloon which belongs to you."

"Personal papers --"

"What's going on?" Cougar demanded, quickly joining the lawman.

Bix Bradley, recently emerged from the back room, clutched a carpetbag in his hand.

"Theft, by the looks of it," Claw said.

Bradley tried his most charming smile. He might have spared himself the effort if he had any awareness what that smile translated to in the minds of the two people before him.

"Nothing of the kind."

Claw remembered his earlier promise that if Bradley won he would find some excuse to arrest him. He retrospectively amended that vow.

If Bradley lost, he would find some excuse to shoot the bastard.

His trigger-finger itched and it took more control than he thought he possessed to refrain from shooting the worm.

"You're through here. I want you on the seven o'clock stage out of Hellhole."

"You can't order me to leave town."

The odds were good Bradley considered himself related to a cat, for he surely used one of his nine lives with that statement.

"I just did. Cougar, take that case. Whatever is in it belongs to you."

She responded immediately, grabbing the carpetbag and removing it a careful distance away before prying open the sides.

"Cash from the safe," she identified. "Papers; contracts."

"I lost the saloon," Bradley protested. "That doesn't mean I gave up my rights to everything in it."

He wasted a second life with that protest.

"Want to bet?"

Claw was not a man who bluffed.

"I'll hire a lawyer --"

"You do that." This time, Cougar spoke. Her entire world had turned upside-down and what would have been unthinkable audacity yesterday became first nature this morning.

"What about my clothes -- my belongings upstairs?"

As the new owner of the Lowdown, Cougar had the right to answer, but Claw's obligation as a lover demanded he make one final denial.

"Nothing upstairs belongs to you. Get out."

Bradley hesitated, then shrugged.

"How can I leave town when I don't have any money to buy a ticket?"

He extinguished his third life faster than a cigar butt tossed into a Saturday night spittoon.

"You're wearing cufflinks and a watch. You also have a right fancy pair of shoes on your feet. Trade them for your ticket."

"You can't mean that."

He reduced himself to five lives and none worth one thin dime.

"Let's go," Claw directed, motioning with his gun. "You can wait outside or you can cool your heels in jail. Makes no difference to me."

Not precisely true, but Bradley wisely did not think to quibble. Walking stiff-legged by the saloon owner, he moved dejectedly through the now empty parlor, brushing past the marshal to make his way through the batwings.

"Thanks," Cougar said to the Law, sending Bradley on his way with a look of pure hatred.

"Just doing my job, ma'am."

She grinned and he grinned. Claw held out his arms and she came to him, her radiance mating with his, until their combined joy equaled the spectacular colors of the dawning Kansas sun.

The fact that he hugged her with the pistol still clutched in his hand was not lost on the ever-present specter of Ada Duvall. She knew it to portend things to come. One night had ended, a new day begun.

Nothing had altered the fact Claw Kiley was a lawman. Not all the winning hands in the world could change that one whit.

Not all the love a woman had to offer, or the discovery of a new friend could stave off destiny.

If she were a gambling woman, Ada Duvall would have recited the oft-expressed prediction that the new marshal would not live out the year.

And then placed her dead husband's life insurance premium on a sure bet.

The End

GSFE

ALSO BY: S.L.KOTAR AND J.E.GESSLER

A character based historical 1950's courtroom based murder mystery entitled "**The Hugh Kerr Mystery Series**"..

- Book I   **The Conundrum of the Decapitated Detective**
- Book II   **The Conundrum of the Absconded Attorney**
- **Book III**   **The Conundrum of the Sins of the Fathers**
- **Book IV**   **The Conundrum of The Two-Sided Lawyer**
- **Book V**   **The Conundrum of the Clueless Counselor**
- **Book VI**   **The Conundrum of the Loveless Marriage**
- **Book VII**   **The Conundrum of the Executed Defendant**
- **Book VIII**   **The Conundrum of the Jettisoned Jury**
- **Book IX**   **The Conundrum of the Perjured Pigeon**
- **Book X**   **The Conundrum of the Haunting Halloween**
  - **Party**
- **Book XI**   **The Conundrum of the Tuneless Tunesmith**
- **Book XII**   **The Conundrum of the Meddling Motorcar**
- **Book XIII**   **The Conundrum of the Blundering Bear**
- **Book XIV**   **The Conundrum of Shooting Fish in a Barrel**
  -
  - **To Be Continued!**

Next a series is "New Beginnings" a 1950's medical drama.

- Book I   **The Believer**
- Book II   **The Heretic**
- Book III   **Arrow Song**
- Book IV   **Peas In A Pod**
-
  - **To Be Continued!**

"the ReproBate saga" is a character-based series in the 1860 American Civil War

- **Book I**   **Beneath the Rose**
- Book II   **skull and cRossBones**
- Book III   **Redefining Bastions**
- Book IV   **thicker than Blood**
- Book V   **prioR Battles**
- Book VI   **Requited Blasphemy**
- Book VII   **The waR Between**
- Book VIII   **To Richmond or Bust**
- Book IX   **carrying Battlescars**
  - ○   **To be Continued**

"the Hellhole saga" is a character-based series from the American West

- Book I   **First Draw**
- Book II   **Audition for a Legend**
- Book III   **Strange Bedfellows**

"The Kansas Pirate Series" is another character-based series from the American West

- Book I   **Pirate Treasure**
- Book II   **Strawberry Fields**
- Book III   **The Drinking Gourd**

Stand-alone novels include:

- **Catman** *He was every man; he was no man*
-
- **ONE** Science Fiction space travel

- **Shepherd of the Kingdom** a modern-day horror classic

Non-Fiction

"**The Kepi Magazine**," A publication specialized in the Civil War and 19th century life.:

- **The Kepi Volume I and II**
- **The Kepi Volumes III and IV**